Celebrations at the Toffee Factory

By Glenda Young

Saga Novels
Belle of the Back Streets
The Tuppenny Child
Pearl of Pit Lane
The Girl with the Scarlet Ribbon
The Paper Mill Girl
The Miner's Lass
A Mother's Christmas Wish
The Sixpenny Orphan

The Toffee Factory Girls
Secrets of the Toffee Factory Girls
Celebrations at the Toffee Factory

Helen Dexter Cosy Crime Mysteries
Murder at the Seaview Hotel
Curtain Call at the Seaview Hotel
Foul Play at the Seaview Hotel
Deadly Dancing at the Seaview Hotel

GLENDA YOUNG

Celebrations at the Toffee Factory

Copyright © 2026 Glenda Young

The right of Glenda Young to be identified as the Author of
the Work has been asserted by her in accordance with the Copyright,
Designs and Patents Act 1988.

First published in 2026 by Headline Publishing Group Limited

1

Apart from any use permitted under UK copyright law, this publication
may only be reproduced, stored, or transmitted, in any form, or by
any means, with prior permission in writing of the publishers or,
in the case of reprographic production, in accordance with the terms
of licences issued by the Copyright Licensing Agency.

All characters – apart from the obvious historical figures – in this
publication are fictitious and any resemblance to real persons,
living or dead, is purely coincidental.

Cataloguing in Publication Data is available from the British Library

Hardback ISBN 978 1 0354 0259 5

Typeset in 12.75/16pt Stempel Garamond LT Std
by Six Red Marbles UK, Thetford, Norfolk

Printed and bound in Great Britain by Clays Ltd, Elcograf S.p.A.

Headline's policy is to use papers that are natural, renewable and recyclable
products and made from wood grown in well-managed forests and other
controlled sources. The logging and manufacturing processes are expected
to conform to the environmental regulations of the country of origin.

Headline Publishing Group Limited
An Hachette UK Company
Carmelite House
50 Victoria Embankment
London EC4Y 0DZ

The authorised representative in the EEA is Hachette Ireland,
8 Castlecourt Centre, Dublin 15, D15 XTP3, Ireland (email: info@hbgi.ie)

www.headline.co.uk
www.hachette.co.uk

To Mam
1939–2024

Author's Note

Please note, in this work of fiction I have used poetic licence to best fit dates to the narrative. If you'd like to discover the real history of Elisabethville, fictionalised in this novel, I highly recommend the books *Who Were the Birtley Belgians?* by Birtley Heritage Group, published by Summerhill Books, and *Of Arms and the Heroes: The Story of the Birtley Belgians* by John G. Bygate, published by History of Education Project.

Acknowledgements

My grateful thanks go to the many local historians who provided their time, advice and help while I researched the history of toffee factories in the north-east. Thank you to Gavin Purdon, local historian in Chester-le-Street and author of the book about Horner's toffee factory, *It Was Grand Toffee*. Thank you to Dorothy Hall and Steve Dodds and everyone at Chester-le-Street Heritage Group. Thank you to Val Greaves, Jean Atkinson, Barry Ross and Joan Hall and everyone at Birtley Heritage Group. Thank you to Dirk Musschoot for allowing me to use his name in the book, and for his book *Belgen Maken Bommen*. Thank you to Sunderland historian Sharon Vincent for her invaluable knowledge of women's social history, and also to Suzanne Green for all her support.

Huge thanks to the very helpful staff at the University of York Borthwick Archives, where I researched toffee factories during World War I. Thank you to the Strachey Trust and the Society of Authors for their financial support with a research travel grant that allowed me to research in York.

Thank you to Graham Soult, retail consultant at CannyInsights.com and a High Streets Task Force expert, along with Phil Reilly, business development manager at Lumley Castle Hotel. Special thanks to the staff and volunteers of Calderdale Industrial Museum in Halifax (aka Toffee Town) for their enthusiasm and support – and for demonstrating their amazing toffee-wrapping machine!

Thank you also to my agents, Caroline Sheldon and Safae El-Ouahabi at RCW Literary Agency, for everything, and to the team at Headline who look after me so well. Finally, thank you to my husband Barry, for fuelling me with tea, coffee and cheese scones when I lock myself away to write.

The Story So Far

The Toffee Factory Girls

and

Secrets of the Toffee Factory Girls

Hetty, Elsie and Anne start work at Jack's toffee factory in the Durham market town of Chester-le-Street when war breaks out in 1914 and men leave to serve in the forces. They don't know each other before they arrive at the factory but soon become firm friends.

Hetty Lawson is the breadwinner at home. She wins a competition at the toffee factory to become the face of the new brand of toffee, named Lady Tina. Hetty lives with Hilda, who gave her the shock news that she is not her real mum. When Hetty's boyfriend Bob goes off to war, Hetty falls for a Belgian man, Dirk, who lives in the nearby village of Elisabethville. She writes to Bob to call off their relationship, but her letter gets lost. Now with war over, Bob is on his way back to propose!

Elsie Cooper has had a rough upbringing. She marries Frankie, but his evil hold over her results in tragic consequences. Meanwhile, Elsie's factory colleague, Stan, will do anything for her, but she is blind to the fact that he's the right man for her. When Elsie's aunt Jean marries and moves to London, Elsie moves in with Hetty and learns how to cook, run a house and be independent for the first time in her life.

Anne Wright starts work in Mr Jack's office as a typist. She is efficient and organised and whips the office – and Mr Jack himself – into shape. However, behind her businesslike facade, she hides a heartbreaking secret. She had a baby out of wedlock and had no choice but to sell him to a wealthy couple. She channels her sorrow and energy into her work and impresses Mr Jack with her energy and enthusiasm so much that he proposes, and she accepts. They now have a child called Dinah. Married to the toffee factory boss, forthright Anne puts her stamp on the business, but not all of her ideas go down well with the men on the management board. She helps steer the factory through the war years, but now that war is over, she faces a fight to stay in her position.

Chapter One

Spring 1919

The morning was warm and bright as two young women walked to work at Jack's toffee factory in the market town of Chester-le-Street. Both girls were dressed in khaki and red overalls. Dark-haired Elsie and her friend Hetty linked arms as they turned into Market Lane. However, Elsie's heart grew heavy as the factory came into sight, her pretty face clouding over.

'Have you heard the rumours?' she asked. 'Some of the girls say we might be laid off now the men are returning from war. Aunt Jean's already lost her job in London. She was driving trams when she first moved there with Alfie. Now she's stuck at home cleaning and cooking while Alfie goes out to work. Her last letter to me said she was bored stiff after the excitement of working on the trams. She misses her friends at work too. And did I tell you what happened to my friend Laurel and the other girls at the munitions factory?'

Hetty shook her head.

'They were sacked as soon as the Armistice was declared. On the eleventh hour of the eleventh day of the eleventh month, all the girls were told to leave. Just like that, no wages, nothing. They were forced out of the factory and haven't worked since. Laurel's rattling around the house now, cooking and cleaning for her brothers and her dad who work down the pit. Doesn't seem fair if you ask me. Why can't we stay in our jobs now that war's over?'

'The men have to get their jobs back. It's the way things are,' Hetty said, resigned.

'It's not like you to be so defeatist, Hetty Lawson. Where's your fighting spirit gone?'

'I've got a lot on my mind,' Hetty huffed.

Elsie pulled her friend closer and began to speak in a whisper. 'Some say the men who've returned from war aren't all there.' She tapped the side of her head. 'They've seen too much; it's destroyed their minds.'

Hetty pushed a stray lock of fair hair behind her ear. 'At least they're home. A lot won't be coming back.'

Elsie dropped her gaze. 'I'm sorry, Hetty. I wasn't thinking. I didn't mean to upset you over Dan.'

They walked in silence for a few moments, both thinking about Hetty's half-brother, who had been killed in action.

'I daren't think what might happen if I lose this job,' Hetty said at last.

Elsie shot her a worried look. 'Me neither. I'm skint.' She could feel Hetty's eyes burning into her and had a feeling she knew what was coming next. She wasn't wrong.

'You wouldn't think about doing . . . you know, what you did before, would you?' Hetty asked nervously.

Elsie shook her head. 'No way. Walking the streets, selling my body to any Jack, Tom or Bobby? No, I learned the hard way how dangerous that was, even if the money was good. Don't worry, I'll never go back to that. But you're one of the lucky ones, why should you worry about money? You've got two jobs.'

Hetty gave a wry smile. 'Working in the kitchen at Lumley Castle doesn't pay as much as my job at the toffee factory. And I need to earn as much as I can so that I can look after Hilda. You know how much the doctor's bills are, and there's the medicine she needs. It costs a small fortune.'

Elsie laid her head on Hetty's shoulder as they walked. 'I'll help as much as I can. It's the least I can do after you and your mum took me in.'

'Hilda's not my mum, remember,' Hetty said sharply.

Elsie bit her tongue. 'Sorry, love. Sometimes the word slips out when I'm not thinking. It happens to you too; I've heard you call her Mum now and then. But look, it was months ago that you found out the truth about her. You're not still angry, are you?'

Hetty slowed her pace and turned to face her friend. 'It seems I'm angry a lot lately. It's stress caused by worry.' She nodded towards the iron gates of the factory, where young girls and women were streaming through. 'If we lose our jobs when the soldiers come home, I might lose the house if I can't pay the rent. Hilda's still poorly and needs looking after. And then there's . . .'

'Man trouble?' Elsie grimaced.

Hetty nodded and gave a small smile. 'Man trouble indeed. Oh, Elsie, I don't know what to do. Dirk says he loves me, but he's leaving to return to Belgium soon. And now Bob's on his way back from war, and in his last letter he said he's going to propose to me the minute he sees me.

One minute I think my future should be here, safe with Bob—'

'Safe but dull,' Elsie chipped in.

Hetty let the comment slide. 'And the next minute I can't bear to think of life without Dirk. But he has to go home, and I can hardly go with him.'

Elsie looked at Hetty with her big brown eyes. 'If I were you, I'd go.'

'To Belgium? Don't be daft. A girl like me doesn't leave Chester-le-Street. Anyway, if I went, I wouldn't know anyone!'

'You'd know Dirk,' Elsie said gently.

Hetty picked up her stride, dragging Elsie with her as they made their way through the factory gates. 'I won't talk about this now,' she said sternly.

'You started it,' Elsie sulked.

'I did not,' Hetty replied.

'Did so,' Elsie said with a smile.

Hetty looked at her and the pair of them burst into giggles.

'Have you seen anything of Anne lately?' Hetty asked once they'd stopping laughing.

'No, I haven't,' Elsie replied. 'You know what things are like since she married Mr Jack and had her baby. We hardly see her outside of work any more. Do you ever wonder what she sees in him?'

An image of Mr Jack popped into Hetty's mind, and she tried to suppress a smile. He was a short man, much shorter than Anne, and the pair of them looked quite comical when they walked around the factory together.

'What does she see in him? You mean apart from him idolising her and being the head of a toffee empire, with enough money to fulfil her heart's desire? Not to mention the big house he provides for her to live in, the gorgeous little girl they have at home, the housekeeper who cooks and cleans, the garden Anne sits in on a sunny day... Need I go on? The last time I saw her, she said she'd asked Mr Jack to teach her how to drive his car.'

Elsie's eyes opened wide with surprise. 'No!' she said. 'I haven't seen a woman driving in Chester-le-Street before. Do you think he really will teach her?'

'I don't think he'll have a choice,' Hetty replied. 'You know what Anne's like; when she wants something, she gets it.'

She nodded towards the long, low buildings that made up the toffee factory. Ahead of them was a tall, thin chimney belching smoke into the air. It loomed high above the railway lines that ran in one direction to Scotland and in the other to London. The logo of Jack's toffee factory was painted high on the chimney for the hundreds of train passengers to see.

'Come on, let's get to work. We don't want a ticking-off from Mrs Perkins for being late.'

They headed towards the slab room, where they worked cutting warm, freshly made toffee into delicious bite-sized pieces. From the slab room the toffees were sent to the wrapping room, where every single toffee was wrapped by hand. And each wrapper had to display the Jack's logo perfectly straight. Before they reached the slab-room door, however, a thickset man appeared pushing a wheelbarrow. It was Stan Chapman, the gardener. He had hands like shovels, a broad chest and strong arms. His face was open and honest, weather beaten and ruddy from years spent outdoors doing the job he adored. His thick brown hair was hidden under his flat cap and his hazel eyes lit up when he saw Elsie.

'Morning, Elsie!' he called.

Hetty tried to peel away, but Elsie held her tight.

'There's your fella, I'll let you go and speak to him,' Hetty said.

'He's not my fella,' Elsie hissed.

'I thought you liked him?' Hetty whispered.

There wasn't time for Elsie to reply, as Stan walked up to her and planted a kiss on her cheek. She kept tight hold of Hetty's arm, not allowing her to enter the slab room without her.

'Morning, Stan,' she said coolly.

Stan nodded at the wheelbarrow. 'It's a big day for me and my team,' he said proudly. 'We're finally putting back the flower beds and digging up the vegetables. It's been a long time without flowers during the war. Now it's time to get the factory garden back to the way it once was.' He raised his cap to Elsie. 'Could I take you out for tea one night? Perhaps tonight after work?'

Elsie bit her lip. 'Not sure I can, Stan. I've got things to do.'

'Another time, then,' he said, and walked off with his wheelbarrow.

Hetty looked askance at her friend. 'I thought you and Stan were courting these days. Why did you give him the brush-off?'

But Elsie didn't reply, her attention focused on two strapping men heading into the sugar-boiling room. As they walked, they kept turning to look at her. She undid the top button of her overall and stuck her hand on her hip. One of the men winked at her and she waved in return.

'Oh, Elsie. Don't say you've started flirting with those fellas again. You'll get a bad reputation. You're still a married woman, remember,' Hetty chided.

Elsie's face clouded over. 'As if I could forget. I wish I'd never met Frankie Ireland.'

'Have you seen him lately?' Hetty asked.

Elsie shook her head. 'No, and I don't want to after what he put me through. I hear things about him from Cathy in the Lambton Arms. She tells me he drinks himself into oblivion most nights then falls down outside the pub. She says if it was up to her she'd leave him there all night, but Jim insists on bringing him indoors. Well, he is his brother. Jim lets him sleep on the pub floor, but he won't have him upstairs in the family's living area. He keeps Frankie away from their boys in case he lashes out at them like he did to me.'

'I'm sorry you went through all of that,' Hetty said.

Elsie shrugged. 'It's water under the bridge now,' she said with a catch in her voice.

Hetty looked at her. 'Well, Stan clearly thinks the world of you.'

'I know he does, and I like him a lot. But I'm scared that if I choose Stan, I might miss out on someone better, more exciting and fun,' Elsie replied, casting another look at the door of the sugar-boiling room.

'You're terrible, Elsie Cooper,' Hetty laughed.

A mischievous smile played around Elsie's lips. 'At least I'd never settle for a dull man, like someone else I could mention,' she replied, raising her eyebrows and throwing a knowing look at her friend.

'That's enough now, Elsie.' Hetty sighed. 'Come on or we'll be late for work.'

Chapter Two

Hetty threaded her arm through Elsie's and they walked into the slab room. From behind them they heard a car engine stutter and knock. The unholy noise was followed by a screech of gears and brakes, and they turned, stunned to see Mr Jack's gleaming black car jolting and jerking through the iron gates. It shuddered to a halt outside the factory reception. By now the car had attracted a curious crowd.

Jacob, the factory receptionist, came running out to greet Mr Jack. It was the first time Hetty had seen him move at anything more than a snail's pace. And his face seemed animated too, which was unusual. She had only seen him looking surly and miserable as he worked on his ledgers whenever she called at reception on an errand for their supervisor.

'Sir, whatever is the problem with your motor?' he called as he ran to the driver's side of the car. However, it wasn't Mr Jack who stepped out from behind the wheel; it was Anne. Hetty watched as Mr Jack slowly unfurled himself from the passenger side, his short legs finally reaching the ground. His normally round and cheerful face was set stern with a worried expression, and he ran a blue linen handkerchief across his bald head, which was covered in perspiration. His trademark bow tie in the same colour blue as the factory logo was skew-whiff.

Anne walked around the car to her husband and straightened his tie. 'I think I managed to park quite well this time, William,' she said cheerfully.

William gulped. 'At least you didn't hit the gate, dear.'

Hetty noticed a scratch on the front of the car, then watched as Jacob and Mr Jack had a discussion about moving the car to a more appropriate space. It was blocking entry through the gates, and women were having to squeeze past on both sides.

'Morning, Anne!' Hetty called.

Anne strode over to the girls. She was dressed in a smart navy jacket with matching skirt and flat shoes. Under her jacket she wore a cream lace blouse and at her neck was a beautiful brooch of blue stones, a present from Mr Jack.

'How are you both?' she asked.

Elsie nodded at Hetty. 'Well, she's down in the dumps, but I'm all right.'

'I've just got a lot on my mind,' Hetty snapped. 'Anyway, she's flirting with the sugar boilers again.'

Anne tutted. 'Oh, Elsie. Haven't you learned your lesson after what happened with Frankie? The sugar boilers are a rough lot, leave them be. Stan's the man for you. Everyone can see it.'

'Everyone but her,' Hetty quipped.

Anne nodded at Elsie's overall, which strained across her ample bust and revealed more cleavage than the girls were allowed to display. 'You might want to fasten that button before Mrs Perkins catches you and tells you off. It's always best to keep on her good side.'

'She hasn't got a good side, she's an old dragon,' Elsie muttered, doing up the button.

'She's not so bad,' Anne said gently. 'You just need to get to know her, that's all.'

Hetty made to leave. 'See you later, Anne. We really must get to work.'

When Elsie hesitated, Hetty saw that her friend's gaze was firmly fixed on Anne's brooch.

'Elsie, come on,' she said, gently pulling Elsie into the slab room to begin their day.

Working in the slab room was hard work, physically tiring, and their muscles ached by the end of the day. But it paid well, and for that Hetty was grateful, yet she constantly worried about how much longer her job would last. She forced a smile as she walked into the room. Mrs Perkins, their supervisor, was sitting at her desk in the corner, and Hetty saw her look up before taking a pencil and marking two ticks on her list, confirming, Hetty knew, that she and Elsie had arrived.

Mrs Perkins was middle aged. Despite her title she was a spinster, although there had been rumours that she'd married once and that her husband had left her for reasons unspecified but much gossiped about by the factory girls. She was older than any of the girls at the factory. Her long brown hair was plaited down her back and she always wore the same blue skirt. Hetty found her firm but fair to work for, yet she knew that Elsie had suffered a few run-ins with her, mainly to do with Elsie disappearing to flirt with the men behind the sugar-boiling room. Hetty and Elsie had worked under Mrs Perkins almost continuously since they'd started at the factory. They'd worked in the wrapping room first, twisting waxed papers around toffees. They'd wrapped thousands each day and their fingers had ended up swollen and sore. Then they'd been transferred to the packing room, away from Mrs Perkins and her strict no-talking rule, but now the supervisor had been moved by Mr Jack to the slab room to oversee the levelling and cutting of warm toffee.

As more girls streamed into the vast space, Mrs Perkins kept looking at the door and ticking names off her list. The slab room was noisy, with the sugar boilers carrying large pans of hot, bubbling toffee to the cooling tables where Hetty and Elsie worked. The sugar boilers were all men; no women were allowed in the sugar-boiling room, such were the dangers of working with hot toffee and heavy pans. Lifting the pans required brute force, a strength that not even Mrs Perkins possessed.

As Hetty took up her position on one side of the cooling slab, she looked across at Elsie opposite her. Her friend was a beauty. She had olive skin, dark eyes and thick black hair piled up on her head and wrapped in a khaki turban. She wore heavy make-up, not just for nights out dancing in town but also for work. Her lips were painted scarlet. However, her smouldering looks often got her into trouble, attracting the wrong kind of man. Hetty shuddered at the thought of Elsie's husband Frankie. He'd once worked as a sugar boiler before he was sacked by Mr Jack for stealing boxes of toffee. Frankie was a violent, evil man whom Elsie had been forced into marrying when she fell pregnant. The worse for drink on their wedding night, he had beaten her so badly that she'd lost the child. Since then, the pair had gone their separate ways, although Frankie had tried to win her back. However, Elsie had stayed strong and was determined not to fall for him again. It had been Stan who'd helped her during that awful time. That was why Hetty couldn't understand why she was shunning him to flirt with the factory men again. She sighed and shook her head. 'It's none of my business,' she muttered under her breath.

From the corner of her eye, she noticed a swish of blue material, and Mrs Perkins appeared.

'Hands, please, Miss Lawson,' the supervisor barked.

Hetty held out her hands for Mrs Perkins to inspect. When the woman was satisfied that they were clean enough to work on the cutting device, she moved on to inspect the next girl, then the next.

Around Hetty the slab room rang with noise and chatter. Mrs Perkins couldn't enforce her no-speaking rule here, as the girls needed to shout instructions about their work to each other to be heard. The room was bustling with sugar boilers coming and going. Some were ex-soldiers who'd already returned from the trenches. The war had brought many problems to the factory, not least sugar rationing, which had caused production to drop to three days a week. There was still no news from Mr Jack about when, or if, this might change. Some of the men were stripped to the waist to deal with the heat of working with boiling sugar. The hot toffee oozed from the pouring spouts of the pans and filled the metal slab where Hetty and Elsie stood waiting. As soon as the pans were emptied, the men returned to the sugar-boiling room to make more delicious creamy toffee.

When Hetty told anyone where she worked, the first thing they asked about was the wonderful smell of toffee. And it was true, the smell was as sweet and welcome as anything she had known. If she stuck out her tongue, she could taste toffee on the air. There was so much sugar in all of the rooms at the factory that it made the floors sticky to walk on, even though they were cleaned at the end of each day. The girls had to wear clogs in case they got stuck to the floor. If that happened, they would be lifted out of them by two strong-armed sugar boilers.

Hetty had worked at the factory for so long now she hardly noticed the smell any more. She'd also grown used to the sticky floors and having to grip her toes to keep her clogs on. She and Elsie had worked at Jack's toffee factory since the outbreak of war. Back then, women had been recruited en masse to replace the men who'd been sent to war. It was the first time women had worked outside of the home, and friendships had soon been forged. Hetty had met Elsie and Anne and now she had two best friends.

Working at the factory had given her confidence. She'd stood up for girls who'd been unfairly treated. She'd helped get gas lamps installed to light up the dangerous lane at the back of the factory where her friend Beattie had been attacked. And she'd even become the face of Lady Tina toffee by winning a competition. Now Lady Tina was the factory's best-selling toffee, and each tin had Hetty's face on the lid.

'How will I manage if I lose my job?' she sighed.

'Are you all right, love?' a voice asked.

Hetty turned to see Beattie watching her quizzically.

'You seem to be talking to yourself a lot this morning,' Beattie said.

'Was I?' Hetty said, distracted.

'Watch out, here it comes.' Beattie handed Hetty a long, flat metal bar. Hetty leaned forward and began smoothing the bubbling toffee with it. She was careful not to let any part of her skin touch the toffee. She'd seen too many girls suffer burns.

Chapter Three

Up and down the rows, on both sides of the slabs, women and girls quickly levelled toffee while it was warm. Leave it too long and it'd go hard and be uneven, consigned to the reject bins. Mr Jack had very high standards.

'Ready!' Beattie called from the top of the slab. She was a strong, sturdy woman whose family ran a farm on the outskirts of town.

The girls stood back as large metal grids were lowered onto the slabs where the toffee was starting to cool. It needed to be at the perfect consistency to be cut into the right size. The cutting grids were made up of small squares with sharp edges and were lowered to the toffee by pulleys from metal bars. Hetty always marvelled when she watched the toffee being cut; it was a magical sight. While she might have grown used to the sweet smell of sugar, seeing the toffees cut into shape and sent off to the wrapping room made her heart swell with joy. She took great pride in her work.

She exchanged a smile with Elsie and the girls got to work scooping the toffees into barrels to be wheeled to the wrapping room. As each slab was cleared, more pans of boiling toffee were carried into the room, and the whole process of pouring, spreading, cooling and cutting was repeated. Delicious scents drifted on the air: peppermint from one corner, strawberry from another. These were welcome aromas that had been missing from the factory during the years while war had raged.

'I smell fruit. More supplies must be getting through at last,' Beattie noted.

'What'll you do once the men return and we have to leave our jobs?' Hetty asked.

'I'll go and work on the farm with my family,' Beattie replied. 'I'll be all right, although I much prefer working here. What will happen to you? Will you look after your mum at home?'

Hetty bit her tongue. She didn't want to talk about Hilda. She shrugged. 'I've still got domestic work at Lumley Castle for two days a week. But it doesn't pay well.'

Beattie stiffened, then tapped the side of her nose. It was the signal that Mrs Perkins was on the prowl.

The offices at the factory were in a separate building, away from where the toffee was made, wrapped and packed. There was a hush in the office building, with deep, soft caramel-coloured carpets laid from wall to wall. The walls were panelled in dark wood and decorated with framed certificates awarded for quality toffee.

Anne worked in a plush corner office that had once belonged to the factory's sales manager, James Burl. Mr Burl was tall and good looking, with fine features and a firm jaw, and he considered himself Mr Jack's right-hand man. However, while there was no denying he was excellent at his job, he treated his office staff badly and was brusque in his manner with everyone he met. Anne had never got along with him. They'd started off on the wrong foot on her first day in her role as Mr Jack's secretary. Back then, Mr Burl had felt certain that his fiancée Miss Brabin would be appointed to the role. When Anne was chosen instead, he never forgave her. He'd been offhand with her since, undermining her at every turn. Or at least trying to, for he hadn't realised just how strong willed and determined she was.

Concerns about Mr Burl's rude behaviour and ill-treatment of his staff had been raised to Anne by his secretary, Meg. Once she knew the truth about what was going on, she had spoken to her husband in private. The upshot of it was that Mr Burl had been moved from his office to a shared room with other senior staff, who could keep their eye on him to ensure his bullying behaviour was kept in check.

Mr Jack's office was along the corridor from Anne's, and had an anteroom where Anne had once worked. Now that room was occupied by Meg, whom Anne had promoted to work for Mr Jack and herself. It was a demanding role, working for two of the most important people at the factory, and Anne often wondered if it was too much for Meg. The girl sometimes became flustered and made silly mistakes when Mr Jack and Anne gave her tasks at the same time. However, Anne always impressed upon her that work from Mr Jack took priority. He was the boss, after all.

Anne's role at the factory involved assisting her husband in every way she could. Working as his secretary had given her an all-round understanding of the way the factory worked. She now took on its day-to-day running, from buying ingredients at the best possible price to ensuring the canteen and cleaning services were well staffed and efficiently run. She also helped manage the factory's gardening and maintenance, and most things in between. William often said that he didn't know how he'd coped before.

She removed her smart jacket and hung it carefully on a hook on the back of her door, then moved to sit behind her desk and set her handbag on the carpet. She sat straight in her chair and pushed her round wire-framed glasses up to the bridge of her nose. Her desk was the colour of chocolate, dark and rich. In a wire basket was a pile of letters and correspondence that Meg had typed for her. She would read these first, then deliver them back to Meg to either correct any mistakes or take them to the post office. By far the most important item on her desk, however, was a framed photograph of a small child, her daughter Dinah, whom she adored.

'I'm doing this for you,' she whispered as she looked at the little girl's sweet face. Oh, there were plenty of people in Chester-le-Street, and in the factory, who told her that she should be at home looking after her daughter. Plenty who said she shouldn't be taking a job at the factory when a man could be working instead. Plenty who dared tell her she was neglecting her child. But Anne knew the truth. Dinah was much loved, and Anne was resolute about working for a living. She also had William's full backing. So no matter what people said, either to her face or behind her back, she knew in her heart she was doing the right thing. Each night at home, she showered her daughter with love and affection, reading her stories and playing games. Weekends were always family time too, which included William's parents, who doted on their granddaughter. But still, from time to time she felt a pang of guilt when she sat at her desk and looked at Dinah's face.

She glanced at the clock on the wall. There were seven hours to go before she would see Dinah again. Until then, the child would be tended to and cared for by Edith Brown, their live-in housekeeper. Edith had become part of Anne's life when she'd first met Mr Jack. She had worked for him for many years and had demonstrated her discretion on the occasions when Anne had stayed overnight at the Deanery before she was wed. Now Anne trusted her with all of her heart, and with her daughter's care.

There was a knock at her door and she forced herself to focus. 'Come in,' she called.

A tall, slim woman entered. Her shoulders were stooped as if she was trying to deflect attention from her height, which only made it obvious that she was embarrassed by her stature. She was an attractive woman, with short, curled brown hair. There was a nervous look about her and she avoided eye contact, looking down at the carpet.

'Good morning, Meg, how are you?' Anne said.

'Good morning, Mrs Jack. I have some papers for your signature.' Meg laid a folder on Anne's desk, then stepped back. 'Would you like a cup of coffee? I'm making a pot for Mr Jack's meeting with the finance team this morning.'

Anne was puzzled. She didn't know anything about a meeting with the finance team and wondered why William hadn't mentioned it. They normally shared everything to do with the factory, especially when it came to finances.

'Has he requested I attend the meeting?' she asked, trying to keep her voice steady.

'No, Mrs Jack,' Meg said. She backed out of the office.

Anne's hand flew to the blue brooch at her throat, her fingers running over its precious stones. It was most unlike William not to keep her up to date. She thought for a moment about storming to his office and demanding to know what was happening. But she stayed in her seat. She knew her husband too well. The best time to tackle him was tonight, at home, after a good dinner cooked by Edith and a brandy warmed by the fire.

She straightened her back and picked up one of the papers that Meg had brought, a standard letter to a supplier about meat for the canteen. She spotted two typing errors and marked them with her pen. Sighing, she wondered again if she and Mr Jack were putting too much on her. The next sheet was a letter to the supplies office at Elisabethville. This was a community in the nearby town of Birtley where thousands of Belgians lived. They'd been brought to England by the British government after the war began to work in the munitions factories, and had built their own village and named it after the Belgian queen. Now Elisabethville was being dismantled and the Belgians were returning home. Anne spotted typing errors in this letter too, not least that Elisabethville had been spelled with a *z* instead of an *s*.

'Meg, you should know better,' she muttered, marking the error. She put the letter to one side, then picked up the next document, which consisted of two sheets clipped together. The top one was a letter to a supplier, with an order for blueberries. Fruit-flavoured toffees had been Anne's suggestion at a recent board meeting now that supplies were coming through from the docks, and she was heartened that more flavours would be available soon. There was a typing error on this letter too, but it was an insignificant one, and so instead of marking it for Meg to retype, she simply corrected it with her pen before turning to the second sheet. She expected this to be related to the blueberry order. But it wasn't. It was a list of figures; a finance report, handwritten by William. She would recognise his writing anywhere.

As she cast her eyes down the sheet, her heart grew heavy. The figures were alarming. It was a list of debts owed, with a final amount so large she couldn't comprehend it. She took a deep breath and decided she couldn't wait until she returned home to talk to William about this. She pushed her chair back and stood, holding the sheet in her left hand while she straightened the brooch at her throat with her right. Then she left her office and began the walk along the corridor to join the finance meeting, whether her husband wanted her there or not.

Chapter Four

When Anne reached William's office, the door was closed. She raised her hand to knock, as she always did before entering. William was her husband, yes, but at work he was Mr Jack, king of the toffee empire. She treated him with the same respect that she would give to any senior member of staff. However, this time was different, and she dropped her hand and pushed the door open.

William's face when he spotted her was a picture of horror. Meg was sitting at his side, taking notes with a pad and pencil. Opposite him sat two men. Their backs were to Anne, but she recognised both immediately: Mr Burl, the sales manager, and Mr Smith, the finance manager. Mr Smith was a stocky man wearing a dark jacket, his waistcoat straining over his hefty chest. Mr Burl turned to look at her, trying to suppress a grin. Anne guessed he was enjoying the spectacle of her being caught on the back foot. She was determined not to give him the pleasure.

She moved to stand next to her husband and laid her hand on his shoulder, feeling him tense beneath her touch. 'I'm sorry I'm late for the meeting,' she said gently. She slipped the list of figures in front of him, making it obvious that she'd seen it, and his shoulder slumped under her hand.

'Meg, pull up a chair for Mrs Jack,' he said.

Meg disappeared to the anteroom and returned with a chair, which she placed next to Mr Burl. Anne sat down, smiling at the man through gritted teeth before turning her attention to her husband.

'Now, what I have missed?'

Mr Burl shifted in his chair. 'I really don't think it's a good idea for Mrs Jack to be included. This is a confidential meeting,' he spluttered.

'Are you saying I can't be trusted?' Anne said, keeping her tone light and playful, which she knew would infuriate him.

'Mrs Jack can stay.' William glanced at Meg. 'Make a note in the minutes that Mrs Jack has joined the meeting, please.' Then he turned back to Anne. 'I'm sorry, dear, that you weren't kept informed.'

Anne gazed steadily at her husband, wondering again why he hadn't told her about the meeting and the alarming figures. His cheeks were turning pink and he seemed unable to hold eye contact. His hand flew to his blue bow tie, a telltale sign that he was feeling anxious, and he twirled it through his fingers before returning his attention to the matter in hand.

'Gentlemen . . .' he began.

Anne coughed, twice. She was the first woman to work at the factory in any capacity other than on the factory floor or as a cleaner, canteen worker or secretary. She knew how much of a novelty she was, and she had to keep reminding the men she worked with, including her husband, that she was vital to the factory's life.

'And Mrs Jack,' he added sheepishily. 'I've called this meeting to alert you to some...' He paused, then straightened in his chair and laid both hands on his desktop, as if to steady himself. 'There are a large number of outgoings that the factory needs to cover. Mr Smith and I have been through the accounts, more than once, and we have uncovered debts that we let slide during the war. These debts are being called in by our suppliers now the country is gearing up to full production once more. Debts, I'm afraid, that we have no choice but to pay. Of course we will honour every single penny, but...'

Anne's heart started going like the clappers. She knew the factory's finances had been precarious during the war, but William had assured her that he and the management board were steering the factory to survival. Now it sounded as if unforeseen problems had reared their ugly head. She leaned forward.

'But what?'

William looked from Mr Smith to Mr Burl then finally at Anne. 'These debts, when paid in full, may cripple the factory and even close us down.'

Mr Burl banged his fist against the desk. 'No!' he yelled, his face full of anger, directed at his colleague seated to his left. 'How the devil did you and your finance team let such a thing happen? This is outrageous!'

William turned to Meg. 'Meg, put your pencil down, please.'

She laid her pencil on top of her pad.

He stood and began to pace. 'We must find a way out of this,' he muttered.

Anne glanced at the handwritten sheet of figures on

the desk. If the figures were a true indication of the state the factory was in, then it was very bad indeed.

'Does the board know about these debts?' she asked.

'Not fully, not yet,' Mr Smith replied, casting a nervous look at William. 'I'm preparing a financial report for discussion. Mr Jack has asked me to arrange an emergency board meeting.'

This was another shock for Anne. She shot William a look, but he ignored it and kept pacing.

Mr Burl turned again to Mr Smith, his eyes burning with anger. 'You're incompetent, not fit for the role of finance manager!'

Finally William returned to his seat. He looked straight at Mr Smith. 'Send the board the date for the emergency meeting as soon as you can. We need to get everyone around the table and we'll be open and honest. It's the Jack's toffee factory way.'

'Yes, sir,' Mr Smith said. He rose from his seat and left the office. Mr Burl remained where he was.

'You may go too, Mr Burl,' William said.

Slowly Mr Burl rose, but he made no move to leave. Placing both hands on the back of his chair, he glared at Anne. 'Since certain changes were brought about in this factory, the place has been run into the ground.'

Anne managed to force a smile. She had an idea where this was going and she wasn't going to make it easy for him. 'What changes, Mr Burl?'

'This was a fine factory once,' he said, his eyes narrowing. 'When the gentlemen of the board knew and trusted one another. When debts were covered and invoices paid. Now we allow women to make decisions, and look where that's brought us!' He turned to William. 'We're on our knees, man!'

William leapt up. 'How dare you speak to my wife in such a manner!'

Anne kept her back straight and her gaze focused on Mr Burl's face. She glanced at her husband and nodded discreetly, a signal for him to stay calm. He was so outraged she was concerned he might punch the man. The idea of it appealed; it was something she'd often thought of doing herself. Instead, she cleared her throat and began to speak.

'Mr Burl, in case you haven't noticed, there's been a war raging across Europe for the last four years. A war that has meant reducing factory production to three days a week. It is this that has brought the factory to the situation in which we find ourselves. However, you seem to suggest otherwise; that it is having two women on the management board that is the source of the problem. If this is so, it is an insult to Mr Jack's mother and myself.'

'Should I write this down, sir?' Meg chipped in.

'No,' William replied.

'Yes,' Anne said at the same time.

Meg glanced from one to the other, unsure what to do.

Mr Burl's face dropped and he looked at William. 'I'm sorry, sir,' he muttered.

William dismissed him with a wave of his hand. 'You may go, Mr Burl. But I warn you now never to speak to my wife like that again or there will be dire consequences. And remember, not a word to anyone in the factory. What has been said in this room today is confidential.'

When Mr Burl had gone, Anne turned to Meg. 'Meg, dear, could you please leave Mr Jack and myself to speak alone?'

'Of course. I'll be in my office,' Meg said. She picked up her pad and pencil and turned towards the anteroom. However, Anne knew from past experience how thin the walls of that room were.

'Would you mind working in my office for a while?' she said. 'I have filing that needs to be done.'

'Yes, Mrs Jack,' Meg said, and she followed Mr Burl out.

Alone with her husband, Anne looked him straight in the eye. 'Care to tell me what on earth's going on?'

At the end of the day, the factory whistle blew and the girls streamed out of work. Hetty and Elsie left arm-in-arm, heads together, gossiping about the day they'd both had.

'Mrs Perkins was cheerful today,' Hetty noted.

'Can't say I noticed,' Elsie replied breezily. 'Got my mind on other things.'

One of the men from the sugar-boiling room cycled past, and Hetty noticed Elsie's gaze following him.

'So I see,' she said.

Elsie poked her gently in the ribs. 'Oh, don't come the innocent with me, Hetty Lawson. I know you like the fellas too. Aren't you seeing Dirk tonight?'

Hetty smiled at the mention of his name. 'He's picking me up and we're going for a walk along the river. Are you sure you don't mind being alone with Hilda?'

Elsie shook her head. 'I'll read to her, she likes that.'

'Sometimes I think you get on better with her than I do,' Hetty said.

Elsie looked at her. 'I know it's not easy living with her, Hetty. She put you through hell for years, always treating you second best to Dan. Finding out that she's not your mum, well, I understand how hard it must be.'

'Do you? I'm not sure I understand it myself,' Hetty said quietly.

'She's an old lady who's not well, and I'm happy to look after her and that's that,' Elsie said firmly. She patted Hetty's hand. 'Let me look after Hilda and you can think about what you're going to wear to meet Dirk tonight. You can borrow my red skirt if you like.'

Hetty laughed. 'I don't have the confidence or the wiggle in my hips that your red skirt deserves. Only you could wear it.'

'True,' Elsie said dreamily. She tapped her forehead. 'I wasn't blessed with much up here, but at least I've got my figure. That's what Aunt Jean used to say. Oh, I hope there's a letter from her when I get home. I miss her since she moved to London.'

But when the girls arrived home, there were no letters from London and Elsie's bottom lip shot out in a sulk. There was a letter for Hetty, however, and her heart dropped at the sight of the familiar army-issue envelope. It was from Bob.

Chapter Five

Hetty stuffed the letter in her coat pocket. Out of sight, out of mind, for now. She'd read it later, after she'd cooked tea with Elsie and been for her walk with Dirk. The thought of him put a smile on her face. It had been days since she'd since him, as he was busy at Elisabeth-ville now the Belgians were leaving. Many of the single men had already left, travelling by train to Hull then by ship to Belgium. However, Dirk had volunteered to help others pack, wanting to spend as much time as possible with Hetty before he left too. It was a parting that Hetty dreaded, as the two of them had grown very close.

She popped her head around the door of the front room, where Hilda lay in bed. Elsie was already there, propping pillows at Hilda's back, then setting the fire in the hearth. Even though the days were getting warmer now that spring was here, Hilda complained she was cold, and the coal fire was lit as soon as the girls returned home. Hilda was a small woman, and thin, all skin and bones, with sparse grey hair.

'Oh, you're back, are you?' she huffed from her bed

when she saw Hetty. Hetty let Hilda's irate tone wash over her; it couldn't hurt her any more.

One drunken night after news had reached Hilda that her beloved son had been killed at war, she'd revealed the truth to Hetty about who she really was. Hetty had always thought of Hilda as her mum; an uncaring, cruel mum, with never a good word for Hetty but loving words for Dan. She had always been made to feel that she wasn't good enough and could never do anything right. Now she knew the truth: that Hilda was her aunt, forced to take her in as a baby after her real mum had died. She had tried her best to understand the hardships that Hilda had endured as a young woman, left to look after her sister's child, and to forgive her for the way she'd treated her. But there was a distance between them that she didn't think could ever mend. Elsie did much of the work where Hilda was concerned, and Hetty was happy to let her. In return, Hilda spoke to Elsie with kindness and respect, whereas she treated Hetty as sternly as ever.

'I suppose you'll be out with your foreign fella tonight!' she barked in Hetty's direction.

Hetty bent to help Elsie with the fire, laying sticks on top of paper before putting a shovelful of coal on top. 'If that's your way of asking if I'm meeting my boyfriend, Dirk, then yes, I am,' she replied evenly.

'It's all wrong,' Hilda sniffed. 'Local girls shouldn't be courting the Belgiums.'

'Belgians,' Hetty muttered under her breath. 'How many times do I have to tell you? And there's nothing wrong with local girls courting them. Only bigots like you think there is.'

'What?' Hilda yelled. 'What's that you're calling me?'

'Nothing,' Hetty mumbled. 'I'll go and cook tea.'

She and Elsie exchanged a smile as Elsie sat by Hilda's bed. Hetty left the room, and as she turned to close the door, she saw Hilda take Elsie's hand.

'Now then, Elsie love. Tell me all about your day.'

Hetty walked into the hall, where her coat hung on its hook with the letter in its pocket. She sighed and shook her head. 'Oh, Bob. Why do you keep writing?' she whispered.

She walked to the coat and ran her fingers over the pocket. She was tempted to read his words there and then, for the sooner she did, the sooner she'd be able to throw the letter on the fire and pretend it had never arrived. She was brought out of her reverie by a knock at the door.

'I'll get it,' she called to Elsie.

She opened the door and was both surprised and pleased to see Dirk standing there. He leaned forward and kissed her on her cheek.

'Hey, I wasn't expecting you until later,' she said.

From behind his back he produced a bouquet of wild flowers.

'For me?' she said, stunned. 'They're beautiful.'

She looked into his piercing blue eyes. He was a slim man who wore a smart black suit with an unusually wide collar. None of the local boys ever wore such a fancy suit. He was kind and polite and treated her in a way that made her feel special, on top of the world.

'They were being thrown out of the village today as people move out. I didn't want them to go to waste. I hope you don't mind that they were not picked especially for you.'

Hetty took the colourful bouquet and stood to one

side, allowing him to enter the house. 'I don't mind at all, they're gorgeous.'

Dirk nodded towards Hilda's room. 'How is she today?'

Hetty gave a wry smile. 'Irascible as ever.'

He hesitated. 'What is this word... irascible?' he asked in his heavy accent.

'Well, you should know Hilda by now. It means she's quick tempered, angry, snappy.'

'Ah, then she's on good form, as you say here.' He laughed. 'Should I knock at her door to ask how she is?'

Hetty gently pulled him away. 'No, she'll not thank you for it. Elsie's with her. It's probably best if you leave them alone.'

In the kitchen, she went to the pantry and found an empty jar to use as a vase. She filled it with water and placed the flowers on the kitchen table.

'How pretty,' she said, admiring them. 'Please, Dirk, take a seat. Would you like to stay for tea? Elsie and I bought ham on the way home. It's coming down in price now. It's such a relief. And there are potatoes. Then we've a tin of best toffee to share.'

But Dirk remained standing. 'I am afraid that I can't stay.'

'But I thought we were going for a walk,' she said, dismayed.

'I need to go back to work.' He stepped forward and held Hetty's hands. 'Things are chaotic at Elisabethville with people leaving. Families need help packing. Children need supervising. I have to manage rotas for the train passengers, give out tickets for journeys by sea. It's never-ending. I must work tonight, for another ship sails in the morning from Hull.'

Hetty let go of his hands. Oh, she knew she was being selfish, but for days she'd been looking forward to seeing Dirk again. She wanted to share news about her life at the toffee factory and her job at Lumley Castle. She sank into a chair and Dirk knelt in front of her and took her hands again.

'Please don't be sad.'

Just then, the kitchen door was flung open and Elsie walked in. 'Oh, pardon me for intruding!' she cried when she saw the scene. She gave Hetty a cheeky wink. 'Crikey, look at him on bended knee. I hope he's popping the question!' She backed out quickly and closed the door.

Hetty was mortified by Elsie's remark and her face flushed red. She looked away from Dirk, unable to face him, embarrassed by what had happened. However, Dirk gently laid his fingers against her cheek and turned her face to his.

'Your friend is never subtle,' he said softly.

'And she'll never change,' Hetty replied. 'I'm sorry about what she said.'

Dirk lifted her hand to his lips. They both stood, then he wrapped his arms around her.

'My Hetty. I will return soon, and we will take the walk I promised. There is much to tell you about Elisabethville.'

'And about going home?' she said softly.

'I'm afraid so. The village will be empty within weeks. But before everyone leaves, there will be one final dance this weekend. The village will throw open its doors to everyone around; all the locals will be invited. Everyone will come. Then all that remains will be for me to deal with the houses and buildings. I have volunteered to stay until the very end. I'm involved in the administration work needed in handing the place over to the district council. But after that...'

His voice faltered, and they stood with their arms around each other, struggling to keep their emotions in check. When they heard a cough behind the kitchen door, they moved apart.

'Come in, Elsie,' Hetty said. She dabbed at her eyes with a handkerchief.

'Sorry to interrupt again, Hetty, but I'm starving, and Hilda needs more tea. Any sign of our ham and potatoes cooking yet?'

Hetty looked at the empty pans on the hearth and a pang of guilt ran through her. 'I haven't even boiled the water,' she confessed.

'Then I must go and let you work,' Dirk said.

Hetty followed him along the hallway, where the door to Hilda's room was open.

'Who's out there? Who is it?' Hilda yelled.

Dirk stepped forward to stand in the doorway. 'It is Dirk, Mrs Lawson. I am here to see Hetty.'

'Oh. It's you,' Hilda said dully, then she turned over in bed so that her back was to Dirk.

'Don't let her upset you,' Hetty whispered.

'I could say the same to you too,' Dirk replied. He kissed her again, this time lightly on the lips as he gently held her face in his hands. 'I will see you soon, Hetty,' he said.

And with that, he was gone. Hetty couldn't help feeling that this was the start of the end for them.

Later that night, after tea, which Elsie cooked to perfection, the two girls chatted in the kitchen by the fire.

Conversation turned to Jet, the little black dog that had once lived with them.

'I miss him sometimes,' Hetty said.

'I don't miss the mess he used to bring in,' Elsie said.

'I wonder where he ran off to?'

Elsie shrugged. 'As long as he stays away, that's all I'm bothered about.'

Hetty yawned and said goodnight, then took her letter upstairs to read in the privacy of her room. Taking a deep breath, she ripped open the envelope. It was another update from Bob on his location. He had arrived in England at last and was on the south coast, where his unit would be stationed for a few weeks before travelling north. The more she read, the worse she felt. For there in Bob's spidery handwriting was his promise, again, to propose as soon as he saw her. His words were of undying love.

She bit her lip to stop herself from crying, for she'd never once given him any indication that she felt the same way about him. When he'd gone off to war, she'd waved him goodbye with a heavy heart, much like a sister saying farewell to her brother or a good friend. But she'd never loved him in the way that he now professed to love her. She'd written to him over a year ago to end their relationship, once she'd met Dirk, but it seemed her letter had never reached him. Then one stormy night his sister had turned up to deliver the news that she'd written to him to tell him about Hetty and Dirk – and that was the worst thing of all. For in his letter to Hetty, he said he forgave her and would let nothing and no one stand in the way of him making her his bride. Hetty threw the letter to the floor.

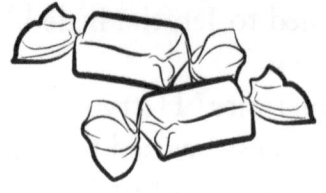

Chapter Six

The next morning Elsie was cooking breakfast when Hetty walked into the kitchen, dressed for her work at Lumley Castle, where she worked in the kitchen as a skivvy: cleaning, scrubbing and serving food. Elsie herself was still in her nightgown, not needing to dress early as the factory was closed that day. Instead she'd tend to Hilda, do the shopping and clean the house.

'A dance?' Her eyes lit up when Hetty told her what Dirk had said the night before. 'Tell me more. You know I love dancing.'

'Well, Elisabethville is throwing open its doors for everyone to join the last dance before the village closes for ever,' Hetty said. 'It's this weekend. Would you like to come?'

'Course I'd like to come. I'll wear my red skirt. I hope there's some decent fellas left to dance with. They can't all have gone home yet.'

'Don't you want to go with Stan?' Hetty asked.

Elsie turned away and began poking a piece of bacon in a pan. 'I suppose I could ask him,' she said, but her tone suggested she'd rather not.

'He'll be upset if you go without him,' Hetty continued.

'But I'll feel trapped if he's with me all night.' Elsie kept her face turned away.

'He thinks the world of you,' Hetty said.

Elsie said nothing, so Hetty changed the subject.

'Dirk told me last night there's only a few weeks to go before he has to leave.'

This time Elsie turned and faced her friend. 'I'm sorry, love,' she said.

Hetty patted her on the shoulder. 'That's why I think you should give Stan a chance. He's here, he adores you and he's not about to disappear to another country. You're lucky.'

There was silence between them for a few moments.

'Did Bob's letter say anything new?' Elsie asked gently.

Hetty bit her lip and gazed out of the window. 'It said what his letters always say: that he'll be back soon to marry me. I'm going to have to break his heart when I see him again. I can't marry someone I don't love. I won't.'

At home in the Deanery, Anne was taking breakfast with her daughter. Edith brought toast to the table with a fresh pot of tea. Anne watched as the housekeeper bustled between kitchen and dining room. When Edith placed a plate on the table, Anne lightly touched her hand.

'How would I ever cope without you?' she said.

Edith smiled kindly, making lines crinkle around her eyes. Her grey hair was swept into a bun. 'I'm just doing my job, Mrs Jack.'

Anne looked around the dining room. 'Edith, have you seen my blue brooch? I seem to have mislaid it. I remember taking it off in my bedroom last night, but I can't find it this morning. Not that I need to wear it today, of course. I'll be visiting William's parents with Dinah. But I'd be grateful if you could keep an eye out for it when you clean the house.'

'Yes, Mrs Jack, I'll be sure to look for it. It can't have gone far.'

Anne changed the subject. 'Have you heard there's to be a dance in the Belgian village this weekend?'

'Yes, Mrs Jack. Talk of it is all over town. It'll be the first time locals have been inside the place. I hear there'll be Chinese lanterns in the community hall. It should be a spectacle to remember for ever.'

Edith scooped up Dinah's used bowl and spoon and walked back to the kitchen. Anne doubted she could persuade William to attend the dance, as dancing was one of his least favourite things. Plus there'd been tension between the two of them since she'd confronted him at work about the factory's debts. She felt hurt, angry and upset, not only at the dire situation the factory was in, but that William had kept the truth from her. It was fair to say that relations between them were frosty.

'Dada?' Dinah cried, as if reading her thoughts.

'Daddy is at the factory, darling,' Anne replied. He worked there even on the two days each week when the factory was closed. Today he'd be running through figures, balance sheets, accounts, desperately trying to work out ways to pay off the debt. He blamed himself for getting the factory into such a dire predicament, and told Anne he needed to get to the bottom of what had gone wrong before he could turn things around. 'And I will, I swear,' he'd added.

Anne wished she felt as confident, but she feared the debt was too deep to climb out of without substantial investment. She recalled the time when she'd first met William. He was engaged at the time to beautiful, wealthy Lucinda Dalton. Lucinda's father Bertram was all set to invest in the factory, but when William called off his engagement after he'd fallen for Anne, Dalton swore he'd never forgive him for the shame he'd brought to his family and withdrew his financial support. The last Anne had heard of Lucinda was that she'd married into landed gentry on the Devon coast.

She shook her head to remove thoughts of the Daltons, consigning them to where they belonged, in the past. She turned her attention to Dinah instead and cut up a slice of toast Edith had brought. Something outside the dining-room window caught Dinah's eye, and she waved her chubby hand. Anne saw the postman walking down the garden path. What a relief it was now that war was over to have regular deliveries again. Anne waved at the postman too, then waited for Edith to collect the mail and bring it to the dining room.

Efficient as ever, Edith brought the mail straight away and laid it on the table. Dinah reached out to touch the letters, and Anne moved them away from her.

'Thank you, Edith,' she said.

'More toast, Mrs Jack?' the housekeeper asked.

Anne shook her head. She picked up the mail and sorted it into two piles – one for herself and one for William. There wasn't much for William, as most of his post went to the factory, where Meg dealt with it. For Anne there was a letter from someone whose handwriting she didn't recognise. There was no return address, no indication as to where it was from. She tore open the envelope and unfolded the sheet of paper inside, her eyes jumping to the last line. Her heart lurched when she saw the name 'Mrs Matthews'. This was the woman who years ago had bought her baby son.

The letter was short, to the point. It simply said that everyone in the family was fine and well. *Everyone*. Her gaze lingered on the word, her legs turning weak. This was the letter she'd never let herself dream she'd ever receive. The boy's new parents had taken him to live with them in Scotland. Anne had never expected to hear from them, but here it was, in her hand. Proof that her boy was alive and well and – she glanced at the letter again – *fine and in good health*.

She quickly folded the sheet of paper. No one must see this. Not Edith, or William. No one. William had no clue she had a son. If he had known she'd fallen pregnant before they'd met, that she'd given birth to a child she couldn't look after because she was unwed, he would have judged her badly. Many times he'd spoken critically about unmarried girls at the factory who'd fallen pregnant and had to leave work. He was disparaging of them, and Anne knew she wouldn't be sitting in the Deanery now, married and wealthy, if she'd ever revealed the truth. She had to protect her past in order to forge her future.

She reached out and stroked Dinah's hair, then glanced out of the dining-room door, terrified in case Edith was watching but relieved to see she was not. Sliding the letter under her pile of mail, she sank back in her seat and tried to help Dinah with her toast and cup of milk, but this time her hands were shaking. She glanced around the room again. She felt unsettled after reading the letter, on top of losing her brooch. Where on earth had it gone?

Later that week, on the night of the dance at Elisabethville, Elsie walked slowly down Front Street. She'd reluctantly, and only at Hetty's insistence, arranged to meet Stan outside the Lambton Arms to head to the dance together. The plan was that they'd take the bus the short distance. The Lambton Arms was run by Jim and Cathy Ireland, who had taken Elsie in after she'd been beaten by Frankie. Elsie was still married to Frankie, as she couldn't afford a divorce and had no clue how to go about getting one, though she'd reverted to using her maiden name of Cooper, never his surname.

Standing outside the pub waiting for Stan, Elsie felt nervous in case Frankie should wander past. However, she took heart that Front Street was busy with people walking to the pubs, cinema and dance hall. How wonderful it was to see folk enjoying themselves again. She watched as two sweethearts snuggled against each other, whispering and giggling. Oh, how she wanted to be part of a loving couple like that.

'Evening, Elsie,' said a voice. It was Stan, standing tall and proud, dressed in a dark jacket and flat cap, which he whipped from his head and held at his heart as he addressed her. 'You're looking gorgeous as always and that's a lovely skirt,' he said, leaning in for a kiss.

Elsie turned her head, so that his lips fell on her cheek rather than her mouth, and gave him a smile. 'You look smart too, Stan,' she said. It was true, he looked every inch the gentleman, just not the one she often dreamed of. She wanted excitement and glamour where Stan was dependable, ordinary and nice. Elsie wanted more than just nice. Stan offered her his arm and she took it as they walked to the bus stop.

At the same time, unseen by Elsie and Stan, two men walked into the Lambton Arms. One was Mr Burl from the toffee factory. The other man's face was half hidden in the shadow of his wide-brimmed hat, and despite the warm evening air, his coat collar was turned up too.

Chapter Seven

Two days later, Anne and William were eating breakfast while Dinah sat on the rug playing with a doll. Anne was dressed in her blue skirt and cream blouse, ready to head to the factory. It promised to be another busy day, with papers to prepare for the emergency board meeting. She wished she could give responsibility for this task to Meg, but she didn't trust her to do it correctly. Instead, she'd work with and supervise her.

As well as the board meeting, there was something else on Anne's mind. Something that had caused her a sleepless night. She buttered a slice of toast, spread it with strawberry jam, cut it into four and handed it on a plate to Dinah. Then she sat up straight and looked at her husband. She still hadn't forgiven him for hiding the truth about the factory debts, and relations between them were still at odds. However, she knew she had to speak up.

'William, I have a confession,' she said.

He looked at her, startled. 'A confession?' he said. He laid down his newspaper.

Anne's hand flew to the collar of her blouse. 'It's my

brooch, the blue one you gave me when we were courting,' she began hesitantly. 'I appear to have lost it.'

William's face dropped. 'Lost it? Are you sure? Has Edith helped you look for it?'

'Yes, we turned the place upside down yesterday. We took the cushions from the sofa, looked under the beds. We even scoured Dinah's room in case she had taken it and hidden it. But it's nowhere to be found.'

He picked up his newspaper again, as if the matter of her missing brooch was of no concern. 'I'm sure it'll turn up. Is it possible you could have lost it at the factory?' he asked.

Anne shook her head. 'No, I distinctly remember unpinning it at home, in our bedroom, when I undressed. I placed it on the dressing table as I always do. But when I went to look for it, it was no longer there. I'm distraught. You know how much it means to me, and I know how expensive it was.'

William laid down his newspaper once more and glared at her. 'How the devil do you know the cost?'

A wry smile played around Anne's lips. 'Because the receipt was in your office. When I worked as your secretary, I was filing papers and came across it. I put it to one side with your personal papers, so it was never mistaken as a factory bill.' She narrowed her eyes. 'You should know by now that I always know what's going on. Well . . . usually. I'm still very upset that you kept the truth from me about the factory debts.'

William refilled their cups from the teapot, then cleared his throat. 'Dear Anne, how many times do I need to apologise and explain?' She detected a tone of exasperation in his voice.

'How many times?' she said, affronted. She realised her own voice was raised as anger surged, and corrected herself, not wanting to upset Dinah. Neither did she want Edith to overhear them arguing. She carried on in a calm, more measured manner. 'If you had told me right from the start how bad things were, you would have nothing to apologise for. I am not just your wife, William, I run the factory with you. You *must* tell me what's going on. How am I to support you at work, and at home, if I don't know what's happening?'

He reached across the table for her hand, but she pulled it back sharply. 'Anne, dear, please let's not argue. Things are hard enough with the factory in such a precarious position.'

'A position that some of your staff knew about, but not me. Don't you understand how hurtful that was?'

'Anne, my darling...' he began, but he stopped short when the dining-room door opened and Edith walked in.

'More tea? More toast?' she asked.

'No thank you, Edith,' Anne said, turning to her. 'I don't suppose there's any sign of my brooch around the house this morning?'

Was she mistaken, or did Edith's gaze quickly flicker to William?

'No, Mrs Jack. I will keep looking.' Edith bustled from the room.

'I'm sorry, Anne. Truly,' William said, looking sheepish.

Anne softened when she saw the sad look on his face. 'And I'm sorry for losing the most precious thing you've ever given me,' she said, touching the neckline of her blouse.

From her spot on the rug, Dinah began singing. Anne laughed out loud.

'That should be the second most precious thing you've ever given me,' she said. 'I think our daughter is reminding us of her place in our lives.'

William dabbed at the side of his mouth with a napkin before leaving the table to sit beside Dinah on the rug. He picked up her doll and pretended to feed it toast, which made the little girl squeal with excitement. Anne watched her husband and daughter playing together, enjoying the moment, lost in her love for them both. Then she remembered the letter she'd received from Mrs Matthews, and a lump rose in her throat as she thought about her son. She'd hidden the letter upstairs in the bureau in her personal study, somewhere she knew William would never look. The study was her room, her sanctuary. Even Edith wasn't allowed inside.

She caught William's gaze and smiled, while inside she wondered if the guilt of keeping her secret would ease over the years. And then, with a lurch, she realised how easily he had kept the secret of the factory debts from her. The factory was their life. It wasn't just their livelihood. It was bigger than both of them. It meant so much to the people of the town. Men and women depended on it for wages. Suppliers up and down the country relied on it to keep their businesses afloat. And yet her own husband had hidden from her how severe the situation was. If she hadn't discovered the truth, when would he have told her? She tried to force another smile.

After breakfast, William gathered his briefcase, kissed Dinah and called a cheery goodbye to Edith. He stepped outside and Anne heard the car engine roar into life. The engine continued ticking over as she hugged and kissed Dinah before handing her over to Edith.

'Goodbye, my angel,' she said, waving to her daughter.

Dinah waved her little hand in return, then blew a kiss to Anne as she walked to the front door.

Outside, she was about to head to the driver's side of the car, but was stunned to see William there. 'I thought I might drive again,' she sulked as she walked to the passenger side instead.

'And I thought we'd travel to work more quickly if I drove,' William replied, engaging the gears. 'This is no time to dilly-dally. It's all systems go at the factory if we're to save the place.'

He pulled the car away from the Deanery and onto the main road for the short drive to the toffee factory. It was when they'd almost reached Front Street that Anne slapped her hand against her forehead.

'I've forgotten my briefcase!' she cried. 'Turn the car around, William. I must return home.'

But William carried on. 'Don't be silly, dear.'

Anne shot him a look. 'Silly? I can't go to work without my papers. I read them all night and made notes for Meg to type.'

William brought the car to a halt by the side of the road. 'If you want to run home, dear, that's up to you. But I'm carrying on to the factory. It needs me right now.'

'And I need my briefcase right now,' Anne replied tersely. 'Are you choosing the factory over me?'

He turned to her with a resigned look on his face. 'Anne, please. I must get to work. If you want your briefcase, it's only a short walk.'

Anne was affronted. 'So you're not going to turn the car around and drive me?'

'No, dear.'

She took a deep breath, opened the car door and stepped onto the pavement, slamming the door behind her. As William drove away, she straightened her shoulders, aware that passers-by on Front Street had seen her leave her husband's car. As wife of the toffee factory owner, she often came under scrutiny in the small town.

'Good morning,' she said politely to a gawping woman.

'Good morning, Mrs Jack,' the woman replied, before scuttling away.

Aware that more people were looking at her now, Anne held her head high and walked on. Her face was burning from the humiliation she felt at William dropping her off at the side of the road as if he was delivering a box of toffee to a shop. She walked faster, taking longer strides, as her mind whirled with thoughts about his odd behaviour. She knew he was worried about the factory, but now he was acting out of character, and that made her concerned. Since the day they'd met, they'd never exchanged a harsh word, and she didn't want the factory debts to drive a wedge between them now.

As she walked, she spotted Elsie and Hetty on the other side of the road, heads together, gossiping. Her heart sank and she hoped they wouldn't notice her. They'd want to know why she wasn't being driven by her husband in his car, and she was in no mood to explain. However, her plan to pass by unobserved didn't work. The two girls crossed the road and headed towards her.

'Morning, Anne. What are you doing on the street? Shouldn't you be in your office by now?' Hetty asked.

Anne could feel her face growing red under her friends' scrutiny. 'I left something at home, and need to return to fetch it,' she said quickly, trying to inch away, hoping the pair would pick up the hint that she needed to go.

'Couldn't Mr Jack drive you?' Elsie asked, as forward as ever.

'He's rather tied up with business this morning,' Anne replied. 'Look, girls, I'm sorry, but I really must dash.' She peeled away and hurried on.

When she reached the Deanery, she pushed open the front door. 'Edith!' she called as she headed into the hallway, but there was no reply. There was also no sign of Edith or Dinah. She walked into the kitchen, Edith's domain, but she wasn't there. She glanced out of the kitchen window, thinking she must be in the garden with Dinah, but she wasn't. She ran up the stairs two at a time.

'Edith!' she called.

It was Dinah who replied. 'Mama!' the girl called excitedly.

Anne walked towards her daughter's voice; it appeared to be coming from her personal study.

There was a noise from within – a scuffle, the sound of scraping, as if a drawer had been closed – and Edith appeared at the study door, blocking Anne's entry.

'Mrs Jack,' she said, looking flustered. 'I wasn't expecting you.'

Anne peered over the housekeeper's shoulder into the room. Dinah was standing there, reaching her arms up. Anne bent low, picked up her daughter and hugged her tightly. Then she fixed Edith with a steely gaze.

'What are you doing in here?'

Chapter Eight

'I was searching for your missing brooch,' Edith replied.

Dinah began wriggling in Anne's arms, so she set her carefully back on the floor then held her hand to stop her from wandering. When she looked at Edith, she saw that her face had flushed pink, which wasn't like the housekeeper at all. She rarely lost her composure. Edith stepped forward, but Anne held her nerve and didn't move out of her way.

'But I've already searched in here, Edith,' she said. 'You know that; I told you.'

'Yes, Mrs Jack, but—'

Anne held up her hand, and Edith took a step back and dropped her gaze.

'Also, this room is my private study, as you well know. I am not happy to find you inside it.'

'I'm sorry, Mrs Jack, I was only trying to help,' Edith muttered.

Anne moved away from the door and indicated for Edith to leave. 'I am sure there are chores you can be getting on with in the kitchen.' The housekeeper hurried from the room.

Anne looked around her study and was relieved to see that nothing appeared to be out of place. Her personal letters and stationery were positioned just so, next to her framed pictures of Dinah and William, and one of her late parents. When she heard Edith's footsteps disappear downstairs, she opened the drawer in her bureau where she'd hidden the letter from Mrs Matthews. Her heart skipped with relief when she saw it was still there, tucked in the pages of a notebook. She placed the notebook at the back of the drawer in case Edith pried again, then sank into the chair in the corner and brought Dinah to her knee.

'Mama!' her daughter cried, delighted by her unexpected visit.

'My darling girl,' Anne murmured against the child's soft skin. She stayed there a few moments, looking around the study, trying again to notice if anything had been moved. She wondered if Edith had been telling the truth about looking for the brooch. There'd been something shifty in her manner that had made Anne feel uncomfortable. Then she shook her head to dismiss the idea. Edith was trustworthy, of course she was. She'd worked for William since before Anne had met him and had been the soul of discretion since. They'd never had any reason to complain.

'I'm just feeling fractious after my run-in with your father, that's all,' she muttered to Dinah. She sighed heavily, trying to release some of the tension in her shoulders, then stood and picked up her briefcase from a corner of the room. She and Dinah descended the stairs together, holding hands.

'Edith?' she called.

Edith bustled from the kitchen. 'Yes, Mrs Jack?'

Dinah took hold of the housekeeper's hand. The child was now holding hands with both Anne and Edith, forming a bond. Anne smiled.

'I'm heading to work now, with my briefcase this time. Please remember our house rules about no access to my study. I'd ask you to respect my request, no matter what it is you're looking for.'

Edith raised her gaze and looked deep into Anne's eyes. 'I apologise again, Mrs Jack.'

Anne turned to walk to the front door, and Edith followed with Dinah.

'Mrs Jack? I understand it'll be four for dinner tonight, is that correct?'

Anne spun around. 'Four? Why on earth would it be four?' she said, confused.

'Mr Jack told me there are two men from the factory joining you this evening,' Edith replied.

This was shock news for Anne, but she was determined not to let Edith know that her husband hadn't consulted her. She felt irritated and angry with him all over again. Why had he not told her? She reached for the door to steady herself.

'Ah yes, of course, the dinner,' she said, as if it was something that had just slipped her mind.

'I plan to cook liver and onions, then a lemon tart for dessert,' Edith said.

'Very good, Edith, thank you,' Anne said, keeping her voice even. She turned to kiss Dinah, then stepped out into the fresh air.

She felt her legs begin to shake as she walked along the street. She headed to a lane away from Front Street, away from people and buses on the road. She didn't want to be seen; she needed time to think. William was keeping too much from her. First it was the factory debts and the meeting with the finance team. Now it was a dinner for two factory men at their home. Whom had he invited and why? He'd never brought anyone from the factory to their house before.

She couldn't think straight. Her mind went from William to Edith, from the factory to her study. She thought about her missing brooch, then leaving William's car that morning in full view of passers-by. She knew she had to speak to him and clear the air, for she couldn't bear such discord. It was upsetting, not just at work but in her marriage too. She hurried along the lane with her briefcase in hand until the chimney of the toffee factory came into view.

She strode through the iron gates, intending to head to William's office. But as she walked across the cobbled yard, a woman's voice called her name. She stopped, shielded her eyes from the sun with her hand and saw Elsie walking towards her. Her friend was carrying a large box. When she bent down to place it on the ground, Anne couldn't miss how her overall strained against her ample hips. Mrs Perkins had already spoken to Anne to complain about Elsie's overall, which was shorter, tighter and had fewer buttons to cover her bosom than those worn by the other girls. She had asked Anne to have a word with Elsie, because anything that she herself said on the subject was ignored. However, now was not the time. Anne was desperate to head indoors and see William, yet Elsie was animated and ready to talk. Her dark eyes were shining and there was a smile on her face.

'Isn't it wonderful news?' she said.

Anne glanced at the door that led to the reception area. She inched forward, not wanting to be rude but needing to get inside.

'It's so exciting!' Elsie cried.

'What is? I'm afraid you've lost me,' Anne said impatiently.

Elsie looked askance. 'I can't believe you don't know. There's to be a celebration; a peace celebration. It's going to be held here in Chester-le-Street, in the grounds of Lumley Castle. There'll be soldiers marching and people cheering at a party to commemorate peace at last.'

This was news that cheered Anne's heart.

'All the towns and cities are organising their own celebrations,' Elsie continued.

Anne thought for a moment. 'Did Hetty tell you the news? I know she works at the castle two days a week. Did she find out about it there?'

Elsie looked at her oddly. 'No, it wasn't Hetty who told me. It was Mr Jack. He told all of us just now. He walked into the slab room first thing this morning and announced it. Then he went to the sugar-boiling room, the dispatch room and everywhere in between to tell everyone the good news.' She leaned in close and spoke in a low voice. 'Do you mean you really didn't know? Mr Jack didn't tell you?'

Anne felt deflated. 'No, he didn't tell me. There's a lot he's not telling me at the moment,' she muttered through gritted teeth. 'Look, I'm sorry, Elsie, but I really must head inside. I've got a mountain of work to do.'

Elsie bent down to pick up the box, giving Anne an unwarranted glimpse of her cleavage.

'Elsie, can I give you some advice?'

The girl stood, balancing the box against her hip.

'Do your buttons up, love, before you get into more trouble with Mrs Perkins.'

Elsie walked off with the box as Anne headed indoors.

'Morning, Jacob!' she called to the man seated behind a desk in the reception area.

The room was open and square, with a high ceiling. Mr Jack had spared no expense in fitting it out with the best furnishings the factory could afford. It was the first room that visitors saw, and making a good impression was important. Especially when those visitors were prospective toffee buyers for the wholesale market. On the wall behind Jacob's desk was a clock, which was always correct, much like Jacob himself. He kept the reception neat, ordered and clean.

'Good morning, Mrs Jack,' he replied.

Anne broke stride to head towards him. 'Jacob, how many times do I need to tell you? Please call me Anne.'

He looked up from the ledger. 'I've struggled with calling you that since you married Mr Jack. The Jack surname commands respect.'

'And I'm your friend, so you can call me Anne.'

Jacob gave a rare smile. 'Isn't it grand news about the peace celebration? I'm going to take Meg,' he added proudly.

Anne gritted her teeth. 'Yes, it's very good news. Did Mr Jack tell you about it this morning?'

'Yes, Mrs . . . I mean, Anne. He told me as soon as he arrived at the factory.'

This was another stab at Anne's heart. Another secret

kept from her when William could easily have told her overnight or on their way to work that morning.

Jacob returned to his work and Anne headed to the door in the corner of the room that led to a narrow hallway. William's office was off to one side. The door was open and she walked inside.

Chapter Nine

William looked up from the paperwork he was reading at his desk and seemed surprised to see Anne there.

'Where's Meg?' she asked.

'Hello, dear. I've just returned from doing my rounds at the factory. What's that about Meg? Oh yes, I've sent her to oversee a shipment that's going to Elisabethville so the departing Belgians can take toffee overseas. It might help to keep their spirits up on the long journey. It was Mr Gerard's idea, and another genius one, of course.'

Mr Gerard was the factory's creative manager and one of the longest-serving employees. He'd worked for William's father Albert, when he set up the toffee empire. Although he was old and his hair had turned white, there was always a glint in his eye that suggested that while his body might be failing, his mind was still sharp. Anne admired and respected him, and they got on well.

She positioned herself at the side of William's desk. 'Will Meg be away for long?'

'I should think a good half-hour at least. Why? Did you want her to do some work for you?' William looked at her closely. 'What is it, dear? You're a little flushed.'

She walked around the desk and sat in the chair opposite her husband. Then she set her briefcase on the carpet, straightened her back and looked him straight in the eye. 'Why didn't you tell me about the peace celebration? I've just found out about it from Elsie Cooper.'

'Elsie Cooper, yes, a most attractive girl. I often wonder if we should have used her likeness on our Lady Tina toffee tins instead of Hetty Lawson,' he mused.

Anne began to grow irritated. 'William!' she snapped.

He almost jumped in his seat.

'Please listen to me, dear. Why are you being so secretive?' she asked more gently, trying to coax him, to handle him the best way she knew. 'First it was the debts—'

'Keep your voice down,' William said. He stood, walked to the door and closed it. When he returned to his seat, Anne continued, counting on her fingers.

'Then I found out from Edith that you've invited two men from the factory to dinner at our home. Which men, and why? And thirdly, you kept the news from me about the town's peace celebration. And this morning, you refused to turn the car around and drive me home when I realised I'd forgotten my briefcase. You're acting so strangely. I'm your wife, for heaven's sake. I deserve to know what's going on.'

William's hand flew to his blue bow tie, but he remained silent.

'Out with it!' she demanded.

When he eventually began to speak, he kept glancing at the office door. 'If Meg returns, we must end this conversation immediately, do you understand?'

Anne nodded, and he carried on.

'I've already explained about the debts, dear. I didn't

want to upset you. I was in turmoil when I found out the truth. I still am. There's no clear way yet of how we can afford to pay them off. It'll be discussed at the emergency board meeting.'

Anne crossed her arms. 'And that's another thing you didn't consult me on, arranging the emergency meeting. What's going on? Why are you keeping things to yourself?'

William stood and began to pace. Anne knew this wasn't a good sign. She waited for him to speak.

'If we can't pay the debts, the factory will have to close.'

She gasped in horror, and he walked to her and took her hands in his. His usual cheerful expression was gone and in its place was a deep sadness.

'Don't you see, Anne? It's all my fault. If the factory closes, it'll be because of me. I am the owner. I should have kept on top of things. I daren't think what my father will say. He gave his life to building this factory. That's why I've been secretive, as you call it, although I like to think I've been protecting you from the worst. I'm at my wits' end and I don't know what to do.'

Anne looked into his eyes and gently squeezed his hands. 'Oh, William . . . let me help. Please, I beg you. We're in this together, please keep me informed.'

He thought for a moment. 'Did I really not tell you about the peace celebration?'

She shook her head. 'No, dear.'

'Then I apologise. I sincerely thought I had. I know I meant to tell you as it was such good news and we need cheering up with everything that's going on. It will be on the front page of the newspaper later today, then everyone in town will know. The mayor told me yesterday, late afternoon, and has asked for the factory to be involved. I'm not sure we can afford it, though. I need to speak to Mr Gerard and Mr Burl.' He looked at her sheepishly.

'What is it?' she said.

'They are the men coming to our home for dinner tonight. Oh, Anne, I'm sorry I didn't seek your approval. My head's in a spin, my mind is confused.'

'Yet you had the presence of mind to speak to Edith about it,' Anne said. She tried to keep the petulant tone from her voice. 'It hurts that you didn't mention it to me.'

'I know, dear and I can't apologise enough. We're going through unprecedented times. If we're not careful, this time next year the factory will be closed and toffee production finished for ever. I don't know whether I'm coming or going, whom I've spoken to or what I've said. I need clarity, focus. That's why I have to speak to my two closest allies, away from the factory, the office and prying eyes. You don't mind too much, do you?'

The thought of letting Mr Burl into her home filled Anne with horror. He was the last person she wanted to eat dinner with.

'Must we really invite that man to the house?' she said.

William nodded. 'I'm afraid so. We'll be speaking of matters that could lead to the factory closing down. It has to be somewhere we won't be overheard.'

Anne stood and brushed down her skirt, then picked up her briefcase. 'Then so be it, but don't expect me to be charming to him. You know we don't get along. And William, please confide in me from now on. I must be kept informed of what is going on. The factory is my livelihood as well as yours, and it's our daughter's future too.'

'Yes, dear,' William said sheepishly.

Anne kissed him on the cheek, then strode to the door. When she pulled it open, Meg was there, looking startled. Anne eyed her cautiously. Had she been eavesdropping?

Across town, at Elm Street, Hilda was alone in the house. She was in bed, coughing, her bad chest wheezing, and she was pale and weak. She kept falling in and out of sleep, and despite the warm spring day was wrapped in blankets and an eiderdown to keep herself warm. Occasionally her neighbour, Pearl, would call in to make a pot of tea and a bite to eat or set the coal fire going. So when there was a knock at the door, Hilda braced herself and called out.

'Come in, Pearl, the door's open.'

The door opened, and she heard footsteps in the hallway.

'My word, Pearl's got heavy boots on today,' she muttered. She struggled to pull herself up in bed, and got there eventually, with a pillow behind her back. She ran a hand through her straggly hair to try to make herself look decent before her friend entered the room. There was a heavy breath, then a voice, a man's voice.

'Hetty?'

Hilda's breath caught in her chest. She tried peering around the door to the hallway, but it was impossible from her position.

'Who's there?' she called. 'Is that you, Dirk? I don't want you in here! You know Hetty's at work.'

A shadow loomed into the room, then a man appeared. A man in a soldier's uniform. His trousers were tucked into long, thick socks and he wore army boots. His jacket was fastened at the collar, and large metal buttons ran down the front. There was something about his steel-grey eyes and gaunt face that Hilda thought familiar, but she couldn't place him. She pulled the eiderdown to her neck, afraid.

'Who is it? What do you want?' she hissed.

The man set his kitbag on the floor. 'Hilda? Is that really you?' he asked, taking a step towards her.

'Get away from me,' she yelled. Her chest complained about the outburst, and she began coughing again. The man rushed to her bed and knelt at her side.

'Hilda, don't be afraid.' He gave a warm smile. 'Don't you recognise me?'

She looked into his eyes, recognition slowly dawning. 'Bob?' she breathed.

He took her hand. 'Yes. It's me. I'm back.'

Hilda was shocked by his appearance. She reached out to touch his cheek and took in his long, drawn face and thin lips. There wasn't a spare ounce of fat on him.

He squeezed her hand. 'My unit returned to Chester-le-Street just an hour ago. I'm not fully discharged yet, but it won't be long before I am. A matter of weeks, they say. I came home as soon as I could with an advance party instead of lingering on the south coast.'

Hilda managed a smile. 'And you came straight here?' she said, confused. 'You should go home to your sister; she'll be desperate to see you.'

Bob pushed his shoulders back. 'My sister can wait. There's someone more important to see.'

Hilda relaxed a little and let the eiderdown drop from where she'd been gripping it under her chin. 'You mean Hetty, I suppose,' she said.

'Is she here?' Bob asked. He looked around the sparsely furnished room as if expecting Hetty to magically appear.

'No. She's at work, at the toffee factory.'

He indicated a chair in the corner of the room. 'May I?'

Hilda nodded her assent, and Bob brought the chair to her bedside. He sat down with his back erect and his feet squarely on the floor.

'Hilda, I need to ask you something,' he said.

'Go on,' she replied.

He placed his hands on his thighs and squared his shoulders. 'I'd like to ask for your blessing, and your consent, to marry your daughter.'

Hilda laid back against her pillow, taking in the news. Finally, in a quiet voice, she replied. 'There's something you should know, lad. The war has changed people, and Hetty and I have become more distant than ever. You don't need my consent to marry her; she does what she wants with her life.'

Bob frowned. 'Of course I need your consent. You're her mother. Is she looking after you well?'

'Her friend Elsie lives here. She looks after me now.'

Bob's brow furrowed. 'Elsie Cooper?' he spat.

Hilda nodded.

'But she's a tart!' he cried. 'You can't let your daughter run around with someone like her.'

'Elsie's a good girl, don't speak of her that way. Besides, there's more that you need to know.' She took a deep breath, which set her chest wheezing again. 'Bob, Hetty isn't my daughter. The truth of it came out when Dan died in the war.'

Bob hung his head and sat in silence for a few moments.

'I'm very sorry to hear about Dan,' he said eventually. 'We lost too many good men and boys.'

'I'd tread carefully where Hetty is concerned,' Hilda warned. 'She's not the girl you left behind. She's involved with a Belgian man.'

Bob closed his eyes and pressed his hands together. 'So it's true,' he muttered. 'My sister wrote and told me, but I didn't want to believe that my Hetty had met someone else.' He stood. 'I'm sorry for barging in like this, Hilda.'

'And I'm sorry you had to hear the truth from me. Hetty should have been the one to tell you.' Hilda offered him her hand. 'Take care, Bob. And good luck with your new life. Enjoy your family and friends. I don't expect we'll see you again.'

Bob's face clouded over. 'On the contrary, Hilda. I intend to do all I can to make Hetty see sense. I swore that she would be my bride, and I will not take no for an answer.'

And with that, he picked up his kitbag and walked out of the house.

Chapter Ten

At work in the slab room, Elsie leaned across the table to level the toffee. Hetty was at her side, both girls working quickly before the toffee cooled and turned hard.

'Would you like to sit out in the sunshine with me at dinner time?' Hetty asked.

Elsie shook her head. 'I can't. I promised Stan I'd meet him. He's been on at me for ages to have a chat. He says he's got something to say. I've put him off too many times and started feeling guilty, so I've finally agreed to see him. I wish I didn't have to, though.' She felt Hetty's gaze on her. 'Oh, don't look at me like that, Hetty Lawson,' she chided.

'Like what?' Hetty said, feigning surprise.

'Like you think you know what's best for me.' Elsie looked at her friend. 'I know Stan's a nice man, he's one of the most decent, kindest fellas I've met. But he's not exciting. You should know how that feels. You always used to complain that Bob was dull when you were courting him. Don't judge me. I know that Stan likes me, and I know I owe him a lot after what Frankie put me through. Back then, I couldn't think straight. That night when I walked to the river, if it hadn't been for Stan, I—'

Hetty gently laid her hand on Elsie's arm. 'You don't need to say any more. I remember what happened.'

'I wish I could forget,' Elsie said dully. 'And now I feel an obligation to him. Let's just say I wouldn't be here now if Stan hadn't turned up when he did. I wasn't myself; I didn't know what I was doing. He saved me and I was so grateful that at first I thought I was in love with him.'

Mrs Perkins appeared, and the girls concentrated on their work, smoothing the toffee. When the supervisor had moved on, they began talking again.

'But the more time I spend time with him and the closer we get, the more I think I'm missing out on something else,' Elsie whispered. 'Someone else. Someone better, who'll take me dancing, bring me flowers, shower me with love and affection and presents. Some day I want a family of my own; it's what I've always craved.'

'You'll get it, love, you'll see,' Hetty said.

Elsie stared dreamily ahead. 'I want a man, Hetty, a strong man who'll scoop me up and carry me off in his arms.'

Hetty began to giggle. 'I don't know about getting carried off, but you're certainly getting carried away,' she said with a wry smile. 'I don't think any man would be romantic enough to come in here and scoop you up in his arms. Well, not unless he was one of the sugar boilers called in to lift you out of your clogs.'

Elsie nodded across the room at Beattie, the largest girl in the room. 'No one will be scooping her up. That girl eats too many toffees. I'm surprised she found an overall to fit.' She noticed Hetty's gaze flicker to her bosom.

'Speaking of overalls fitting properly . . .' Hetty began.

Elsie did up her top button. 'Yes, all right, I know.

Mrs Perkins has already had a go at me today about showing too much cleavage... again. Even Anne said something about it this morning. But what's a girl to do? We're stuck in this factory three days a week and I hardly see any fellas on my days off. So when the chance to make an impression arises, I want to be sure I'm showing my best side.'

'You're showing a lot more than that,' Hetty said. 'When did you speak to Anne?' she added.

'When I was delivering a box of toffee to the warehouse. She was looking a bit flustered. And she was confused when I told her about the peace celebration; she said she didn't know. Mr Jack hadn't told her.'

Hetty raised her eyebrows. 'How odd that he couldn't wait to tell everyone at the factory but he hadn't told his own wife. I thought they told each other everything. Well, I guess you never know what goes on behind closed doors. Anyway, enough about Anne. What do you think Stan wants to talk to you about at dinner time?'

Elsie shrugged. 'I don't know, but there's only one way to find out.'

When dinner time came, Hetty went to the canteen while Elsie headed to the spot where she'd agreed to meet Stan. It was a wooden bench on a path in the factory grounds. In front of the bench was a rose bush planted in memory of Anabel, a factory girl who'd died in an accident in the slab room. Anabel's brother, Gavin, had chosen the colour, a vibrant red, Anabel's favourite.

Elsie sat on the bench with an apple and a sandwich. As she waited, she looked around the grounds. Before the war, the garden had been full of flowers, pink and white roses with a wonderful scent. During the war, however, apart from Anabel's rose bush, it had been dug over and replanted with vegetables. Now Stan and his team were turning the soil and preparing for the floral displays to return. Elsie saw Stan walking towards her, and she shimmied along the bench, making a space for him. He raised his cap in greeting, then sat down, placing his cap on the arm of the bench. Elsie noticed that he hadn't brought anything to eat.

'Have you already had your dinner today?' she asked.

Stan stared ahead. 'I don't have time to eat during the day, I'm too busy with the gardens,' he said.

'Oh, you should always stop at dinner time for something to eat, Stan, it's important, especially when you're working so hard in the garden.'

Stan rubbed the back of his neck, then looked at Elsie and changed the subject. 'How's your morning been?'

'Oh, busy as usual.' She indicated the garden. 'Looks like you're ready to start planting.'

Stan surveyed his domain proudly. 'We're going to get the rose bushes in this week. It should look perfect by the summer. Did you hear the news about the peace celebration?'

'I did, and it's wonderful.'

He sat up straight in his seat. 'I was wondering something, Elsie. If you'd like to . . . I mean, perhaps if you're free, and I wouldn't like to impose, of course . . . but if you want to, is there a chance that we could go together? To the peace celebration, I mean.'

Elsie looked at him from the corner of her eye. He was staring ahead again. 'I don't know, Stan,' she said.

'I might be going with Hetty and Anne. And if Hilda's well enough, we'll take her too.'

Stan's face dropped. 'Oh, I see,' he said quietly.

They sat in silence for a while. Finally Elsie could take it no more.

'Stan... I need to say something.'

'Elsie, I want you to know—' Stan said at the same time.

Elsie looked into his hazel eyes.

'You go first,' he said.

She took a deep breath. 'This isn't going to be easy...'

'I'm a tough lad, you can tell me anything,' he said, attempting a smile.

'I'm not sure you'll want to hear what I have to say,' she began.

Stan reached for her hands, and Elsie let him hold them. Then, in a hesitant voice, she revealed her heart.

'I'll always be grateful, Stan. Always. You saved me when I didn't want to live any more. You helped me to heal, and you've offered me nothing but kindness and love ever since.'

He let one of her hands go. She reached up to his face and gently caressed his cheek.

'You're one in a million, Stan Chapman. But I need more.'

His lip quivered. 'Then tell me what you need and it's yours. I'll give you anything, Elsie, you know that,' he said softly.

'I want...' Elsie looked away and indicated the factory grounds with her free hand. 'I want more than this. More than toffee. More than Chester-le-Street. More than being stuck in a tiny house on Elm Street with Hetty and Hilda.' Her words tumbled out. 'I want excitement.

I want to see the world. I want to visit Newcastle. Durham. Sunderland. I need to get away from my bad marriage, the past and Frankie. There are places out there to explore. Places I want to experience and people I want to meet.'

Stan looked shocked. Elsie let her hand drop from his face. He pulled away from her and moved along the bench.

'I see,' he said, although his expression suggested otherwise. 'And these people you want to meet, I presume you mean other men?'

His tone had taken on a wariness. Elsie picked up on it and was reluctant to continue. However, she'd said too much already and knew she had to carry on. It was wrong to keep Stan dangling, thinking he was in with a chance. She dropped her gaze and bit her lip.

'I'm too young to be tied down,' she said. 'I should never have married Frankie, and if that experience has taught me anything, it's to be free and live life to the full. I'm not a bad person, Stan. I know I'm stuck with Frankie, but he can't touch me now and if I can get away from here, he'll never find me again.'

She saw tears reach Stan's eyes, and a lump formed in her throat. She felt truly dreadful, racked with guilt, but also relieved that the truth was out. She tried to reach for his hand, but he slowly pulled it back. She knew she'd hurt him deeply.

'I'm sorry, Stan. I had to tell you. It's not fair leading you on.'

He moved away to the end of the bench. 'I won't stand in your way,' he said quietly. 'If you want to experience life, that's exactly what you should do. But if you ever change your mind, I'll be here.'

Elsie leaned across the bench and kissed him gently on his cheek, then she rose and slowly walked away. She bit the inside of her cheek, trying not to cry, wondering why, after she'd opened her heart and told Stan the truth, she felt so terrible... and so wrong.

Chapter Eleven

That evening at the Deanery, Anne settled Dinah into bed after reading her a story. She'd also searched her daughter's room again for her missing brooch, but to no avail. Downstairs in the kitchen, Edith was cooking liver and onions. Anne laid the dining table with her best linen and tableware, a wedding gift from William's parents. Satisfied that the table looked good, she walked into the living room. William was seated in his armchair reading a file of papers he'd brought from work. She leaned over and kissed him on the top of his head just as there was a knock at the door.

'That'll be Mr Gerard and Mr Burl,' he said.

Edith bustled to the front door and Anne heard her welcome the men inside, offering to take coats and hats. Then she led the visitors into the living room, where Anne and William waited, standing side by side. Anne felt very uncomfortable having Mr Burl in her house. But for William's sake, and for the sake of the factory, she smiled through gritted teeth and tried not to let her displeasure show.

William stepped forward and shook Mr Burl's hand,

then Mr Gerard's. Mr Burl's face was set firm, without a smile. He was all business, with a ruthlessness to his manner that Anne had never liked. In contrast, she adored Mr Gerard and greeted him like an old friend. The factory's creative manager was elderly, with a long, thin face. Wisps of white hair stuck out at odd angles, and he had bushy white eyebrows. Anne brought him to her in a warm hug, and he kissed her cheek. Then she stiffly held out her hand to Mr Burl and they exchanged a brief handshake. Anne nodded to Edith to indicate she could return to the kitchen, and the housekeeper scuttled away. She felt William's reassuring hand at her back.

'Gentlemen, please, follow me, we'll go into the dining room. The sooner we eat, the sooner we can talk business. We can't make any decisions on an empty stomach.'

William took his seat at the head of the table with Anne at the opposite end. Mr Burl and Mr Gerard took the remaining seats. Small talk began about the business of the day. Anne knew this was nothing more than a preamble to the serious discussion ahead. She pressed her shoes into the carpet to steady herself against what was to come. William brought a bottle of good red wine to the table and poured four glasses. Polite chit-chat continued, starting with news of the peace celebration. Mr Gerard suggested that a new line of toffee could be created to launch at the event.

'We could call them Sweets of Peace!' he said excitedly. 'I'll get my creative team involved right away making up a wrapper for your approval, William.'

'Don't talk nonsense!' growled Mr Burl. 'We can't plan new sweets with the factory running itself into the ground.'

Anne laid her hand on Mr Gerard's, noting how cold his skin was, and how thin. 'Let's not get carried away until we know if the factory has a future,' she said gently.

William held up his glass of wine. 'Well, I think Mr Gerard's got a point. We need to think about the future and the peace celebration. Maybe a new sweet line is just what we need to pull us out of the dire situation we find ourselves in. We could put the likeness of a factory girl on the tin, as we did for Lady Tina. This time we could use Elsie Cooper, the dark-eyed beauty who works in the slab room.'

Anne saw a mischievous glint in her husband's eye. His enthusiasm for Elsie troubled her. It also concerned her that this was the second time he'd mentioned Elsie of late. He seemed to be more interested in her friend's smouldering looks than in her own. Telling herself not to be petty, she smoothed a strand of hair behind her ear and sat up straight.

'William, we need to be realistic,' she said. 'We can't plan a new line of toffee. You know the factory is on the verge of collapse. Isn't that what we're here tonight to discuss?'

Conversation ended abruptly when Edith entered the room. With each course the housekeeper served, Anne felt her anxiety heighten. Talk of the factory's future was to be left until after dinner, when they were all relaxed with a glass of brandy. Instead, they began discussing the number of soldiers returning from war and how best to assimilate them into the jobs they'd once held. But the subject only reminded everyone at the table of the more serious discussion to be had once the meal was done. The future of the factory hung in the balance, and unspoken words hung in the air.

Once dessert was finished, Anne dabbed her mouth with her napkin and suggested they move to the living room for coffee and brandy. The men stood in silence, aware of what was to come. In the living room a low fire burned in the hearth to keep away the chill of the night. Anne indicated for Mr Gerard and Mr Burl to sit on the sofa. William took his usual armchair and Anne sat opposite. The living-room door remained closed. Anne had expressly warned Edith not to enter after she'd brought in the coffee pot.

William raised his glass of brandy. 'To Jack's toffee factory,' he said.

The others echoed the toast.

'Gentlemen...' he began, sitting forward. 'And dear Anne,' he added, looking at her. 'I wanted to speak to you tonight, here in our home, away from work and its distractions.'

Anne noticed Mr Burl lift his brandy and drain his glass in a single gulp. She looked at William, aghast, but if he'd noticed, he didn't let on. She took a sip from her own glass, letting the spirit warm her, then turned her attention to her husband.

'The board meeting is arranged for next week,' he continued.

'Yes, we know,' Mr Burl said impatiently.

Undeterred, William carried on. 'That's why I wanted to speak to you now, in private and in confidence. My parents will attend the board meeting too, and as voting members they will support my proposal. But I need you both on my side as well. You're the two longest-serving men at the factory.'

'Tell us more,' Mr Gerard said kindly.

'William swirled his brandy in his glass, a delaying tactic that Anne knew well. She'd seen him do it many times and knew he was gathering his thoughts, trying to figure out how to present his point of view in the clearest way possible. Finally he continued.

'I will propose at the meeting that we ask our creditors to hold the debts for a year, or even two years, to see if we can struggle through. However, if we do this, there are risks. Our reputation could suffer once everyone knows what a dire position the factory is in. Suppliers and buyers may start to steer clear, knowing we're a bad bet. We may lose business.'

Mr Burl placed his empty glass on a side table. 'Surely the best thing to do is cut our losses and close the factory down!' he said forcefully. He banged his fist against the arm of the sofa, making Anne jump.

There was silence in the room. The unspoken words had finally been thrust into the air. Anne felt tears prick her eyes, but she blinked hard and looked at Mr Burl.

'I disagree. Surely the best thing to do is listen to William's idea,' she said.

'Thank you, dear,' William said, smiling. 'Mr Gerard, what do you think?'

Mr Gerard lifted his brandy glass as if examining the spirit inside. The amber liquid caught the light from the fire. Finally he brought the glass to his lips and took a drink.

'I think the image of Elsie Cooper would be ideal to include on our new line of Sweets of Peace.'

Mr Burl looked at him as if he'd gone mad. 'How many times do I need to tell you? We can't afford to manufacture a new toffee line. Our only option is to close the place down. We don't have a future. Sweets of Peace? Don't be such a damn fool!'

But William held up his hand, cutting Mr Burl short. 'Let him speak. Carry on, Mr Gerard.'

The elderly man leaned forward, his eyes sparkling, and looked from Anne to William, then at Mr Burl. 'Yes, the factory is in debt, worse than ever before. In all my years there, we've never been in such peril. But these are unprecedented times. There's been a war, and everyone's suffered. Jack's toffee has not been immune. We're still limping along on three days' production each week. So I say we vote to ask our creditors to hold off if they can. Yes, William, I agree that our reputation *could* suffer. But likewise, it might not. You also said that suppliers and buyers *may* start to steer clear, but again, our honesty may bring us closer to them. And instead of being pessimistic and thinking we will lose business if we ask our creditors to help us out of this mess, just think what would happen if business increased. Why, we could pay them off quicker than expected. We could even think about expanding the factory, rather than closing down.'

Mr Burl banged the arm of the sofa again and Anne shot him a hard look. She'd spent a fortune on the fabric. 'What tosh!' he cried. He turned to William, pleading. 'You can't take this idea seriously!'

'At this moment, I'm prepared to take all ideas seriously,' William replied.

Mr Burl stood, nodding sharply at William but ignoring Anne. 'Then I think it's time I left. I can't believe what I'm hearing. We can't stagger into the future with a proposal based on a new packet of sweets. I've heard enough of this rubbish.'

He opened the door to leave, but neither Anne nor William stood to show him out. They sat in silence with Mr Gerard, listening to the sound of the front door as it opened and closed. Then William sank back in his armchair, cradling his brandy glass in both hands. Far from being perturbed at Mr Burl's outburst, there was a soft smile on his face. Perhaps it was the brandy helping the mood seem more mellow, thought Anne, or the light from the dying embers, but the lines of worry etched onto his face seemed to have softened.

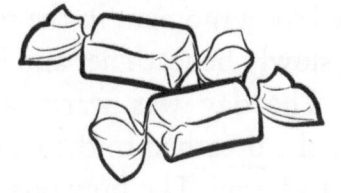

Chapter Twelve

Early the next morning, Hetty walked to work at Lumley Castle. To reach the castle from her home on Elm Street, she headed away from Chester-le-Street town centre. She thought about Dirk as she walked. He'd made her happy for such a long time and had opened up to her a world of love, respect and trust. He'd even told her that he loved her, and she had replied the same way, meaning every word she'd said with all of her heart. Dirk was everything that dull, dependable, buttoned-up Bob wasn't. He treated her better than Bob ever had, showing her nothing but kindness, and his kisses . . . oh, the mere thought of them caused her stomach to flutter. But now too often when she thought of Dirk, she felt a sadness creep into her heart. She couldn't bear the thought of losing him when he returned overseas. She felt a lump rise in her throat.

'Come on, Hetty, pull yourself together,' she muttered. 'There's nothing you can do. He has to leave; you always knew that.' Her bottom lip began to tremble, and she turned her face to the sky. 'Then why does it hurt so much?' she whispered.

She crossed the River Wear on the newly built Lumley

Bridge and paused for a moment in the middle, watching the river flowing slowly beneath her and listening to birdsong in the air. The day was warm and still, with a cloudless sky. As she breathed in the clean, fresh air, her thoughts turned to home. The previous night, when she had popped her head around the door to check on Hilda, the woman hadn't stirred. And this morning, before Hetty left the house, she found her asleep again. She knew Elsie would look after her and didn't worry further.

As she carried on up the hill, she thought of the chores that lay ahead at the castle, cleaning the large kitchen and swilling down the yard, skivvying for Mrs Doughty, the housekeeper. At least it wasn't dangerous work; no risk of being scalded by hot toffee or having a finger chopped off.

As Hetty made her way to the castle, a man dressed in the uniform of the Durham Light Infantry was walking along Front Street. He passed the Lambton Arms pub, then turned right onto narrow Market Lane. From there he headed towards the tall chimney of the toffee factory, but was surprised not to see smoke belching from its top. He rubbed his chin, looking around. He wondered where the workforce was, the thousands of women and girls he'd heard about who'd started work at the factory, replacing men like him who'd gone off to war. Where were the strong, burly men who worked as sugar boilers, the men who lifted heavy pots of molten sugar, butter and cream? Why were there no delivery carts? Where were the vans he'd heard about from his sister in her letters while he'd been at the front? He approached the iron gates, but it was obvious to him, even before he reached them, that they were locked. Nevertheless, he rattled them and called out.

As he turned to walk away, wondering what to do next, he heard a woman's voice. 'Can I help you, sir?'

He turned and saw a slim, attractive woman standing inside the gates. She wore wire-framed glasses and her fair hair was gathered into a bun. Her looks were delicate, her skin porcelain, and when she smiled, her eyes sparkled. She was dressed in a blue skirt and short-sleeved blouse with a silver bracelet at her wrist.

'I'm Mrs Jack, the factory owner's wife. Do you have business here, sir?'

'Good morning,' he replied politely. 'My name is Robert Grayson, but everyone calls me Bob. I was hoping to find a girl.'

Mrs Jack's eyes opened wide in concern while Bob's face blushed pink.

'I'm sorry, that came out wrong. What I mean is . . .' Delving into the kitbag that was slung over his shoulder, he brought out a toffee tin and pointed at the picture. 'This is the girl I hoped to find. She's my fiancée, you see.'

Anne rocked back on her heels. 'Your fiancée?' she said, confused. She knew Hetty was courting Dirk, a Belgian man who lived in Elisabethville. She eyed the soldier cautiously. She'd heard that some men back from war had been damaged in both body and mind. She wondered if the man in front of her had taken leave of his senses. And then a name came back to her. Hetty had told her about a man called Bob whom she'd courted before he went off to war. Was this Bob in front of her now?

'Could I come in to look for her?' he pleaded.

Anne stood her ground. 'I'm sorry, sir, the factory is closed, and no one is allowed in. My husband and I are the only ones here.'

This wasn't entirely true, but Anne didn't feel the need to reveal to him that their secretary was also indoors. She had asked Meg if she would help finish preparing the board papers on a day that the factory was quiet. There was also someone else here. Dinah was currently sitting on William's office floor, drawing with pencils. Anne had pushed William to agree that they'd bring their daughter with them to the factory on days when there was no production.

'May I return when it reopens?' the man asked.

Anne tilted her chin. 'I'm afraid that won't be possible. The factory only allows those who work here to enter. Now it would be best if you left, sir.'

He gripped the gate with his free hand, while in the other he held tight to the tin of toffee. 'I must see Hetty Lawson, I must!' he cried.

'That is our Lady Tina brand of toffee,' she said, trying to deflect him. She was beginning to feel a little anxious about his agitated state. Automatically her hand flew to her collar, where she normally wore her blue brooch. Her fingers felt the lack of it, another reminder that it still hadn't been found. 'I'm sorry, sir, I really must ask you to leave,' she added firmly.

'I need to see her!' he pleaded, then he began to call out. 'Hetty! Hetty, I know you're in there! It's Bob. Please, Hetty!'

Anne stepped back from the gate. 'Sir, please . . .' she said forcefully.

He dropped his gaze to the cobbled ground. 'I'm sorry,

Mrs Jack,' he mumbled. Then he seemed to gather himself. He squared his shoulders, stuffed the tin of Lady Tina into his kitbag and nodded sharply. 'Please tell Miss Lawson I was here. It's Bob. Bob Grayson.'

Anne watched him march away, feeling relieved he was leaving and hoping he wouldn't return. She headed into the office building, through the empty reception room, along the hushed corridor and into William's office.

'Everything all right, dear?' he asked, without looking up from his paperwork.

Anne didn't feel he'd appreciate being told about what had happened while his mind worked on figures and accounts.

'Everything's fine,' she said.

William pushed his chair back, stood and walked from the room, muttering about not yet having had his morning coffee. Anne scooped Dinah into her arms and carried her into Meg's office, where the secretary was arranging sheets of papers on her desk.

'That's the agenda done. I'm just waiting for the rest of the papers, then I'll take them to the post office today,' she said.

'Very good, Meg,' Anne replied.

She walked to the window with Dinah and looked out at the factory gardens, beginning to feel calmer after her run-in with the soldier at the gate. She pointed outside and Dinah's gaze followed her finger.

'One day, my darling, all of this will be yours. Daddy will keep the factory running, you'll see,' she said. But still she crossed her fingers for luck, just in case.

Chapter Thirteen

When Hetty returned home from Lumley Castle, she collapsed into a chair at the hearth. 'I'm exhausted,' she moaned.

Elsie was busy at the fire, lifting the kettle, filling the teapot, slicing potatoes for tea. 'I've been busy too, you know,' she replied. 'Hilda's been awake most of the day. She's been asking for you. Says she's got something to say.'

'Oh, crumbs,' Hetty moaned. She stretched her arms above her head. 'I suppose I should go and see her.'

Elsie shot her a look. 'Didn't you pop your head around her door when you came in?'

Hetty's shoulders slumped. 'All right, I'll go and look in on her now.' She knew she sounded like a spoiled child, but the animosity between her and Hilda had built up over years, and being petulant was a hard habit to break.

She paused at Hilda's room, where the door was ajar, and gently knocked.

'Come in,' Hilda said.

Hetty pushed the door. The fire was burning and the room felt stuffy. The smoke made the air thick. 'Would you like me to open the window?' she asked.

'If I wanted the window open, I'd have asked Elsie to do it,' Hilda said abruptly. 'Now sit down and listen.'

Hetty sat on a wooden chair at the side of Hilda's bed. The woman in front of her was all skin and bone, wrapped in a thick dressing gown, sitting up in bed with pillows at her back. She looked at Hetty for a few moments.

'I want a word with you,' she said.

While she looked weak, lying in her bed, rarely leaving her room, she sounded as full of fire as always.

'Your fella came here,' she went on.

'Dirk?' Hetty said, confused.

'I don't mean the foreign fella,' Hilda spat. 'I mean the other one, Bob.'

Hetty felt as if the wind had been knocked out of her. She gripped the chair seat with both hands. 'Bob was here? Today?' she cried, incredulous.

Hilda shook her head. 'He came yesterday. This is the first time I've seen you since.'

'But . . . but his last letter said he was on the south coast with his unit.'

'Are you calling me a liar?' Hilda snapped.

Hetty's mind was reeling. 'What did he want?'

Hilda tutted. 'What do you think he wanted? To see you, of course! Although why he wants anything to do with you after you've been seeing another man, I don't know.'

Hetty chose to ignore the cutting remark. 'What did he say?'

Hilda sneered at her. 'My word, you really are gormless, lass.'

Hetty held her nerve. 'What did he say?' she repeated.

Hilda's watery eyes locked onto Hetty's face. 'He wants to marry you, that's what he said.'

Hetty's legs began to shake. She gripped the chair tighter. 'No . . . I won't do it.'

'Well, he's determined you will,' Hilda said matter-of-factly. 'Besides, what choice have you got? Your Belgian lad's not going to hang around once Elisabethville is empty. He'll want to return to his own kind. You'll be left on your own. If you ask me, you'd do well to snap up a catch like Bob. You'd be lucky to have him.'

Hetty's mouth went dry. 'How . . . how was he?' she managed.

'Looked well enough, I suppose, after what he must have been through. Bit too thin, but nothing that home cooking can't help with. He needs feeding up. Speaking of which, you should ask Elsie to teach you how to cook properly. You're going to need kitchen skills when you marry. Elsie's a much better cook than you'll ever be, you could learn a lot from her. The leek soup you made the other week turned my stomach. It makes me feel sick each time I think about it.'

Hilda's words rattled around the room without fully landing on Hetty. She was still in shock, processing the fact that not only was Bob back in town, he'd also visited her home.

'Is he coming back?' she dared to ask.

Hilda gave a wry smile. 'You'll be lucky if he does. I told him about your Belgian man, but he already seemed to know. Says his sister told him.'

Hetty's body seemed to collapse into itself. Her shoulders rounded, and she dropped her gaze to the floor. She clasped her hands in her lap as Hilda continued.

'He wasn't happy to hear Elsie lives here with us now. He called her a tart, although I put him straight. She's a lot better since her aunt moved away. I reckon Jean was a bad influence on her.'

Slowly and carefully, Hetty pushed herself to her feet. She waited a moment, holding onto the chair back, while her legs steadied against the shock of the news, then began to walk out of the room.

'Hey! Where do you think you're going? I'm not finished with you yet!' Hilda called, but Hetty let the words fall behind her as she walked back to the kitchen.

'You look as white as a sheet. What's up?' Elsie asked.

Hetty fell into at a chair at the table. 'Bob's been here,' she said in a quiet voice.

Elsie's eyes opened wide in surprise. 'Bob? Here? When?'

'Yesterday. He spoke to Hilda. Said he's determined to marry me.'

Elsie sat in the chair next to her. 'And you're determined not to, right?' she said.

'Of course I won't marry him. I don't love him, and I never have. But the poor lad's just back from the war, and he . . .' Hetty closed her eyes. 'I can't imagine the horrors he's been through. I can't bear the thought of adding to his distress.'

'You need to think about yourself,' Elsie said sagely. 'Besides, you'd be doing him no favours marrying him when you don't love him.'

Hetty swallowed hard, then straightened in her seat and pushed a lock of hair behind her ear. 'You're right. I need to see him and tell him the truth. I need to put him out of his misery and set him free so he can look for someone else.'

'Are you certain about this?' Elsie said.

Hetty nodded. 'It's not Bob I want.'

Elsie reached over and squeezed her hand. 'We both know your heart lies with Dirk. But be warned. You're going to have to say goodbye to him soon. Prepare yourself for heartbreak, Hetty.'

On the hearth, a pan of water began bubbling and splashing, and Elsie rose and removed it from the flames. Hetty put her elbows on the table, joined her hands and leaned her chin on them, thinking.

'What time's Dirk coming to take you out tonight?' Elsie asked, breaking into her reverie.

Hetty glanced at the clock on the wall. 'Not for another hour. Do you think I should tell him about Bob turning up today?'

Elsie busied herself with a small joint of beef roasting in a pan. 'It's up to you,' she replied.

Hetty leaned forward in her seat. 'Elsie, what would you do?'

Elsie paused with a basting spoon in her hand. 'I'd be honest, it's the only way,' she said at last. 'I had a heart-to-heart with Stan this week to call things off with him. I thought it was best to get it over and done with and not keep stringing him along. It wasn't easy, but we both know where we stand now.'

'You said there was something Stan wanted to tell you. Did he say what it was?' Hetty asked.

Elsie thought for a moment. 'He asked me to go with him to the peace celebration.'

'What did you say?'

She shrugged. 'I never gave him a reply; we started talking about other things.'

'Oh, Elsie,' Hetty said. 'What a pair we make. We're

both working girls, earning our own wages at the factory and me up at the castle, and yet neither of us knows where our future lies. You're holding out for a man who'll sweep you off your feet, and I've got Dirk, whom I care for deeply, but he's leaving the country soon. Then there's Bob, who I don't feel anything for, but he's professing marriage and love. What are we going to do?'

She stood and stepped towards Elsie, and the two girls hugged for a very long time.

That evening, when Dirk called for Hetty, she answered the door and went straight out onto the street, already dressed in her coat.

'Is everything all right?' he asked, concerned.

Hetty pulled the door closed and began walking briskly away. 'Hurry up, Dirk,' she ordered.

He ran to catch her, and they soon fell into step. Hetty slid her arm through his and they slowed their pace. Dirk was dressed in a smart grey suit with wide lapels. Hetty glanced at him and thought he'd never looked as handsome as he did that night. His blue eyes sparkled in the evening light.

'Why the rush to get away from your house?' he asked once they'd left Elm Street.

'There's something I need to say,' Hetty said. 'I didn't want to tell you at home, where Hilda might hear or Elsie might get in the way. I wanted it to be just us.'

They walked in silence to the riverside, where wooden benches were placed to sit overlooking the water. In the distance, the towers of Lumley Castle rose beyond the trees.

'Let's sit here,' she said, indicating an empty bench.

Dirk stopped and pulled out a large, folded handkerchief from his jacket pocket. He carefully opened it, then swept it over the bench.

'Thank you,' Hetty said. She could never imagine Bob being so thoughtful. She snuggled into Dirk's side, feeling the reassuring weight of his arm around her shoulders.

'It is beautiful here,' he said.

'How are things at Elisabethville?' she asked. She braced herself for the answer, not wanting to hear how close Dirk was to leaving but needing to know all the same.

'Almost empty now,' he said, then he turned to her. 'But I have news that may be good for your aunt.'

'News for Hilda?'

'It hasn't been released officially, so please keep it under your helmet.'

Hetty smiled. 'It's *hat*, Dirk. The phrase is *under your hat*.'

'Ah yes, I learn so much from you, Hetty. My English has improved leaps and bounds, as they say. Well, the news has been discussed today with your town council. It's about the accommodation at Elisabethville.'

'The houses? What of them?'

'They will be given to local people to rent. They were newly built when your government brought the Belgians to work at the munitions factories. They have electricity and running water, things the local houses don't have.'

Hetty looked at Dirk's kind, open face. 'I don't understand. What does this have to do with Hilda?'

'Don't you see?' he said gently. 'I know she is not well and your house on Elm Street is damp, dark and cold. I could ask if she could take one of the houses at

Elisabethville, put in a good word for her. She will have an indoor privy, Hetty, no more going to the yard in her poorly condition. No more climbing the stairs with her bad chest; the houses are on one level.'

Hetty felt a rush for love for the man at her side. 'You'd really do that for Hilda?' she said.

'I'd do anything to help you and your family,' he replied.

Hetty squeezed his hand. 'Thank you, that would mean the world to us all.'

'Now, what did you have to tell me?' Dirk said.

Hetty took a deep breath and began to tell him the news about Bob.

Chapter Fourteen

The next day, the recent run of warm, sunny weather broke, and the sky was moody and grey. Dark clouds scudded overhead and a stiff breeze whipped through the trees. Hetty and Elsie huddled together, arm-in-arm, as they walked to work. Their topic of conversation turned, as it so often did, to men.

'What did Dirk say when you told him that Bob was back?' Elsie asked.

Hetty's face broke into a smile. 'He offered to fight for me,' she said.

'Fight?' Elsie cried. 'Oh, Hetty. You've got two men fighting over you. If only my life could have so much drama, I'd be a happy girl.'

Hetty gently shoved her in the ribs. 'I don't think he was being serious. But he did say that if Bob caused any problems for me, he'd be on hand to help.'

Elsie shook her head. 'Bob won't cause you any problems. From everything you've told me about him, he doesn't sound like that type of man. As for fighting, one hard look from Dirk would send him scuttling away in fear. Are you going to meet him to tell him to leave you alone? He can't keep turning up at the house and bothering Hilda while we're at work. You know she's not well.'

Hetty remembered what Dirk had told her about the Belgian village. 'Dirk said he could arrange for Hilda to move into a new home at Elisabethville if she wanted to. The houses that are being left empty are being taken over by the council. They've got electricity, Elsie, running water, two bedrooms and a garden. Just think how easy her life would be if she lived there. They're on one level too.'

Elsie was quiet a moment. 'If we all move to a house with two bedrooms it means that you and I would have to share. Plus, I'm not sure Hilda's up to being moved; she's very frail, you know. But we could at least ask her and see what she says. A garden would be lovely. She could sit outside in the sun instead of being stuck in bed all day.'

A gust of wind caught them, and they huddled together again.

When they reached the factory, they saw Anne step out of the driver's side of Mr Jack's black car. They watched in awe as she smoothed down her skirt, picked up her briefcase from the back seat and strode towards them.

'You managed to park today without hitting anything,' Hetty laughed.

'Oh, I'm definitely getting better,' Anne said confidently. 'William says he might allow me to drive on my own soon, without his supervision.' She leaned towards the girls. 'Perhaps I could take you both for a spin? We could spend the day in Durham and have afternoon tea by the river. We could take Edith and Dinah too.'

'That'd be wonderful,' Elsie replied.

The wind howled around them, and Anne indicated the door to reception. Hetty and Elsie followed her inside. Anne pushed up her glasses to the bridge of her nose then turned to Hetty.

'Hetty, there was a man at the factory asking for you. He said he was called—'

'Bob,' Hetty said dully.

'Why, yes,' Anne said. 'He claimed to be your fiancé. Is that true? I thought you were courting the Belgian man, Dirk.'

Hetty's face fell. 'Bob *was* my boyfriend before I met Dirk. I know I mentioned him to you before. I said goodbye to him at the station four years ago and haven't seen him since. But the truth is, I never loved him. I wasn't even that keen on him. It was just sort of taken for granted that we'd end up together.'

'And now he's back and wants to propose,' Elsie chipped in.

'Did he say he was coming back to the factory?' Hetty asked, concerned.

Anne shook her head. 'I gave him short shrift and sent him packing. I'll ask Jacob to do the same if he turns up again.'

'Thanks, Anne,' Hetty said. 'Look, we really should head to work. Mrs Perkins won't be happy if we're late.'

As the girls turned to leave, Mr Jack walked in. 'Ah! Elsie Cooper!' he cried. 'Just the girl I want to see.'

'Me? Have I done something wrong, sir?' Elsie asked, alarmed.

'Follow me to my office, now,' he ordered.

She did as instructed, leaving Anne and Hetty together.

'What's going on?' Hetty asked. She saw that Anne's face had flushed bright red.

'I don't know,' Anne replied. 'He's been acting very oddly lately, and I'm determined to find out why.'

Anne hurried along the hallway to her husband's office. The door was closed, but she wasn't going to let that deter her. She tapped, then walked in. William was seated at his desk, Elsie in the chair opposite. Anne walked forward and stood behind Elsie as William looked up to acknowledge her. He didn't appear too surprised.

'Ah, Anne, dear. Could you bring a pot of coffee for us, please?' he said.

Anne was embarrassed by the request. She hadn't been asked to make coffee since she'd given up her job as his secretary. It was a task she'd happily delegated as soon as she'd taken on her more strategic role. Her job now was to help keep the factory running, not boil water and spend time in the kitchen. While she would have happily made a pot of coffee at home, she found the request at work patronising. It was as if William was trying to put her in her place, and she didn't like it one bit.

'Isn't Meg available?' she said.

'No. I've sent her on a mission to find Mr Burl. It appears he's missing this morning. Damn fellow. I wanted a word with him too. I dare say he'll be around somewhere and Meg will hunt him out. Now then, if you don't mind, hurry along and bring the coffee, will you.'

Anne couldn't believe how he was speaking to her – and in front of Elsie, too. 'William, I rather think it would be better to wait for Meg to bring the refreshments,' she replied firmly. 'That way, I can join you with Elsie... Miss Cooper in this impromptu meeting.'

'There's no need to join us, dear. You can probably guess what our meeting is about, after hearing Mr Gerard's suggestion for the new toffee line.'

'A new toffee line?' Elsie said excitedly.

'It's just a suggestion at the moment,' Anne said, shooting her husband a look.

'Yes, well... I suppose we could wait for Meg to return,' he agreed.

'It is her job, after all,' Anne said with a practised smile.

William looked at her. 'Anne, dear, would you mind very much if I held this meeting with Miss Cooper alone?'

Anne dug her heels into the carpet. Of course she minded, very much. Why was he shutting her out? However, she didn't want to let on to Elsie that there was anything wrong.

'Mind, dear? Why would I mind?' she said, forcing out her words. 'I've got a mountain of paperwork on my desk to attend to.'

She turned and walked out of the office with a heavy heart. She knew things were bad at the factory, and the board meeting was hanging over them all. But really, how rude William had been to ask her to make coffee then tell her to leave! What must Elsie think? She closed the door behind her and waited a moment with her ear to the door, listening.

'Mrs Jack?'

She spun around to see Meg standing in the corridor. She jumped away from the door and tried to regain her composure.

'Ah, good morning, Meg. When you have a moment, Mr Jack would like a pot of coffee, enough for two. And I think I could do with some too. Did you find Mr Burl?'

Meg shook her head. 'I've looked for him everywhere. No one knows where he is. I spoke to the men in his office, who said he hadn't given any indication that he was coming in late. However, what I did hear . . .' she leaned close to Anne, 'was that some of the workers aren't happy. Rumours are going around that the factory's closing down. One man's already been for an interview at Mayfair Toffee in Sunderland, afraid he'll lose his job here.'

Anne's heart sank. 'This is dreadful. We must put a stop to these rumours and find out who's spreading them. Let me know once William's meeting with Elsie Cooper has ended.'

'Elsie Cooper?' Meg said, surprised. 'I didn't put a meeting in his diary with any of the factory girls today. Besides, dealing with the girls is your domain now.'

There was a beat of silence.

'Please let me know when she's gone,' Anne said.

She walked to her office, furious and disappointed with William. She was also concerned over the rumours flying around the factory. She opened her office door, set her briefcase on the carpet, took off her coat and hung it on the coat stand. Glancing out of the window at the grounds, she saw Stan Chapman and his men busy at work with wheelbarrows and plant pots. They were preparing for the factory's future, while the truth of it was that she didn't know how long the place might survive.

'It has to continue, for Dinah,' she whispered.

She was so lost in her thoughts about the debts, the

board meeting and William's preoccupation with Elsie that she hadn't realised how much time had passed until there was a knock at her door.

'Come in,' she called. She looked up to see Meg standing in the doorway holding a tray with an empty coffee pot and two mugs on it.

'Miss Cooper is leaving,' she said.

As Meg headed to the kitchen with the tray, Anne walked in the other direction. When she reached William's office, she saw Elsie coming out. She was stuffing something in her overall pocket. Anne saw a flash of blue and silver, the exact colours of her missing brooch.

Chapter Fifteen

'Elsie?'

Elsie spun around and her face dropped. Her hand hovered protectively over her pocket.

'What's in there?' asked Anne.

Elsie blanched. 'Where?'

'Come on, Elsie, don't play games. What's in your pocket?'

The girl backed away. 'I don't know what you're talking about.'

'I saw you put something in your pocket.'

Elsie smiled widely. 'Ah, you mean these,' she said. She dipped her hand into her pocket and pulled out two Lady Tina toffees in silver and blue wrappers.

Suddenly Anne felt a fool for imagining that her friend might have her precious brooch. 'I'm sorry, Elsie. I didn't mean to sound abrupt. I'm not thinking straight at the moment; there's a lot of pressure on me . . .'

She stopped. It was no business of Elsie's to know what was going on behind the scenes, either at the factory or in her marriage. 'Well, I'm sorry, that's all,' she finished.

Elsie patted her pocket and cast a sly glance at William's

office door. She leaned close to Anne and whispered, 'Don't tell Mr Jack, but I took these toffees from his office when he wasn't looking. That's why I didn't want you to know what I had in my pocket. I can't resist Lady Tinas; they're my favourite. We're not allowed to eat in the slab room. Mrs Perkins comes down hard on us if she catches us. I was going to keep these for dinner time and share them with Hetty.'

'I won't say anything,' Anne promised. 'You should probably run along now, or else Mrs Perkins will be after you.'

Elsie nodded. 'Thanks, Anne,' she said, and walked away.

Anne braced herself before entering William's office.

'Did you have a good meeting with Miss Cooper?' she asked, trying to keep her tone even, which was hard as she still felt vexed. She strode towards his desk and sat down.

'It was very productive,' he said, without looking up.

She let a moment's silence pass before she carried on.

'William, why more secrets? I'm as worried as you are about the future of the factory, but keeping me locked out of meetings and negotiations will distance us. I beg you again to please keep me informed.'

'Very well, dear,' he said dully. 'I expect you want to know why I spoke to Miss Cooper.'

'Of course I do.'

'It was about becoming the face of the new Sweets of Peace that Mr Gerard has proposed. If there is to be a factory girl featured on a new toffee brand, Miss Cooper would be ideal. But it won't do to talk about the future of the factory until a decision is made at the board meeting next week. I have sworn Miss Cooper to secrecy.'

William laid down his papers and looked at Anne. She noticed how tired he seemed. His usually cheerful expression had been replaced with a look of grave concern. She let his words sink in. There was something about his tone and his manner that didn't seem right. She put it down to the stress of what was happening at work. Then she remembered what she'd heard from Meg.

'Rumours are already going around that the factory might close,' she said.

William's hand flew to his blue bow tie and he fiddled with it nervously. 'That's bad news indeed,' he replied. In that moment, he looked crumpled, done in. Anne stood and walked around the desk to stand at his side.

'Should we call a staff meeting in order to quash the rumours?' she suggested, but even as the words left her lips, she knew it was a bad idea. 'Maybe we should wait until after the board meeting, when we have a clearer picture of the factory's future,' she added quickly.

William patted her hand. 'Have you seen Mr Burl this morning?' he asked.

'No,' Anne replied.

He sighed heavily. 'Where the devil could he be? He knows how much I need him, especially at a time like this.'

'Perhaps he's ill, at home,' Anne suggested.

William shook his head. 'He's never had a day's illness in all the years he's worked here.'

Meg walked into the room to place a folder of papers on William's desk. Anne turned and left the office, feeling very unsettled indeed.

That evening, Elsie stood outside the Lambton Arms. She was waiting for a man named Malcolm. He was one of the sugar boilers and she'd been relentlessly flirting with him for a few days. Finally her persistence had paid off and he'd asked her out for a drink. She glanced impatiently at her watch, disappointed that he was late.

'I'll wait fifteen minutes, then I'm off,' she muttered.

As the minutes ticked away, she grew irritated.

'Five minutes, that's all I'm giving you,' she said out loud.

She was about to return home to Hetty and Hilda when she saw Malcolm sauntering towards the pub along Front Street with a cheeky grin on his face.

'You all right, Elsie?' he said as he approached.

'You're late. I was about to give up,' she replied tersely.

He gave her a wink. 'I'm always worth waiting for,' he said.

Elsie hoped he was right. She was wearing her best red skirt, and a black velvet hat borrowed from Hetty.

'Are we going in, then?' she said, indicating the pub.

Malcolm held out his arm, which she accepted, and together they walked inside. The pub was smoky, busy and noisy with men's voices and laughter. She saw her brother-in-law, Jim, and his wife Cathy working hard behind the bar, pulling pints, taking orders and handing over change. Elsie was jostled by men passing behind her and pulled her handbag close.

'You go and find a table and I'll get the drinks. What would you like?' Malcolm asked.

'I'll have a small beer, please,' she said.

She looked around, trying to find a free table, but the pub was packed full. Men leered at her as she walked.

'Hey, darling, come and sit beside me!' one of them yelled. Elsie ignored him. Her gaze landed on a man she thought she recognised from the factory. He saw her too, and they locked eyes for a moment. Elsie could have sworn it was Mr Burl. She was puzzled. Surely not, she thought. What would he be doing in a rough pub like the Lambton Arms? She tried to see whom he was sitting with, curious in case it was one of the factory girls, but there were no women at the table, only men.

Suddenly she felt herself being shoved, and an almighty row started up behind her. She retreated to the side of the room, scared she'd be caught up in the fight if she stayed where she was.

'It's Jim's brother,' she heard a man say.

She stopped dead. 'Frankie?' she gasped.

'I've got him!' another man yelled.

'Jim, be careful!' Cathy called.

Elsie elbowed her way through to the bar. 'What's going on?'

'It's Frankie, causing bother again,' Cathy told her. 'He's drunk, as usual. Some of the lads have thrown him out and Jim's gone to help.'

'Should I go and help too?' Elsie asked.

Cathy shook her head. 'He's not your problem any more.'

'I'm still married to him,' Elsie said miserably.

'You're better off without him,' Cathy replied.

The row outside quietened and men returned to the pub. Jim walked back to the bar, and Elsie was surprised to see he was followed by Stan, who caught her eye and smiled.

'Hello, Elsie. You weren't caught up in that fight, were you?'

'I'm fine, Stan, thanks,' she replied politely.

Stan looked around, concerned. 'Are you here on your own?'

Elsie stood on her tiptoes, looking for Malcolm. 'No, I'm with someone,' she said. 'But I can't seem to find him.'

'He's left, love,' Jim told her. 'You came in with Malcolm the sugar boiler, didn't you? Well, he's gone.'

Elsie couldn't believe her ears. 'Gone? Where?'

'He said he wasn't sticking around while there was a fight on. He's a coward, if you ask me. Not like Stan here. He helped get Frankie out of the pub. In fact, if it hadn't been for Stan, Frankie wouldn't have calmed down as quick as he did. Let me show my appreciation, Stan, and pull you a pint on the house. What'll it be?'

Elsie looked at Stan. He had a small cut on his cheek. She dug in her handbag and pulled out a handkerchief. 'Here, you're bleeding,' she said, handing it over.

Stan took it from her and gently dabbed his cheek.

'Did Frankie do that?' she asked.

He nodded. 'It's nothing. It doesn't hurt.'

Jim reached for a beer pump. 'Pint of mild, Stan?' he said.

'That'd be lovely, Jim, but really there's no need. I was just doing what anyone would have done in the situation.'

'Well, Malcolm didn't, did he?' Jim said, casting a look at Elsie. She felt embarrassed, stranded by her date, who'd run away at the first sign of trouble.

Stan delved into his pocket and pulled out coins, which he placed on the bar. 'Let me pay for this beer, Jim. And for whatever Elsie's having.'

'No, Stan, I can't stay,' she said quickly. She didn't want to get his hopes up by joining him.

They were jostled at the bar, and men's laughter rang out. For a moment, Elsie and Stan were thrust together by the surging crowd. Elsie was in danger of losing her balance, and she held onto her hat.

'One at a time, gentlemen, please!' Cathy yelled angrily.

Elsie was rocked this way and that by the crowd squeezing into the pub. The fight seemed to have fired up energy in the room, and the laughter turned raucous. She tried to squeeze away from Stan but was caught between two men pushing to the bar. Stan laid a steadying arm around her shoulders and glared at the men.

'Come on, fellas, take it easy, there's a lady here,' he said. Elsie felt the pressure ease off and was grateful for his help. Then he turned his hazel eyes to her. 'Are you sure you won't stay for a drink?'

She looked into his kind face and realised he still had his arm around her shoulders, and she took comfort from that in the chaos of the pub. How easy it would be, she thought, to chat and fall into easy laughter with him.

In front of her, Jim set a pint of mild on the bar. 'Elsie, what would you like?' he asked.

Elsie looked from Stan to Jim, then shook her head. 'I'm sorry, I have to go.'

Quickly she pushed her way through the crowded pub. When she reached the pavement outside, she looked around for Malcolm, but he was nowhere to be seen.

Chapter Sixteen

When the day of the board meeting dawned, Anne woke with a knot in her stomach. She turned over in bed, reaching for the comfort of William's body, but all she found was an empty space. She got out of bed, pulled on her dressing gown and walked along the hallway to her daughter's room. There was a gentle night light glowing inside, and she paused by the open door. She saw William at Dinah's bedside, and heard him talking to her. At first she thought he was reading her a story, but as she listened to his words, she realised they weren't coming from a book; they were coming straight from his heart.

'Darling Dinah, the factory will be yours one day, if we vote to keep it running. Daddy has an important meeting today with Mummy and lots of other people that you don't know. Perhaps one day you will. I'm not a religious man, child, but I'll happily pray for the factory today. Grandma and Grandpa will be at the meeting too, and I know I can count on them for their support. As for the other board members, who knows how they will vote? If we do manage to keep it going, even if we struggle, then one day you will be in charge. Oh, you might want to change the Lady Tina toffees when you take over. I daresay they'll appear old fashioned by then. And if we do produce a new line called Sweets of Peace, well, you might want to change their name too, because, my dear child, war will be a distant memory when you are a grown-up. The war to end all wars is over, Dinah. There will never be fighting like it again.'

Anne watched as he stood, then leaned down to Dinah's small bed and gently kissed her on her cheek. He turned to leave the room and she had to swallow the lump in her throat. William gave an amused smile when he saw her.

'I expect you heard most of that, which is more than Dinah did, as she's still fast asleep,' he said.

He reached for Anne and wrapped his arms around her slim waist, pulling her to him and resting his head on her shoulder. They snuggled together outside Dinah's room for a very long time, slowly moving side to side as if to a silent tune only they could hear.

'It's going to be a tough day, Anne. Are you ready?'

'As ready as I'll ever be,' she replied. She gently pulled away. 'I'll ask Edith to prepare a hearty breakfast before we leave for work. We need sustenance to keep up our strength.'

William turned his face to her, and she saw again how tired and worried he looked. 'Thank you, Anne. I'll take my bath now. Edith has prepared the hot water. What would we do without her?'

Anne felt slightly uneasy at the mention of Edith's name, recalling how she'd found her rummaging in her study a few days ago.

'Yes, she is irreplaceable, I'm sure,' she replied. The missing brooch went through her mind again. Surely it wasn't possible that Edith had taken it. Anne closed her eyes and tried to force the ridiculous notion away.

After a breakfast of bacon and eggs, then toast with marmalade and coffee, Anne and William kissed Dinah goodbye and prepared to leave. As William headed outside to the car, Anne hung back to speak to Edith.

'I don't suppose my brooch has appeared, has it?' she asked.

Edith's face was stern. 'No, Mrs Jack. I would tell you immediately if it had. Are you sure you didn't lose it at the factory?'

Anne was certain she had taken off the brooch in her bedroom and placed it on her dressing table. She'd been over this many times. Now her thoughts were jumbled. Perhaps it *had* fallen off at work and she hadn't noticed? Perhaps it had been stolen? Perhaps . . . and here her mind went again to seeing Elsie coming out of William's office, and the flash of blue and silver in her hand. She shook her head to dismiss the nonsense idea of Elsie or Edith being a thief.

'I know I took it off at home,' she replied.

'Then I'll keep looking for it,' Edith said.

Anne headed outside to join her husband. She'd been hoping to drive the car again, and was disappointed to see William in the driver's seat. She slid into the passenger seat and set her briefcase at her feet. William started the engine and revved the car into life.

The board meeting was scheduled for ten o'clock. When Anne and William arrived at work, Meg was looking flustered.

'Calm down, dear,' Anne said with what she hoped was a reassuring smile.

Meg's hands fluttered at her heart. 'There's so much to do, Mrs Jack! I've got to prepare the boardroom and refreshments. Should I put a plate of Lady Tina toffees on the table? Do I bring in the coffee pots at the start of the meeting or halfway through? Oh, I hope I remember to make all the right notes. Where should I seat Mr Jack's parents?'

Anne gently took hold of Meg's arm and guided her into her office. 'Take a seat,' she said kindly.

Meg did as she was told.

'Now breathe in deeply.'

She took a deep breath, keeping her eyes on Anne.

'And breathe out slowly.'

She let the air go noisily through her mouth.

'Keep breathing, Meg, nice and easy, you'll calm down in a minute.'

Meg slumped in her chair. 'Oh, Mrs Jack, I'm all in a flap. It's such an important day. What if the board vote against Mr Jack's proposal to keep going? We could be closing down by the end of the week.'

Anne walked to her and gently laid her hands on her shoulders. 'Look at me, Meg,' she said.

Meg looked into her face.

'You're capable of getting through today,' Anne said firmly.

'I'm capable,' Meg repeated.

'Mr Jack and I are depending on you.'

'I'm dependable, Mrs Jack.'

'I'm pleased to hear it,' Anne said, taking her hands from Meg's shoulders. 'Now, I want you to remain sitting here for a while, in silence. When you feel calm, you can set up the boardroom. If you need help, ask Mr Burl's secretary. I'll square things with him if he complains.'

'Thank you, Mrs Jack.'

Anne walked into William's office, leaving Meg sitting in her chair breathing deeply, in, and then out again.

'Meg seemed flustered when we arrived,' William said.

'She'll be fine,' Anne said. She glanced at the clock on the wall. 'I must go, dear. I have a meeting with Mrs Perkins. She's asked to see me before the board meeting.'

William shot her a look. 'Really? What does she want?'

Anne shrugged. 'She wouldn't say.'

She walked to her own office, hung up her coat then opened her briefcase. She was lifting a folder of papers to her desk when there was a knock at the door.

'Come in,' she called.

It was Meg. 'Mrs Perkins is waiting in reception to see you.'

'Send her in, Meg, thank you.'

Anne settled herself behind her desk and straightened her spine. A moment later, Mrs Perkins entered the room. As usual, she wore her long brown hair plaited down her back, and she looked serious and businesslike. Anne stood and held out her hand.

'Pearl, dear. How are you?' she said warmly. She knew Mrs Perkins well; the supervisor lived with Mrs Fortune, who'd been Anne's landlady when she'd rented a room in the days before she married William.

Mrs Perkins gripped Anne's hand with both of her own and shook it heartily. 'I'm very well, Anne, thank you. How's little Dinah?'

At the mention of her daughter's name, Anne's face

brightened. 'Oh, she's as gorgeous as ever,' she said brightly. 'I'll tell her that her favourite lady was asking after her. Please, have a seat.'

Mrs Perkins sat, then smoothed her blue skirt with her hands.

'What is it, Pearl?' Anne asked.

The supervisor dropped her gaze to the floor, then slowly lifted her head. 'I'm afraid it's not good news. What I have to say is something I don't think you'll want to hear.'

Anne's shoulders slumped. What now? 'Try me, I'm tougher than I look,' she said with an attempt at a smile.

'Well . . .' Mrs Perkins began hesitantly. She dipped her hand into her handbag and brought out a folded sheet of paper, which she placed on Anne's desk. 'I think you should know that I intend to leave. I've given my notice in writing, as I'm obliged. You'll find all the details there.' Her face began to colour.

'Leave?' Anne cried. 'But you can't . . . I mean, you're one of the best supervisors we have.'

She leapt out of her seat and walked around to the other side of the desk. Mrs Perkins crossed her arms, as if in defence of her personal space.

'Oh, Pearl, dear. You're more than a supervisor, you're a friend. I'll miss you terribly. Why are you leaving and where will you go?'

Mrs Perkins slowly uncrossed her arms and looked Anne straight in the eye. 'As you know, Avril Fortune and I have grown close, and she is leaving to live in Durham. She has a sister there who needs looking after and she's asked me to go with her. Her sister's generous provision is such that Avril no longer needs to work for her living, and she has made an allowance for me too.'

Anne let the shock news sink in. 'I see. Then of course you must go. Yes, it's the right thing to do. When will you leave?'

'I'll go this summer, if I may be released that soon. I trust this will give you plenty of time to find a replacement. I'll do all I can to help the factory recruit the best supervisor. She's out there somewhere, I'm sure.'

Anne rubbed her chin and thought about the board meeting due to take place in less than an hour's time. There might be no recruitment taking place at all if William's proposal to keep the factory going was voted against. However, she had to remain stoic and professional. She gave a brief smile.

'Pearl, thank you for letting me know. I would of course appreciate your help in the recruitment process. I'll arrange for your discharge papers to be drawn up, with a leaving date in the summer.'

Mrs Perkins laughed. 'Discharge papers? You make it sound like the end of the world.'

Anne swallowed hard and thought again of the looming board meeting. Mrs Perkins had no idea how accurate her words might be.

Chapter Seventeen

Once Mrs Perkins had left, Anne sank into her chair. On the desk in front of her was her set of papers for the board meeting. There was only one item on the agenda: William's proposal to keep the factory going for as long as possible, paying off its debts gradually rather than all at once, which would put the business at risk. She eyed the clock on the wall; the minutes were ticking down until the meeting began.

She busied herself with paperwork, opening her mail, all the while Mrs Perkins' words about leaving ringing in her ears. How would she ever find a supervisor as diligent and experienced to replace her? But the thought of recruiting staff made her heart sink, for if the vote went against William today, people would be laid off instead of taken on. She buried her head in her hands, then set her pen down, stood and walked to the window. She gazed out at the grounds, where Stan Chapman and the gardeners were digging, wheeling barrows and planting shrubs. Once more, the irony wasn't lost on her. The factory grounds were being planted for the future, but there was a real danger that no one would be around to see the roses bloom.

She returned to her desk and carried on reading her mail. Most of the envelopes had been opened by Meg, who dealt with everything she could or passed it on to other departments within the factory to handle. However, she never opened anything marked *Confidential*; such letters were left for Anne herself. And today there was such a letter. She picked up the sealed envelope and recognised the logo and brand name. It had been sent from Mayfair Toffee in Sunderland, where she'd once worked. The envelope was typed, addressed to her as Mrs Jack, and she thought it might be a character reference request for the worker Meg had mentioned who'd applied to Mayfair for a job.

She slit the envelope open and pulled out the letter. As she read it, her heart skipped. It wasn't a character reference at all. It was an invitation to discuss the possibility of a job offer. The letter said the managing director was impressed with the work she'd carried out at Jack's toffee factory and wondered if he might tempt her back to Mayfair Toffee in what he described as a challenging role. Anne was gobsmacked but didn't have more time to think about it as her door burst open and William walked in with his elderly parents, Albert and Clara. She quickly stuffed the letter into her desk drawer and tried to cover her surprise with an over-bright smile.

Albert wore a long black overcoat with a black hat. He was a short man, like his son, with a narrow, long face and a tidy white moustache and beard. Clara was dressed in a soft cream jacket that fell around her in folds. Her greying hair was immaculately styled and she wore heavy powder on her face. Anne leapt out of her seat, her heart going like the clappers. She quickly scanned William's face, looking for a clue that he might have caught her reading the letter from Mayfair Toffee, but he appeared not to have seen. Relieved, she approached Clara and kissed her on her powdered cheek, then hugged Albert too.

While Anne made small talk with Clara, Albert began muttering to William about a funeral he'd attended that morning. Anne caught fragments of their conversation.

'The death of Sir Michael's father has left him with a large estate with lots of land he intends to sell. He should make quite a fortune if he sells it all,' Albert said. He turned to Anne, and she noticed that his blue eyes were twinkling. 'Are you ready for battle, my girl?' he asked.

Clara stared at him, aghast. 'It's not a fight, Albert, it's a board meeting. Please, show some decorum.'

Anne nodded to Clara. 'I'm more than ready. But I fear Albert might be right. We have to fight to win the vote today. William's proposal must pass if we're to have a chance of keeping the factory going.'

Albert strode to the door with Clara in his wake. 'Then let's go into battle!' he declared.

Anne and William shared a smile. Anne picked up her papers, making sure that her desk drawer was closed and the letter hidden from sight. What was Mayfair Toffee thinking, sending such a letter to her? It was shocking.

As she walked towards the door, William caught her gently by the arm. 'Whatever happens in the meeting, Anne, we'll face the future together,' he said.

Anne crossed fingers on both hands. 'Come on, dear, let's go in and fight to save the factory.'

* * *

Elsie was making a delivery in the factory grounds. Mrs Perkins had sent her on an errand to hand a tin of Lady Tina toffee to Stan Chapman and his gardening team.

'Why pick me?' Elsie had sulked. The last thing she wanted was to speak to Stan. She hadn't seen him since the awful night at the Lambton Arms when she'd been abandoned by Malcolm. Ever since, she'd deliberately kept out of his way, too embarrassed to face him. Also, she didn't want to seem over friendly with him, for she knew it would be all to easy to fall back into the comfortable way they had together.

Mrs Perkins put her hands on her hips and glared at her. 'Elsie Cooper, if I have to ask you once more, I'll complain to Mrs Jack.'

Elsie's bottom lip shot out. 'It's not fair,' she muttered.

Hetty had sidled up to her. 'I could deliver the tin instead, Mrs Perkins,' she'd offered.

Mrs Perkins looked at both girls as if she was considering this, but then shook her head. 'Elsie needs to learn to do as she's told,' she said firmly.

Elsie had snatched the tin of toffee from the supervisor's hand.

'Elsie!' Hetty chided, but Elsie pretended not to hear and stormed from the slab room. She walked across the cobbled yard, past the reception, trailing her hand along the stone walls of the office building. Through one of the windows she could see a meeting taking place. A lot of straight-backed gentlemen sat around a table, all with stern expressions on their faces. Then she caught sight of Anne and Meg, and another woman, older, whom she didn't recognise. She raised her hand and waved at Anne, but couldn't seem to catch her eye.

As she walked on into the factory gardens, she saw Stan and his men working in the far corner. She slowed her pace, trying to work out how best to approach him. 'Keep calm and distant,' she told herself.

Stan looked up when he saw her and smiled. He said something to the three lads with him, and they nodded, put down their spades and walked off. Elsie's heart dropped. It meant she'd be speaking to him alone. This wasn't what she wanted. She braced herself.

Stan leaned on the handle of his spade and beamed at her. 'Morning, Elsie, what a lovely surprise to see you.'

Elsie thrust the tin of Lady Tina toffee in his direction. 'This is from Perky Perkins in the slab room.'

Stan looked at it, then scratched his head. 'Old Perky's sent a tin of toffee for me?'

'Well, it's for you and your lads. She thought you could do with a sweetener after all the hard work you've been doing in the garden.'

Stan wiped his palms on his trousers and reached for the tin. Elsie saw that his large hands were encrusted with dirt, and there was soil under his nails. How many times had she told Hetty that she wanted a man who'd caress her soft skin with clean, delicate hands? And yet she felt something tug at her heart. There was something honest about Stan, solid and true. His were hard-working hands. Hands that nurtured and cared.

She shook her head to stop herself getting carried away, then turned to leave. 'I've got to get back to work.'

Stan raised the toffee tin. 'Say thank you to Perky from me and my lads. And take care of yourself, Elsie,' he added.

* * *

Inside the boardroom, the air was tense as William presented his proposal.

'My plan is to keep the factory going under the most difficult challenges it has ever faced,' he said seriously.

Much discussion took place, with arguments going this way and that. Some members of the board wished to settle the factory's losses and pay off its debts immediately to protect its good name. However, William pointed out that if this happened, the factory would suffer, and might have to close. He repeated, time after time, his proposal to pay off the debts carefully, cautiously, and to work with their creditors to enhance any goodwill that was left. After a bruising hour of debate, finally a vote was taken. Of the twelve members of the board, seven were in favour of paying off the debts slowly and working with their suppliers. William's proposal was carried, and Anne breathed a sigh of relief. She reached for his hand under the table, and when her fingers met his, she gave them a squeeze.

However, Mr Burl had been one of the men who had voted against him, and he wasn't about to give in without a fight.

Anne looked hard at him. He'd never explained where he'd disappeared off to, and she didn't trust him an inch. 'We'll regret this, you'll see!' he yelled.

Mr Gerard, seated beside him, shot him a look. 'Calm down, Mr Burl. Our future will be secure with...' He paused for dramatic effect. All eyes were on him. 'Eggs!'

Mr Burl's eyebrows shot up. 'Eggs? What are you on about, man? Have you completely lost your mind? Everyone knows you're a creative genius, but your unusual ideas have gone too far this time.'

At Anne's side, Meg was furiously scribbling notes,

but now she almost dropped her pencil. 'Did I hear right? Did Mr Gerard say *eggs*?' she whispered to Anne.

Around the table, the board members stared at the creative manager. Many of them nodded, as if in agreement with Mr Burl. Anne saw William's parents give each other a worried look. She leaned forward.

'Eggs, Mr Gerard? Please explain what you mean.'

The elderly man had stunned everyone into silence with his strange outburst. Slowly he pushed himself up from his chair, gripping the edge of the table for support.

'Mr Gerard, are you well?' Albert asked at last. 'What is this talk of eggs?'

Mr Gerard looked round the table. Meg's pencil was poised mid-air ready to make notes as soon as he began speaking again.

'There is no doubt that there is hard work ahead,' he began. 'We have voted to accept William's proposal to keep the factory open, continuing our three-day-week production schedule. It is not ideal, I know.'

Here he cast a look at Mr Burl, who was red in the face, apoplectic with rage.

'Some of you already know of my suggestion for a new line of toffees called Sweets of Peace.'

'It's a terrible idea, under the financial circumstances,' Mr Burl muttered.

'Carry on, Mr Gerard,' William said, ignoring Mr Burl.

Mr Gerard steadied himself against the table.

'Do you need to sit down, dear?' Clara asked.

Mr Gerard shook his head and held firm. 'Forget the Sweets of Peace, because more than ever, we need to look to the future to secure the factory. That's why I wish to suggest a different line of toffee to be launched next year.

But this will be no ordinary line. It will not even be sold in a tin.' There were gasps around the table, and he leaned forward, his eyes sparkling with mischief. 'Gentlemen and ladies of the board, I suggest a new novelty line to sell at Easter next year. Our very own toffee eggs.'

Anne's mouth dropped open with shock.

Chapter Eighteen

Mr Burl banged his fist on the table. 'I've never heard such rot. Toffee eggs? They'll never take off. Who in their right mind would want a confectionery egg?'

William raised his hand to quieten him and looked at Mr Gerard with concern. 'This is certainly an odd proposal, Mr Gerard. I'd go so far as to say it is the most unusual you've ever presented.' He looked around the room. 'As always with our board meetings, whatever is said here goes no further. Whatever Mr Gerard tells us now must remain in strict confidence.'

Mr Burl crossed his arms. 'You mean you don't want this leaking to our competitors because we'd become a laughing stock,' he said. He glowered at William, challenging him. Anne noticed the exchange with interest and felt her heart swell with pride at her husband for not backing down.

'Mr Gerard, carry on,' William said.

Mr Gerard's face lit up as he outlined his plan. 'The Swiss chocolatiers already have a novelty line of eggs that go on sale for the Easter market and sell very well. I suggest that we take up the mantle and become the first in this country to manufacture toffee eggs.'

'But—' Mr Burl began, but William shook his head.

'Let him continue,' he said firmly.

'Thank you, sir,' Mr Gerard replied. 'We are not in a position to plan for a new novelty toffee for this coming Christmas – it's too late. Also, we need to see out the rest of this year with caution and proceed slowly as we pay off our debts. However, looking beyond the end of the year, I suggest we maximise the potential of the commercialisation of Easter. It's become a confectionery manufacturer's dream for the chocolatiers in Europe. If we begin to produce soft toffee-filled chocolate eggs, it would put Jack's toffee factory on the map. We'd be unique in their production. No one else in the country does this.'

'That's because it's foolish,' Mr Burl muttered.

Everyone ignored him and waited for Mr Gerard to say more.

'We can sell the toffee eggs at a popular price. The customer will know exactly what they're getting inside. There'll be no nasty surprise, just a pure toffee treat. We could offer display stands to confectionery shops to sell the eggs with the Jack's logo on the front. There could be a range of eggs with novelty wrapping, marzipan flower decorations and extremely attractive packaging. Gentlemen . . .' he looked to Anne, then Clara, and smiled, 'and ladies of the board. I have had my team draw up ideas and designs. And I have worked with the finance team on costings for the new toffee eggs. I will give these to Mr Jack after the meeting.'

'Please give the papers to Meg,' William said. 'I have another meeting after this and will look at them later.'

Anne wondered what meeting William had, and with whom.

'Novelty toffee will never take off,' Mr Burl complained.

The finance manager sitting opposite also shook his head. 'I have to say I have reservations too. Any new line, be it eggs, giraffes or bumblebees...' a titter went up around the table, 'needs serious consideration, especially when we are struggling to keep the factory afloat. We can't rush into creating a new line of toffee, however laudable the sentiment.'

However, Mr Gerard remained firm. 'And neither can we, or should we, stand still and do nothing. The factory needs a future, a focus, and this new novelty line could be the one that saves us all.'

Muttering broke out, and Anne noticed Meg struggling to capture the men's comments in her notes.

'Gentlemen, please, for the record of the meeting, it is imperative that you speak one at a time and not over each other,' she said firmly.

A lengthy discussion then took place that had Anne's head spinning, and she was glad when the meeting finally ended.

She gave William's parents a hug and invited them over for dinner at the Deanery one night, then went to her office and closed the door, relieved to be alone. Sitting at her desk, she closed her eyes, but Mr Burl's face came to mind. He'd stormed out of the meeting when it had finished, muttering dark words about the foolishness of producing novelty toffee. She took a few deep breaths, feeling the stress of the meeting finally leaving her. Then she remembered the letter from Mayfair Toffee. The board meeting had pushed all thoughts of it away.

She glanced at her office door, aware that William would be furious to know that she'd been approached by a rival with an offer of work. Anne, however, was intrigued. She took the letter out and reread it. She felt flattered and curious, interested to know why they had sought her out, and in such a confidential way. The letter was clearly not for William's eyes, but of course Mayfair Toffee would assume that, as William's wife, she would tell him about it sooner or later. How odd it all was.

She folded the letter and slid it into the envelope, then placed it back in the drawer. She knew she should tell William, yet he had enough on his mind with the difficulties at the factory, and for that reason alone, she decided to keep quiet for now. Rising to her feet, she walked to the window in her office and looked at the gardens again. Stan Chapman and his men were turning the soil and planting more roses. She laid her hand on the window pane as she looked out.

'Perhaps the factory might survive after all,' she said.

She watched a group of factory girls in their khaki and red overalls walking in the garden, sitting on benches in the sunshine.

'It's dinner time already?' she muttered, casting a glance at the clock on her wall. Time had marched on in the board meeting, and she realised she was hungry, despite the hearty breakfast.

She saw Hetty and Elsie heading arm-in-arm to a bench near to where Stan was working. Elsie and Stan exchanged a smile, and Stan raised his cap in greeting, before Hetty and Elsie tucked into the food they carried in paper bags. Anne was about to turn from the window and head to the canteen when she saw William outside too. Intrigued, she watched him walk towards Elsie and Hetty. What on earth was he doing? She couldn't believe her eyes. She watched as he spoke to the two girls. Then Elsie rose and walked with him out of the gardens.

Anne's stomach turned over. William hadn't mentioned that he wanted to speak to Elsie again, so why would he seek her out? Was he talking to her about Sweets of Peace, to tell her the idea was now shelved? She shivered despite the warmth of her office. She peered out of the window as far as she could see, but William and Elsie had disappeared. She had to find out what was going on.

She walked quickly out of her office, along the hallway to the reception. Jacob was working at his desk. The room was quiet, warm and calm.

'Do you know where has my husband gone?' she demanded.

Jacob, startled by her outburst, looked up from his ledger. He opened his mouth to reply, but Anne flew past him, out to the cobbled yard. Around her, factory girls were walking to the gardens, or out to the café and shops on Front Street. Everyone wanted to make the most of their hour of freedom from the factory, and no one paid her any notice. She walked to the railway sidings at the back of the factory, asking the men there if they'd seen William. Everyone shook their heads.

'He's not been here this morning, Mrs Jack,' they said.

When she spotted Stan Chapman heading to the canteen, she stopped him and asked him if he'd seen Elsie.

'I did see her, yes,' he said nervously. 'But I wasn't slacking in my work, Mrs Jack, I never do. You can ask any of the lads in my team.'

'It's all right, Stan. I know what a hard worker you are.

I wondered if you'd noticed in which direction she headed when she left the gardens?'

Stan shook his head and apologised. Despondent, Anne walked back to reception. Nothing seemed to make sense.

'Mrs Jack?' Jacob called as soon as she stepped into the room.

She approached his desk and wasn't too surprised to see Meg with him. The pair had been courting for some time after Anne's friendly intervention had brought the lovebirds together.

'Yes, what is it?' she said.

She saw Jacob gently nudge Meg. 'Tell her, she'll understand,' he whispered.

'Meg?' Anne said kindly.

The woman blushed pink. 'It's the notes from Mr Gerard about the design and costing of the . . .' She glanced at Jacob. 'The, er, novelty item that was suggested at the board meeting.'

'Yes, what about it?' Anne said, her patience wearing thin.

'Well, the thing is, Mrs Jack, you see . . .'

'Tell her, be honest,' Jacob whispered.

Meg took heart from his encouragement. 'Mr Gerard's proposal was on my desk after Mr Jack left his office at dinner time. I went to the kitchen to make myself a cup of coffee, and when I returned . . .' She shifted nervously. 'When I returned, the proposal had gone.'

Chapter Nineteen

It was later that week, and Hetty and Elsie were almost ready to set off from Elm Street for work. Before they left the house, Elsie popped her head around Hilda's door.

'Anything you need before we leave?' she called.

But Hilda was sleeping, and so Elsie gently closed the door.

'You know, if we still had our little dog Jet, Hilda would have company when she wakes up,' she said. 'I still wonder why he ran away and who is looking after him now.'

Hetty shrugged. 'Maybe she could get a new dog if she moves to Elisabethville.'

They left the house and closed the door. Hetty slipped her arm through Elsie's.

'Think of the garden we could have if we move there, Hetty!' Elsie said. 'We'd be able to hang our washing on a clothes line, and our drawers can dry flapping in the wind instead of in a poky back yard. Ooh! Just think of electric lights in every room and water running out of our own taps. It'd be a palace compared to Elm Street.'

Hetty gently nudged her in the ribs. 'Do you mind?

That's my home you're talking about, the place I grew up in.'

Elsie looked at her seriously. 'And is a poky back street where you want to grow old and die?'

Hetty avoided her friend's gaze. Thinking about moving to a new house in Elisabethville meant thinking about Dirk leaving, and she didn't want to dwell on such a painful topic. They walked in silence for a few moments before she decided to change the subject.

'Where did you go with Mr Jack the other day?'

'Sorry, what?' Elsie said, distracted.

Hetty looked at her as they walked. 'You still haven't told me what happened or where you went. It's not like you to keep a secret. I thought we told each other everything. Where did Mr Jack take you when he interrupted our dinner at work?'

'Oh, that,' Elsie said dismissively. 'He wanted to speak to me about becoming the face of a new line of toffee.'

'But he'd already spoken to you about that,' Hetty said. 'When I was made the face of Lady Tina, I never got special treatment. I had a sitting with Mr Gerard and his team, who painted my likeness, then the next thing I knew my face was on the tins. There were no secret meetings between me and the factory owner.'

'It wasn't a secret meeting,' Elsie snapped.

Hetty stared at her. It wasn't like Elsie to lose her temper.

'I'm sorry, I'm a bit tired,' Elsie explained. She gave a weak smile. 'Now where were we? Oh yes, let's talk about moving to Elisabethville.'

Up at Lumley Castle, there was a knock at the kitchen door. Mrs Doughty, the cook and housekeeper, wasn't pleased with the interruption, as she was in the middle of rolling pastry. She didn't like having her routine disturbed. She was a stout woman with a cheerful round face. She wore a flour-covered apron over a long-sleeved black blouse. Her feet were clad in flat black shoes and her legs in black stockings. Her hair was uncovered, done up in a bun, from which strands of grey hair fell around her chubby cheeks.

'Can someone answer the door!' she yelled, hoping that one of the scullery maids or the kitchen staff, or even the Earl's butler, would go. When no one did, she dusted off her hands, tutted loudly, then marched to the door and pulled it open.

She was greeted by a dull-looking man she was sure she'd never set eyes on before. She noticed he carried a small bunch of wild flowers tied with scarlet ribbon. She narrowed her eyes at him. 'What do you want?'

The man stood to attention and attempted a smile. 'My name is Robert Grayson and I'm here to see Hetty. I understand from my sister that she works here on the days when she's not at the toffee factory.' He held out the flowers. 'I would like to give her these.'

Mrs Doughty put her floury hands on her hips and glared at him. 'Hetty? She's not here, love. And even if she was, you've got no right coming here demanding to see her. When she's here, she's at work. She can't be disturbed. I run an efficient kitchen and won't allow my girls to stop at the drop of a hat, or the knock at the door when a stranger arrives.' She made a move to close the door. 'Now if you don't mind, I've got work to do. The pastry won't make itself.'

The man stuck his foot in the doorway so that the

door wouldn't close. 'If she isn't here, does that mean I'll find her at the toffee factory today?'

Mrs Doughty shook her head. 'It's not my place to say where she might be. I'll be sure to tell her you called. Now if you'll just remove your foot . . .' And she pressed her own foot hard against his, bringing her weight down. He grimaced and stepped back. 'Good day, sir,' she said, then she slammed the door, floured her hands again and went back to rolling pastry.

Elsie and Hetty joined a throng of women and girls streaming in through the factory gates. The tall chimney next to the railway sidings was already belching smoke, signalling that toffee production had begun.

'Hey, there's Anne getting out of Mr Jack's car,' Elsie said, indicating the sleek black motor.

'She looks a bit frazzled this morning,' Hetty noted.

'I don't know what she's got to be frazzled about,' Elsie huffed. 'She's got everything on a plate, that one. A gorgeous little girl, a loving husband, a car, a housekeeper. Oh, I wish I had all that. See, Hetty, that's what I want in my life. I don't want boring and dull.'

Hetty raised an eyebrow. 'You mean you don't want Stan.'

Elsie shrugged. 'Stan's all right. He's a nice man, but you know I crave excitement.'

'You want the world on a stick, Elsie Cooper.'

Elsie laughed out loud. 'You know me too well, dear friend.'

As Anne walked towards reception, she called out to Elsie. 'Can I have a word, Elsie, please?'

'I wonder what she wants?' Hetty whispered.

'There's only one way to find out,' Elsie replied.

Anne led the way through reception, along the hall and into her office. She indicated a chair at her desk, and Elsie sat, while Anne remained standing, still wearing her coat.

'What's going on between you and my husband?' she demanded without preamble.

Elsie rocked back in her seat with shock. This wasn't what she'd expected. 'What? Going on where? What on earth do you mean?'

'You've met him twice, meetings I knew nothing about.'

Elsie felt her face begin to burn. 'Have you asked him?' she said.

Anne's face fell. 'Of course I've asked him. I'm not stupid.'

'Anne, please—' Elsie began, but Anne cut her off.

'He says he's been talking to you about becoming the face of the new Sweets of Peace, but I know that can't be true. The board hasn't voted in favour of any new line of toffee. So come on, out with it. I demand you tell me now.'

Elsie swallowed hard. She forced herself to look into Anne's determined face and gripped her hands in her lap as she gave her reply. 'It's exactly as Mr Jack says, Anne. He was fired up about a new toffee line. He wanted to talk to me about using my likeness for the tin. I can't say any more than that, because there's nothing else to tell.' She felt Anne's eyes boring into her, but she kept her nerve and held her head up.

Finally Anne gave a loud sigh, her shoulders sank and she began to undo the buttons on her coat. 'I'm sorry, Elsie. Look, if Mrs Perkins complains about you being late in the slab room, tell her I called you into my office. I don't want you getting in trouble for something that's not your fault.'

Elsie rose and began to walk from the room.

'Elsie?' Anne said.

Elsie spun around. She looked into Anne's face, illuminated by the light from the office window. She thought her friend looked exhausted, and her heart went out to her.

'I'm sorry if it sounded as if I was accusing you of something other than being chosen for the new toffee line. I've got an awful lot on my mind at the moment, and nothing makes sense. I lost something special recently, then something important went missing from Meg's office after the board meeting. My mind is jumbled, and I seem to be jumping to conclusions, seeing things that aren't there.'

'Perhaps you're in need of a rest,' Elsie suggested.

Anne nodded gravely. 'You might be right.'

Elsie opened the door and walked out into the hallway. She had to lean against the wall for a moment to steady herself as her legs turned to jelly and her heart began to pound.

Bob arrived at the factory gates, still clutching the bunch of wilting wild flowers. He walked to reception and stood in front of Jacob, who ignored him completely. Finally he could take no more. He coughed loudly and Jacob looked up.

'Good morning, sir, how may I help you?'

Bob stepped forward. 'I'm here to see one of the toffee factory girls; her name is Hetty Lawson.'

Jacob eyed him coolly. 'I'm afraid it's not possible to

visit any of our staff during working hours. You'll need to come back at dinner time or after work tonight.'

'But she's here today, yes?' Bob asked.

'I'm sure if she wished you to know where she was, she would tell you,' Jacob replied sternly. 'Now please, sir, this is a place of work, and I would appreciate it if you would leave.'

'Can't I wait for her here?' Bob pleaded.

One look from Jacob gave him his answer.

'All right, I'll go,' he said sadly, and turned to leave.

When she'd finally pulled herself together, Elsie walked out of reception, ignoring Jacob at his desk. She noticed a man carrying a bunch of wild flowers, but paid him no mind as he walked towards the factory gates. Out in the fresh air at last, she took a deep breath and pushed a lock of dark hair behind her ear. She straightened her overall, then popped open the top button and headed to the slab room. Before she reached it, however, she heard a commotion in the garden. She saw Stan's team of men, then her heart dropped when she spotted Stan lying on the ground. She ran to him and threw herself down at his side.

'What happened?' she cried.

'He collapsed,' one of the men replied. 'I've sent a lad to fetch the doctor.'

'He was fine when he arrived this morning, but then he went down like a sack of spuds,' another added.

Elsie looked at Stan's face. His skin, normally ruddy from the years spent working outdoors, was ashen and pale.

Chapter Twenty

'Stan? Can you hear me? It's Elsie.'

'Elsie?' he whispered.

'It's all right, Stan, don't worry. Help's coming.' She reached out and took his hand.

The factory doctor was soon on the scene. Elsie stood and moved away to allow him to kneel at Stan's side. She watched as he expertly examined Stan, listening to his heart and chest and checking his vital signs. Then he nodded to the men and together they got him to his feet. Stan laid one arm around the doctor's shoulders and the other around one of his men, and they helped him to the sick bay. Elsie followed with concern etched on her face. She'd only ever known Stan as robust and healthy. To see him stricken like that, lying on the ground barely breathing, was hard to take in.

She stood at the door of the sick bay, watching as the doctor brought him a glass of water. Stan was slumped in a chair; he seemed unable to focus or pull himself up.

'Does he need the hospital, Doc?' one of the gardeners asked.

The doctor busied himself putting away his stethoscope

after listening to Stan's heart again. 'No, thankfully. But he does need to go home to rest. Does he live far? Could one of you take him?'

One of the lads stepped forward. 'I'll take him. I know where he lives, it's only a few streets away. He might need a cup of tea bringing from the canteen.'

'Fetch him something to eat too, a slice of pie or cake, whatever you can get your hands on,' the doctor added.

'I'll do that,' another lad said, and disappeared from the room.

Elsie took the opportunity to step inside and sit next to Stan. She reached for his hand again. 'I'll come to your house after I finish work tonight,' she said softly. 'To check how you are. I could take Patch for his evening walk along the river if you're not feeling up to it.'

'Thanks, Elsie,' he managed to say. His breathing was shallow and weak.

Elsie looked at the doctor with concern. 'What's wrong with him? Why did he collapse?'

The doctor stood up straight and eyed Stan directly. 'Are you eating properly?' he said.

Stan dropped his gaze to the floor. 'As well as I can,' he muttered.

'You need to look after yourself better. We can't have you passing out at work, especially when you're working with sharp blades in the garden. You need feeding up, lad.'

'Yes, Doc,' Stan mumbled.

The doctor looked at Elsie's hand wrapped around Stan's. She noticed his gaze, felt uneasy and pulled away.

'I'm just a friend,' she said.

He nodded. 'I see. Well, someone needs to make sure he looks after himself.'

Elsie remembered Stan's words about not having time to eat during the day, and wondered if he had been pushing himself too hard at work, running on little energy.

'I'll do my best,' she said.

The lad appeared at the door with a mug of hot tea and a slice of toffee cake, which he handed to Stan.

'There's three sugars in your tea, just how you like it.'

'Thanks, lad,' Stan replied.

Elsie stood. 'I need to go back to work, otherwise Mrs Perkins will be after me. But I'll pop by your house tonight, straight after work. I'll call at the butcher on Front Street and bring a beef pie.'

Stan reached for her hand. She felt comforted by his touch. Neither of them was in a hurry to let the other go.

'Until tonight, Stan. Take care of yourself and rest.'

'Aye, lass, I'll be fine. You'll see,' he said.

Elsie hated leaving him there, looking so ill and pale, and wished there was more she could do.

When work ended that day, Elsie and Hetty walked out of the slab room and headed to the factory gates.

'I'm going to Stan's house to check on him. I'll be home later,' Elsie said.

Hetty nodded. 'Well I might not be there when you get back. I'm going to Elisabethville with Dirk to help him clear the schoolroom.'

Elsie gently laid her hand on Hetty's arm. 'That must be heartbreaking for you. As if it's not enough that he's leaving soon, he's got you working at the Belgian village.'

Hetty shook her head. 'He didn't ask me to do it. I offered. I want to spend as much time with him as I can before he leaves, even if that means packing boxes at Elisabethville. I can't bear to think about losing him, Elsie. I honestly don't know what I'm going to do after he's gone.'

Elsie leaned into her and hugged her tight. But as she looked over Hetty's shoulder, she saw a man walking towards them with a determined look on his face.

'Hetty?' she whispered.

'What is it, love?'

'Do you know a tall lad, thin, with a long face? He's heading our way.'

Hetty stiffened. 'Oh crikey, it sounds just like Bob. Where is he?' she whispered.

'Behind you,' Elsie replied. 'Do you want me to stay?'

Hetty shook her head.

'Are you sure?'

'I'll be fine. It's about time I faced him. He needs to know where we stand.'

Hetty took a deep breath before slowly turning around. As she came face to face with Bob for the first time in more than four years, the shock hit her hard. The last time they'd seen each other had been on the day Bob had gone off to war. She'd walked with him to the railway station, where he'd boarded the train but hadn't kissed her goodbye. Back then, it had been taken for granted that the two of them would wed when he returned. But that had been before she'd had her head turned and her heart stolen by Dirk.

Now she looked at the man in front of her. He was

thinner than she'd seen him last, his face gaunt and his gaze vacant. However, rather than seeming happy to see her, he appeared angry. Hetty steadied herself for what she guessed was to come.

'You never answered my letters!' he cried.

'Sorry?' she said at last, trying to focus. She hadn't heard his voice in so long, she'd forgotten what it sounded like. There had been no 'Hello, Hetty' or 'How are you?' but then she hadn't expected much else. Bob had always been blunt. That was one of his many traits that she disliked.

'My letters, Hetty. You never replied to them,' he snapped. 'Then I learned from my sister that you'd got yourself another man. Well, that certainly explains the lack of correspondence. But I'm prepared to overlook it, Hetty Lawson. Now that I'm back, things will be different.'

Hetty was shoved from the side by two girls walking out of the factory gates. 'We need to go somewhere quiet to have this conversation,' she said. She was in a state of shock at seeing Bob, and she had to press her feet into the pavement to steady herself. He held out his arm for her to take, but she shook her head. She had to hold her nerve.

'We'll go to the river and sit for a while,' he said.

'No, not there,' she cried. The riverside had become her special place where she went with Dirk.

Bob looked at her, startled. 'Then I insist on walking you home. We'll walk slowly and talk on the way.'

Hetty agreed, knowing she owed him an explanation. The truth was the least he deserved. They headed along Front Street in silence, but instead of going home to Elm Street, Hetty had an idea. She turned a corner and made for the railway station.

Celebrations at the Toffee Factory

'There are seats on the platform, we can talk in privacy,' she said.

When they reached the station, they found an empty bench. Hetty sat on one end and Bob on the other, with a space between them. The station was quiet; a train had just left and was steaming away in the distance.

So much had happened since the last time they were on the railway platform together. Hetty was different now, no longer the timid girl Bob had left without so much as a goodbye kiss. She was more confident and sure of herself. She knew what she wanted... and what she didn't. When they began to talk, they both spoke at once.

'Bob, I need to be honest with you—'

'Hetty, I have something to say—'

'Let me speak first,' Hetty said firmly. She was acutely aware from Bob's letters and from what Hilda had told her about his visit to Elm Street that he was intent on proposing. She needed to nip things in the bud. She looked him square in the eye, trying to keep her voice calm while her heart hammered with fear of upsetting him.

'Your sister was right. There is someone else in my life, someone I'm very keen on. Someone, in fact, that I love.' She felt a lump rise in her throat thinking about Dirk and knowing she was set to lose him. 'I'm sorry to be blunt, Bob. I wrote to you and told you all about this. But I found out from your sister that the letter didn't arrive. When you kept on writing to me, I couldn't figure out why.'

Bob stiffened. 'Yes, well, least said, soonest mended. You'll listen to me now, Hetty. I even brought you flowers.'

'Flowers?' she cried. Bob had never given her flowers, and she saw his hands were empty now.

'My sister gave them to me this morning, she thought you might like them. But they wilted so much I threw them away. Anyway, war's over, Hetty, and I'm back. I went away as a boy, but I've come back a man, and I want to claim what's rightfully mine. You can say goodbye to your other chap now,' he added formally.

Hetty kept her hands in her lap and stared ahead. 'No, Bob, you can't tell me what to do. When you went off to war, I was a girl, but now I'm a woman and I know my own mind. Claim what's rightfully yours? How dare you! I'm not a piece of furniture you can pick up and take home. I'm sorry, but I've got strong feelings for Dirk, and I don't want to say goodbye to him.'

Her heart fell as the words left her lips, because saying goodbye to Dirk was exactly what she'd need to do soon. Tears pricked her eyes at the thought of life without him. Dirk made her laugh, took her dancing, and had supported her through the agony of Dan's death and finding out Hilda wasn't her mum. Even when he went back to Belgium and she was left on her own, she knew she could never settle for Bob. After meeting Dirk, she knew what love was. And she'd never felt that way with Bob.

'No, Bob, it's over between us. But then it never really began, did it?' she added softly.

'How can you say that?' he demanded.

'Because it's true. You and I grew up together, and we became close, we were friends. Your sister and Hilda assumed we'd get married, and so did you. But it wasn't what I wanted. When you went off to war, we didn't even know what love was.' She knew she was wounding him with each word, but he had to be told. He had to know they had no future. 'Can't you see? I'm setting you free.

There are lots of lovely girls in Chester-le-Street who'd be lucky to have a man like you.'

'But I don't want just any girl. I want you,' he declared.

Hetty stood and reached for his hand, but it wasn't to caress it. She shook it heartily, hoping to give him a final goodbye.

'It's over between us. I should go. Hilda will be wondering where I am.'

She turned to leave, but Bob gripped her arm, and she cried out in pain. She shook his hand away angrily and looked at his face. His eyes had narrowed with anger.

'You can't walk away from me, Hetty Lawson. I won't give up without a fight.'

Chapter Twenty-One

Elsie found Stan's house without a problem; it was at the end of a terraced row close to the factory. She appraised it as she walked towards it. The windows sparkled and the door was freshly painted. And the front garden, although small, was magnificent. It was a riot of colour, with flowers spilling onto the path. She breathed in their sweet scent as she knocked on the door. When there was no reply, she opened the letter box.

'Stan? Are you in there?'

'Come in, Elsie,' he replied.

She pushed open the door. Despite the warm day outside, the house felt cold.

'I'm in the back room,' he called.

Elsie walked along the hallway to a room at the back where a coal fire burned. She stood on the threshold, unsure how much further she should go.

'I called to see if you were all right,' she said. She thrust her hand into her handbag. 'And I brought the beef pie I promised. It'll taste better if you heat it.'

She stepped forward and laid the pie in its paper bag on a sideboard. Stan was sitting at the kitchen table, in front of a large window that overlooked a garden at the back. The flowers here too caught Elsie's eye, and she moved forward for a closer look.

'Why, it's beautiful,' she said.

'Aye, it is that,' Stan replied. 'My garden's just about the only thing that gives me pleasure these days.'

His dog Patch uncurled himself from under the table and stood to attention at Elsie's side.

'And Patch here, of course,' Stan added with a wry smile. 'Sit yourself down, Elsie. Would you like a cup of tea?'

Elsie slid into a seat at the table and began to stroke Patch's head. 'I'd love one, thank you. How are you feeling now?'

Stan laid his hand on her shoulder. 'Thanks for asking, lass. It's good to know someone cares.'

As he busied himself with a small kettle and teapot, Elsie turned to look at him properly. 'You've got a bit more colour in your cheeks now,' she said.

'I'm feeling better, lass. Today was a one-off. It'll never happen again.'

'I overheard the doc say that you weren't eating properly,' Elsie began softly.

Stan took his time to reply, and when he did, he kept his gaze on his beloved garden. 'I'm a proud man, Elsie, and I don't like asking for help. I've managed to cope on my own so far in life, and I'll continue to do so. But the truth is, I'm not a good cook and I guess I've been lazy with mealtimes at home. I've been so busy at work; I threw myself into renovating the gardens and lost myself in the pleasure of it all. It means I didn't think much about food and haven't been eating as well as I should. I've been skipping meals, not eating breakfast, and working through dinner at work. I guess fatigue overtook me in the end.'

Elsie reached for his hand. He turned his face to her, and she looked deep into his hazel eyes. 'Oh, Stan,' she said softly.

He moved away, seeming to want to put an end to the topic, but Elsie carried on.

'Let me help you. You were so good to me when I suffered that awful business with Frankie. It's the least I can do . . . as a friend.'

He set the kettle on the coals, then sat next to her at the table. 'And as a friend, I'd like to say thank you for bringing the beef pie. It looks good and I'll eat it tonight.'

'What else can I do?' she asked, but he waved his hand dismissively.

'I'll be all right, lass. I'm sure you've got better things to do than think about me.'

But thinking about Stan was something that Elsie had been doing a lot that day.

She thought of the evening that lay ahead. She had the tea to cook, then she'd be left at home with Hilda while Hetty went to meet Dirk. Even if she was only helping him to clear the schoolroom, it was more exciting and interesting than anything Elsie had planned that night, or any night for that matter. Sitting at the table next to Stan, looking out of the window at flowers, shrubs and neat rows of vegetables, made her feel settled and happy. She began to unbutton her coat.

'It's nice and cosy in here with the fire. Mind if I take off my coat?'

'Make yourself at home,' Stan replied with a warm smile.

* * *

The next morning at the factory, Anne sat in her office with much on her mind. William was still being secretive at home and at work, and both of them were stressed and anxious. Plus, the missing notes about the toffee eggs had still not turned up. Neither had her blue and silver brooch, and each time she thought of this, her stomach turned over.

She opened a folder of correspondence that Meg had typed for her and read each sheet carefully. Some of the letters contained errors, and she sighed as she circled these for Meg to type again. She was worried about the woman, who'd been in a state of panic ever since the confidential notes had been taken from her office. She knew Meg wasn't the most organised secretary, so perhaps she'd simply mislaid the pages, or misfiled them. She felt certain they'd turn up soon. Still, it was very concerning. The last thing Anne and William needed was for details of their proposed new line to fall into a rival confectioner's hands.

With correspondence read, she stood from her desk, picked up the folder and walked along the hallway to William's office. She expected him to be there, knowing he had a mountain of administration to work through that morning. There were letters to be sent to all their creditors promising that the factory would pay its debts and asking them to allow this to be done carefully and slowly so as not to put the factory at risk. The letters needed to be carefully worded, and each one sent with a sweetener of a tin of best toffee.

She pushed open the door and was surprised to see William's chair empty. Thinking he was perhaps with Meg, she strode confidently to the anteroom. However,

Meg was sitting at her desk alone, collating papers. Anne looked around the door as if William might be hiding behind it.

'Good morning, Mrs Jack,' Meg said, looking up.

'Where's my husband?' Anne asked.

'Isn't he in his office?'

'Would I be asking you if he was?' she replied snappily, then regretted her tone. It wasn't Meg's fault that she felt so wretched. She attempted a smile as Meg flicked through the appointments diary.

'He's not due to meet the sugar boilers until dinner time. He should be in his office. Perhaps he's just stepped out to . . .'

Anne didn't hear the rest of Meg's words. She knew exactly where William was. She could see him clearly through the office window. He was walking with his arm around Elsie Cooper's shoulders. The two of them had their heads together, as if discussing something private.

'How dare he!' she hissed.

'Mrs Jack?' Meg said, alarmed.

Anne slammed the folder onto the desk and strode from the room. She hurried along the hallway and into reception.

'Mrs Jack, wait!' Jacob called, but she brushed him off in her rush to get out and ran across the cobbled yard to the gardens. William and Elsie were ahead, with their backs to her, but she heard Elsie laugh and William chuckle. She was about to call her husband's name, to ask him what in the name of their marriage he was playing at, when something happened that stopped her dead. He leaned in to Elsie and kissed her.

Chapter Twenty-Two

Anne was distraught. She was desperate to know what was going on, but there were factory girls in the gardens, delivery men walking to the warehouse and too many others around. She clenched her fists and screwed her eyes tight to stop the tears from falling. Then she took a deep breath and forced herself to turn around and head back to reception. It was one of the most difficult things she'd ever done, but she had too much pride to make a scene in front of staff, not least in front of Elsie. She would keep her dignity and tackle William alone. She held her head high as she walked back to reception, and slowly, with each step she took, an idea began to form.

'Mrs Jack? Are you all right? You look a little flustered,' Jacob called as she walked past his desk.

Anne was so completely gripped by her idea, she didn't hear him. She walked to her office, put on her coat and picked up her briefcase. Then she removed her black velvet hat from the coat stand and placed it on her head. She wanted to look as smart as she could for what lay ahead. Opening her desk drawer, she took out the letter from Mayfair Toffee. She still hadn't mentioned it to William, as there'd been so much going on at the factory after the board meeting. She hadn't seen the need to bother him about it, and now she was glad that she'd kept it a secret. She thrust it into her briefcase and marched back through reception.

'I'm going out, Jacob,' she called as she walked from the room, her coat tails flying behind her.

'If Mr Jack asks where you've gone, what would you like me to tell him?' Jacob replied.

'Tell him I've gone out on business.'

Outside, she kept her gaze forward, not allowing herself to check to see if William and Elsie were still there. She needed to stay focused on the task in hand. She saw William's car on the road outside the factory gates and was tempted to drive herself to Sunderland, but she'd never driven on a major road yet. So she kept on walking to the bus stop. It would be a long journey to Sunderland, with a change of bus too. But it wasn't something to be scared of. Indeed, it felt as if nothing could scare her in the mood she was in. After what she'd just witnessed, she was ready to rip the world to shreds. How could she not have known that William was having an affair? How could Elsie have betrayed her? She felt furious with them both, and berated herself with each step she took.

Once on the bus, she went over in her mind the events of the last few weeks. The missing brooch, the flash of blue and silver in Elsie's hand. Had William really given her beloved brooch to Elsie? She felt sick at the thought. She'd poured everything into William and the factory. Everything. All her time and energy had gone into her work, and for what? She'd been rewarded with a slap in the face from the man she loved, and from her friend. She and Elsie had shared confidences. Anne had bent the rules at the factory to allow Elsie to stay at work when she'd fallen pregnant with Frankie's child. And she'd pleaded with Mrs Perkins many times to give Elsie another chance after the supervisor complained about her work.

She felt tears threaten and turned her face to the window so that no one would see her cry. She took a linen handkerchief from her pocket and dabbed her eyes. Then she straightened in her seat and took a deep breath. She resolved to tackle William as soon as she returned home. If he admitted that he loved Elsie and wanted to end their marriage, she wouldn't beg him to reconsider. She'd pack her bags, scoop Dinah into her arms and leave. Where she'd go was another matter. Perhaps there were rooms available for women like her, although taking her child with her would make things difficult, if not impossible. Plans and options ran through her mind, but none of them were what she wanted. What she wanted was to go home to her husband and their daughter, enjoy a hearty meal cooked by Edith and talk about the day's events. Instead, she was being forced to think about her future alone.

How she'd do it, she didn't know, but she was determined not to return to her philandering husband. Each time she thought of him walking with Elsie in the grounds, heads together, arm around Elsie's shoulder . . . and that kiss . . . oh, that kiss turned her stomach. What a fool she was not to have noticed the signs! But then they'd been as good as living apart under the same roof for a long time as problems at the factory had intruded into their home.

Finally the bus arrived in Sunderland and Anne alighted. Once there, she remembered the route to Durham Road and the Mayfair Toffee factory. It was a solid building on a main road, nothing like Jack's factory and nowhere as big. There was no chimney at the back and no railway sidings. It looked more like a grand office with tall windows at the front. Anne took a small mirror from her briefcase and checked her reflection. She dabbed her eyes with her handkerchief, aware that they must surely look red and puffy from her tears. She pushed a lock of hair under her velvet hat and replaced the mirror. Then, as confidently as she could, she marched into Mayfair Toffee.

Two hours later, sitting on the bus heading back to Chester-le-Street, Anne felt more sure of her future after being given a firm job offer, to start at a date of her choice. However, she hadn't yet accepted. Just knowing she had the option should she and William separate gave her a morale boost. She would have her own office, and her own secretary too, a cheerful woman called Gwen whom she'd met and been impressed with during the meeting with the factory owner. However, not everything he'd told her was good news. Her role there, if she accepted it, would be to help close down the factory, firing employees and putting others on a short working week. Mayfair Toffee, it transpired, was failing, and they needed Anne's professional help and advice.

It was a poisoned chalice of a role, one that wouldn't last longer than a year. The salary wouldn't be high, but it would be enough to pay rent on rooms on Eden House Road, around the corner from the factory, and of course she'd need to hire someone to look after Dinah too. She ran through the practicalities. This was where her strength lay, and the reason she'd been taken on by Mr Jack, who'd been impressed with her logic and good sense. But as the bus neared Chester-le-Street, her emotions threated to overwhelm her.

She forced herself to stand when the bus reached Front Street, gripping the back of the seat for support. Her legs felt like lead. Dread of what lay ahead at home scared her, but she knew she had to be strong. She ran through in her mind all the things she would say, all the words she would use, and kept repeating them as she walked to the Deanery. She paused on the doorstep, thinking this might be the last time she ever entered the place she'd come to love as her home. Then the door opened, and she almost fell inside. William, Edith and Dinah were there, all with worried expressions on their faces.

'Anne, my darling! Where have you been?' exclaimed William.

'Mama!' cried Dinah.

'Mrs Jack, if you're not coming home for dinner in future, could you kindly let me know in advance? The pie ended up burned after spending so long in the oven!' Edith said sternly.

Anne picked up Dinah and soothed her worried brow. 'It's all right, darling. Mama's home.'

'Thank goodness for that,' Edith declared, and walked off to the kitchen.

'Anne, where did you go?' William asked. 'I've had Meg looking for you all afternoon. Jacob said you'd gone out on business, but there was nothing in the diary. I've been worried sick.'

Anne placed Dinah on the ground and the child toddled

after Edith. She removed her hat and coat and placed her briefcase under the coat stand in the hall. Then she glared at her husband. 'I saw you today, with Elsie Cooper,' she said, keeping her gaze firm and her voice even.

William looked along the hallway at the open kitchen door. 'Keep your voice down, Edith might hear,' he urged.

Anne walked into the living room. William followed, and she slammed the door shut. 'Don't you dare tell me to keep quiet,' she said. She poked him hard in the chest with her forefinger. 'I know what's going on. You and Elsie Cooper. You had me fooled for a while. Well, I won't be fooled any more. I'm taking Dinah and I'm leaving. If you want Elsie, you can have her. Or are you making your way around all the factory girls? Is it Elsie Cooper this week, Hetty Lawson next week and Mrs Perkins after that? How stupid I've been not to notice what's going on under my nose.'

'Anne, please,' William begged. He tried to reach for her hands, but she stepped away.

'I'm leaving. I will not stay in a marriage where my husband not only doesn't love me, but openly canoodles with other women right in front of my eyes.'

'Anne, no!' he cried.

'Move out of my way,' she said.

William began protesting, pleading with her to stay, but Anne's mind was set. She opened the living-room door, walked upstairs and began to pack a trunk. He followed her, telling her she was wrong, swearing there was nothing going on with Elsie, or anyone else. But Anne had seen the truth with her own eyes, and she wouldn't listen, no matter how hard he pleaded.

'Leave me alone!' she demanded. Finally, reluctantly, he went downstairs.

Anne placed clothes for her and Dinah, enough for a couple of nights, into a trunk. Two nights in a hotel, perhaps, would give her time to think. She began to struggle downstairs with the trunk, but it proved too heavy.

When William saw her, he rushed upstairs to help. 'Anne, you can't leave me!' he begged.

'Well I certainly can't stay, William. You've given me no option. Another woman, someone weaker, might stay, but not me. You've picked the wrong person to mess with.'

'I love you, Anne,' he cried. 'Don't go. You've got it all wrong!'

Chapter Twenty-Three

Anne went to the kitchen, looking for Dinah. William followed her.

'Where will you go?' he asked.

'A hotel, I expect, for now.'

'Then let me drive you. If it's time away from here ... from me that you want, I'll try to understand and respect your decision. You can have as much time as you need, then we'll talk. I will not let you walk out of our marriage when I've done nothing wrong.'

Anne heard Edith gasp. She narrowed her eyes at William. 'Nothing wrong? I saw you kiss Elsie Cooper!'

Edith's hand shot to her heart.

'Anyway, I don't need you to drive me anywhere. I can take the car myself.'

'Anne, I can't let you go. You've got it all wrong,' William said again.

'I know what I saw with my own eyes,' she replied.

Dinah began to cry, and Edith brought the girl to her in a hug. Anne lugged the trunk to the car, batting away William's offers of help. She managed to get it onto the back seat, then returned to the house for her daughter. But William blocked her way.

'I don't love Elsie; neither do I want her. It's you I love, Anne, only you.'

'I saw you with your arm around her shoulders.' Anne was determined not to let him change her mind.

'She was helping me with something, that's all. A little task.'

Anne lifted Dinah into her arms, then spun around towards William. 'I won't argue any more. I'm tired and going to bed.'

She stormed out of the room, as William continued to plead with her to listen. However, Anne was too headstrong. Her pride wouldn't allow her to yield. William's words fell behind her as she left the room.

In the middle of the night, Anne decided she could take no more of William and Elsie tangled in her mind. She needed to think things through, away from William, and decided the only thing she could do was leave.

Quietly and carefully, she placed her daughter in the car, drying her tears, trying her best to reassure her that everything was all right, then climbed into the driver's seat. She remembered what William had taught her about starting the car, and slowly pulled away from the kerb.

She drove carefully. Dinah had stopped crying and now thought the car ride an adventure. Anne kept calm and collected as she manoeuvred onto Front Street. She'd thought of heading to Durham to find a hotel, but the road was one she'd never driven on before, and she was unsure of finding her way. Then a sign caught her eye. It pointed to the village of Lumley, where William's parents lived. Could she . . . should she go there at this time of night? If she did, she knew she'd have to explain what had happened. She mulled it over for a second, but with nowhere else to go, she decided it was her best option. She felt sure of this road, as she'd driven it with William many times before. She glanced at Dinah, who was fast asleep.

Albert and Clara's house was set in its own grounds. Anne pulled up on the gravel drive and brought Dinah into her arms. She left the trunk in the car, walked to the impressive stone archway over the door and raised the door knocker. After a few minutes, she heard Clara's voice within.

'I'll answer it, Albert.'

Anne braced herself. She knew Clara would be surprised by this unexpected visit, and shocked when she heard the reason.

The door opened, and Clara's face showed immediate concern when she saw Anne and Dinah. She was visibly shocked and Anne felt a stab of guilt at disturbing her so late.

'What on earth are you doing here at this time of night?' Clara asked.

Anne hugged Dinah tight. 'May I come in, Clara? There's been an incident at home.'

Clara's mouth opened in shock. 'Is it William? Is he all right? Oh, please tell me my boy is all right.'

'He's fine, don't worry,' Anne reassured her.

Albert appeared, and Anne acknowledged him, managing a weak smile.

'Come in, girl,' he said, opening the door wide. 'Don't just stand there, Clara, let them in.'

Anne stepped into the house. 'Dinah's asleep. May I put her to bed upstairs before we speak?' she asked.

Clara nodded her assent. 'You can put her in William's old room, she'll be warm enough in there.'

Anne did as instructed, then returned downstairs. When she walked into the living room, Albert poured whisky into three glasses.

'Clara's on the telephone to William to let him know you've arrived.'

Anne's heart fell. 'He won't turn up here, will he? I can't bear to face him.'

Albert handed her a glass of whisky, and when she took it, she realised her hand was shaking.

'No, he won't come. Clara's firm on that. She'll tell him to stay at home. She's guessed that something's happened between you. Care to tell us what it was?'

Clara came into the room and took a glass of whisky from the sideboard. Anne sat on the sofa and faced the two of them.

'There's no easy way to say this,' she began. She could feel Clara and Albert's eyes on her. 'I've left William.'

Albert downed his whisky in a single gulp. Clara placed her glass on a side table, then walked across the room to sit beside Anne. She gently placed her hand on Anne's arm.

'Whatever has happened, my dear?'

Anne's eyes brimmed with tears at the kindness of her parents-in-law. But she also knew she had to be careful with what she said next. William was their son, and their loyalty lay with him. She decided not to tell them about Elsie.

'There's, um ... there's been a problem and it's

insurmountable, I'm afraid. I've taken the car, and Dinah. I didn't know where else to go.'

'You did the right thing coming here. We'll take care of you and the child,' Albert said. He shot Clara a look. 'Won't we, dear?'

Clara's eyes filled with tears. 'You can stay for as long as you need. Are you sure you won't tell us what the problem is?'

Anne sipped her whisky, stalling for time. 'I can't,' she said at last. 'It should remain between William and me.'

'Will you speak to him if he comes here?' Albert asked.

Anne had a great deal of respect for her father-in-law. Like her, he was practical and straight thinking.

'I must, in time. But not tonight, please. I can't bear to see him for a few days.' She looked from Albert to Clara. 'I'm very grateful for your support. I'm sorry, truly I am, for turning up unannounced and laying my problems at your door. I had nowhere else to go.'

'Will you let your friends Hetty and Elsie know what's happened?'

Anne winced at the sound of Elsie's name. 'I don't know when I'll see them next,' she said softly. Sinking back against the soft cushions on the sofa, she closed her eyes and pressed away tears.

Albert and Clara had the decency not to ask too many more questions and, once Albert had brought in her trunk, they ushered Anne upstairs. She checked on Dinah in William's old room and was relieved to find her asleep although she knew the child would be confused when she woke in the unfamiliar room. She'd never stayed overnight at her grandparents' house.

The room she'd been given by Clara was next door to Dinah. It was cosy, with a floral print on the wall and a matching eiderdown. As soon as she got undressed and climbed into bed, she too fell asleep.

Anne awoke shortly afterwards to the sound of banging at the front door.

'Steady on, you'll have the knocker off its hinges!' Albert called.

Anne froze. Surely it couldn't be William after he'd been told by his mother not to come here. But who else could it be at this time in the morning? She listened as Albert opened the door. She heard him speak to someone, then he called her name.

'Anne? You have a visitor. A woman is asking to see you.'

A woman? Anne's heart skipped a beat. She walked to the landing and peered over the banister, stunned to see Elsie there.

Chapter Twenty-Four

With her heart pounding, Anne dressed quickly and forced herself to walk down the stairs, holding tight to the banister. She felt as if her legs might give way, but she'd be damned if she was going to let Elsie know how shaken she was.

'Anne, would you like to use the parlour to talk?' Albert asked.

'Thank you,' she replied.

Without looking at Elsie, she walked to the parlour door and pushed it open. A coal fire was still burning within. She turned around and saw Elsie behind her.

'Close the door,' she ordered.

Elsie did so. Anne stood beside the hearth and felt the warmth of the fire against her skin.

'Sit down,' she said.

Elsie sat in a high-backed chair at the fireplace. Anne took time to compose herself, then began to speak.

'I expect William has sent you,' she said.

Elsie leapt from her seat and ran to her. 'Anne, please, you have to listen. Your husband and I . . . there's nothing going on. He came to my house in the early hours of this morning. He walked all the way there to tell me you were here. He's out of his mind with worry. He said you wouldn't listen to him when he tried to explain. Please, Anne, will you listen to *me*?'

Anne turned her face away.

'Anne, you have to know the truth,' Elsie pleaded.

'I saw the truth with my own eyes. You kissed my husband. That's all the truth I need. I'm hurt and angry, not just with William but also with you. I thought you were my friend.'

'I *am* your friend,' Elsie cried.

Anne looked at her. Caught by the light from the fire, she saw that Elsie's face was tear stained. She faltered for a moment, and a dreadful thought ran through her mind.

'How did you get here? William's not outside, is he?'

'No, Stan Chapman brought me in the factory van. Please don't be mad at Stan. I begged him. I didn't know how else to get here. I had to see you alone to try to make you see sense.'

Elsie reached for Anne's hands, but Anne stepped away. She walked to a sofa and sat down, facing the fire. Elsie sat on the other end of the sofa. A clock in the room ticked the minutes away, then hesitantly Elsie began to speak.

'It's true that Mr Jack kissed me. And it's true I've been spending a little time with him lately. But none of it is what you think. He is utterly devoted to you. He's your husband and you're my friend. There's no way I'd get involved with a married man, never mind the owner of a toffee factory.' She gave a wry smile. 'I've got enough of a reputation around town. Can you imagine the gossips wagging their tongues if they thought I was running around with your husband? Besides, there's someone else I'm fond of.' Her voice trailed away.

Anne looked at her again. 'Go on,' she said.

Elsie looked deep into the flames as she continued. 'Mr Jack's been a fool, Anne. He'll admit that himself as soon as you let him speak. We began to meet after he chose me to become the face of Sweets of Peace. We met in his office, as you know, and when I was with him, he asked me something else – a personal favour.'

Anne's eyebrows rose. 'What favour?'

Elsie dropped her gaze, gathered her hands to her lap and avoided eye contact.

'What favour?' Anne repeated, more sternly.

Elsie raised her eyes to meet Anne's, and Anne saw again how wretched she looked, her normally made-up face blotchy and pale. Elsie bit her lip. 'It was a favour about your missing brooch.'

Anne's mouth dropped open in shock. 'So it *was* my brooch you had in your hand at the factory! I knew it! You lied to me, Elsie. You lied!'

Tears began streaming down Elsie's face. 'I'm sorry, Anne. I didn't steal the brooch. I'd never do that. Mr Jack trusted me with it because . . .' She took a deep breath, then pulled a handkerchief from her jacket pocket and wiped her eyes. 'He wanted me to find a matching necklace. A present for you.'

Anne tried to make sense of what she was hearing. 'Why couldn't he have gone shopping himself? That's how he bought the brooch.'

Elsie shook her head. 'He said he had to concentrate on the factory; he mentioned some problems he had. He didn't tell me what they were, and it's not my place to ask. But he handed me the brooch and made me swear on my life that I would look after it. He sent me to Durham one day when the factory was closed, and I went to the jeweller he recommended. He wanted a necklace made up of the same blue and silver stones.'

Anne's mind reeled from what she heard. 'But I saw him with his arm around you. And that kiss!'

Elsie hung her head again. 'I'm sorry, Anne. We had to be secretive at the factory when I returned the brooch with the necklace. We had to choose our moment carefully. We couldn't meet in his office because you or Meg might realise what was up, so we met in the factory grounds. He put his arm around me that day as a gesture of thanks, nothing more.'

Anne's eyes narrowed. 'And the kiss?' she asked.

Elsie's face blushed red. 'It was meant to be a peck on my cheek to say thank you. But I couldn't resist, Anne. You know what I'm like. Elsie the good-time girl. Isn't that what everyone calls me? I turned my head at the last minute and he caught me full on the lips. It was supposed to be a joke, but I'm the only one who thought it funny. Mr Jack was mortified.'

'As am I,' Anne said, glaring at her. She sank back against the sofa. 'I've been such a fool,' she muttered, trying to take it all in.

Elsie reached for her hands again, and this time Anne let her take them. She found she was shaking.

'Do you know how much I wanted to tell you?' Elsie said. 'It has killed me keeping this a secret, but William made me swear not to say anything.'

Anne banged the sofa with her fist. 'Then why didn't

he tell me all of this himself last night when I confronted him? He could have stopped me from leaving the house.'

'He wanted the necklace to be a surprise, Anne. He said it was for something special.'

'Special? We don't have an anniversary or a birthday coming up. Damn him! He could have told me the truth instead of sending you here to fire his bullets for him.'

'He didn't send me; I wanted to come. I needed to see you as soon as I heard you'd walked out.'

Anne's head was reeling. 'I almost blamed my housekeeper for stealing the brooch,' she said, running recent events through her mind. 'I've turned the house upside down, and my office at the factory. And all that time you had it.'

They sat in silence for a few moments, Anne trying to process all that she'd learned. With the back of her hand, she wiped away her tears.

'Will you go home to Mr Jack now you know the truth?' Elsie asked.

Anne shook her head. 'Not yet, I won't wake Dinah. We'll stay here until later today. It'll be a valuable lesson to him never to do anything like this again if he doesn't want to risk losing me. What about you, Elsie? How will you get home?'

Elsie looked at the clock. 'Stan said he'd return an hour after he dropped me off.'

Anne stood and walked to the sideboard, where a decanter of brandy stood next to a tray of glasses. 'I know it's early but you have time for a quick drink before he arrives. I think we deserve this. I know I could do with one.'

She poured two small brandies and handed one to Elsie. She sat closer to her on the sofa this time.

'Never keep secrets from me again, Elsie, even if my husband asks you to.'

Elsie raised her glass. 'I promise, Anne. I had no idea something so innocent would lead to this. I can't bear to think what might have happened.'

Anne raised her glass too. 'None of it is your fault, Elsie. My husband should never have got you involved. Here's to no more secrets between us.'

They clinked glasses and raised a toast.

At breakfast later that morning, Anne announced to Albert and Clara that she was returning home with Dinah.

'But, my dear, I thought you needed to spend time away from William to gather your thoughts?' Clara said.

Anne tapped the top off a boiled egg for Dinah. 'My friend Elsie shed new light on the situation,' she replied.

She noticed Albert and Clara share a look, but they said no more, for which she was grateful.

After breakfast, she kissed them goodbye and thanked them for their support. As she headed to the car with Dinah, Albert followed with the trunk. He leaned to Anne, out of earshot of his wife.

'Elsie Cooper is an attractive girl, and so I won't ask you any questions that you don't want to answer. But if that son of mine gives you any more trouble, you come straight to me, you hear? I'll sort him out.'

'Thank you, Albert,' she replied. 'But I think it's all been a huge misunderstanding.'

Once in the car, Anne started up the engine. She turned to wave at Albert and Clara, then slowly and carefully drove back to town. It was one of the days when the factory was closed. However, she knew that William would be in his office, as always, working out how best to save the factory and pay off its debts. She parked the car on Front Street, then, taking Dinah by the hand, walked through the factory gates. All around her was quiet and still. No factory girls bustled past; no sugar boilers swaggered. She heard the toot of a whistle as a train snaked along the tracks.

'Run inside and see Dada,' she told Dinah, who dutifully obliged.

When Anne arrived at William's office, she found him with Dinah in his arms and a stricken look on his face.

'My darling child, I've been so worried about you,' he was saying.

When he saw Anne, he walked towards her in silence, still carrying Dinah. They met in the centre of the room, Dinah between them. William wrapped his free hand around Anne's waist and pulled her close.

'I'm so sorry, darling Anne. I've been so stupid. I hope Elsie explained everything,' he breathed against her face.

Anne gently removed his hand from her waist and looked into his eyes. 'Elsie shouldn't have had anything to explain,' she said tersely. 'You should never have kept secrets from me. Poor Edith, I almost blamed her for stealing the brooch.'

William hung his head. 'I can't apologise enough, my dear,' he said. 'I would like to explain about the necklace.'

'There's no need, darling. Elsie told me the truth, that you'd sent her on an errand to the jeweller. I'm surprised you trusted her after the incident with Frankie Ireland. You were all for sacking her then.'

'Well, I changed my mind about her after seeing how

well she coped with that terrible part of her life.' He leaned forward. 'I bought the necklace to celebrate a special occasion.'

Anne smiled at him. 'But our anniversary and my birthday are behind us, and Christmas is far away. What occasion were you thinking of?'

'I wanted to present it on a special day later this year, when the factory is back on its feet. When we're back to full production and the worries of the war years are behind us. Would you mind waiting for such a day?'

'Of course not, my dear,' she said. She looked around the office. 'And my brooch, is it here? Edith has been looking for it at home.'

William shook his head. 'Poor Edith, she believed the brooch was lost. I had to confess to her after she told me you'd caught her looking in the study and weren't pleased to find her there. Your brooch is at home, safely locked away with the family papers. I'll retrieve it for you tonight.'

'Promise me again that you'll never do anything so secretive,' Anne said.

'I promise,' he replied.

He gently placed Dinah on the floor, and she ran off to play in Meg's office. Then he caught Anne again in his arms and brought her face to his. They were lost in an embrace for a very long time, and only pulled apart when a noise caught their attention. It was Dinah, who'd jumped onto Meg's chair.

'Looks like our daughter is ready to begin work,' William said.

Anne immediately snapped into business mode. 'Then so must we. We have much to discuss.' She held out her hand, and William shook it, both of them laughing out loud.

She took off her velvet hat and her coat and placed both on an empty chair, then began counting off on her fingers.

'There's the factory contribution to the peace celebration. This, I suggest, should be followed by a victory dance. We can hold it at the factory, invite our creditors and their wives, show them we mean business and are ready to take them seriously. Sending a letter is one thing, inviting them inside the factory is another.'

William sat at his desk and began scribbling notes. 'That's a genius idea.'

Anne's eyes twinkled as she continued. This was what she loved, working in harmony with William, running the factory, looking to their future. Through the connecting door from Meg's office, Dinah watched her parents intently.

'We'll also honour the factory men who died in the war. I propose a memorial stone be placed in the garden next to Anabel's rose. We'll read out a roll call of names at the start of the victory dance.'

'That's wonderful, yes, we must,' William said, making another note.

Anne remembered the meeting with Mayfair Toffee from the previous day. With everything else that had happened last night, it had almost slipped her mind.

'William, there is one more thing I'd like you to know.'

As Dinah played next door, Anne told her husband all that she'd learned about the failing toffee factory.

Chapter Twenty-Five

William began pacing his office floor. 'How interesting,' he muttered.

'I will write to them, of course, to decline their job offer,' Anne said.

William blanched. 'You can't really have considered taking it, surely?'

Anne took her time to reply. 'William, you have to understand that yesterday I was seriously thinking of leaving you. You should know by now I'm not a woman who waits for life to fall into place. I had to take measures to ensure that I could earn my own money, if needed, to look after myself and Dinah.'

William nodded in understanding. 'You always were the mistress of your own destiny. However, I suggest you keep lines of communication open with Mayfair Toffee. Find out more. Ask questions. How long are they hoping to stay open? Which toffee lines will be phased out first?'

Anne nodded. 'I'll be as subtle as I can.'

But then William's face darkened. 'It's worrying. If a company like Mayfair Toffee can't sustain their level of production, I'm concerned what their closure might mean for us.'

'Ah, but we have a secret weapon in our arsenal,' Anne said with a mischievous glint in her eye. 'We have the toffee eggs and more novelty confectionery ideas from Mr Gerard and his team.'

In the days that followed, Anne and William settled back into their happy domestic routine. Edith was relieved to have the warring couple back together, and she cooked Anne's favourite dishes for a whole week.

Life at the factory went by in a flurry of activity. Warm days began to shimmer with glorious sunshine. William and the management team went full steam ahead in courting their creditors, making amends and presenting financial plans to pay off the debts. However, the missing notes about the toffee eggs never surfaced as Anne had hoped. She and Meg went through each folder and file in Meg's office, but they were nowhere to be found. Mr Gerard rewrote his proposal and presented it to William again. This time, Anne made sure that a spare set of papers was locked in her office.

During this time, as the toffee factory limped carefully out of the war years, Mr Gerard's idea for the proposed Sweets of Peace was officially shelved. William made the difficult decision after calculating that there was only enough money to invest in one new line, and he had his heart set on the toffee egg. Anne hadn't been keen at first on the novelty idea, thinking it childish. But when she'd seen the sales figures from the European companies who were already selling toffee and chocolate eggs, she realised how lucrative the product would be and soon changed her mind.

Celebrations at the Toffee Factory

When news about the Sweets of Peace was given to Elsie, she put on a brave front. 'I never did want my face on all the tins,' she told Hetty.

But Hetty noticed disappointment in her voice.

Through the warm days of summer, Hetty and Dirk spent all of their free time together, making the most of the few weeks they had left. Such moments were bittersweet. Seeing Dirk smile made Hetty light up inside. Sitting by the river, hearing him talk about his home in Belgium, his parents and his sister, she hung on every word. But she had known for too long that their relationship would have to end.

On a rare free day off work from both the toffee factory and the castle, they took a picnic to the river. Hetty had brought a blanket for them to sit on and sandwiches to eat, while Dirk brought lemonade. However, she was concerned that he seemed distant that day.

'What is it, Dirk?' she asked.

Dirk looked ahead to where the river gently flowed. Birds flew around them, chirping from the trees. He took his time to reply, and when he did, he could barely look at her.

'I've been told that I will receive my leaving date soon.'

Hetty's heart fell. 'How soon?' she asked.

'On the day of the peace celebrations.'

She gasped, and dropped her sandwich onto the blanket. She'd always known he would return home, of course, but had hoped they might have a little more time with each other.

'I know, it's a day we've been dreading,' he said, defeated.

'There is little for me to do now at the Belgian village. Everything has been packed up and shipped overseas. Apart from a small group of us who are there to help the men from the council, everyone else has gone home.'

'What are the men from the council doing?' Hetty asked.

Dirk shrugged. 'Getting the accommodation ready for local people to move into. Would you like to bring Hilda to see if one of the houses might be suitable?'

'I'd like that, thank you. Elsie and I have talked to her about it, and she perked up when she learned there was a garden.'

Dirk was silent for a few moments, and when he eventually spoke, Hetty saw tears in his eyes.

'I don't want to leave.'

She felt a lump build in her throat. She wanted to throw herself into his arms and tell him . . . no, beg him, to stay. But she couldn't. She wouldn't. Dirk often talked lovingly about his ailing parents and their chocolate shop in Ghent. Hetty would never be so selfish as to stop him reuniting with his family, no matter how she felt herself. She reached for his hands.

'Your parents need you,' she said gently.

'And I need *you*,' he quickly replied.

Hetty felt butterflies in her stomach. 'Dirk, what are you saying?' she asked.

'I'm saying that I want to stay with you, Hetty, but I also want to go home. I've been torn over this for months. If I'm honest with myself, I've been torn since the day we first met. I've always known you were special. As soon as I met you, I felt something in here . . .' His hand flew to his heart. 'Do you remember the day?'

Hetty smiled as the memory flooded back. 'How could I forget? You brought a little black dog to me and dropped him in my arms. You thought he was mine, but I'd never seen him before. We named him Jet. Yes, the day we met was the day . . .' She paused, unwilling to carry on and mention Bob.

'Tell me, Hetty, please,' Dirk encouraged.

'Well, I met you after I'd just said goodbye to my old boyfriend Bob at the railway station. He'd gone off to fight with the Durham Light Infantry. And now he's back and wants to take up with me again.'

Dirk's face clouded over. 'And do you want to take up with *him*?'

'Heavens, no!' Hetty cried. She looked into Dirk's piercing blue eyes. 'Before I met you, I didn't know what love was. I've never felt as comfortable with anyone as I do with you.'

'I feel it too, Hetty.'

Dirk shuffled along the blanket to sit at Hetty's side, then wrapped his arm around her shoulders. They snuggled together and Hetty laid her head against his broad chest.

'The future is too difficult to think about,' he said softly.

'If only Belgium wasn't so far away,' Hetty replied.

Dirk turned his face towards her, and she willingly responded, brushing her lips against his.

Elsie was at home with Hilda, tending to her needs. Hilda was being more crotchety than normal and was testing Elsie's patience.

'When am I moving to the new house?' she called.

'We need to take you to see it first. You might not like it. You might decide to stay here instead.'

Hilda tutted loudly. 'I can't wait to get out of this rotten old place. It's brought me nothing but bad luck.'

Elsie had heard this many times before. She gritted her teeth and carried on cleaning the hearth.

'Where's Hetty today?' Hilda asked.

'She's with Dirk.'

'Oh, is she now? If you ask me, she'd be better off with Bob instead of running around with a foreigner.'

'That's not fair, Hilda. Dirk's a smashing lad,' Elsie said.

But Hilda wasn't finished. 'Smashing or not, it'll end in tears when he ships back off to Belgium.'

Elsie's heart sank, because on this, Hilda was right.

Once Elsie had finished her chores, cooked dinner for Hilda and made sure she was settled, she began to get herself ready to enjoy the rest of her day. She'd promised to visit Stan at home to teach him how to make a casserole and a pie, basic dishes she felt he could manage. As she carefully put on her make-up and styled her hair, she realised she was looking forward to spending the day with him. No, he wasn't the most exciting man she'd ever met, or the best looking, but she felt safe and protected with him. She slipped on a blue cotton dress with short sleeves that had once belonged to her aunt Jean. Turning this way and that, making the dress float around her shapely calves, she admired her reflection in the mirror. Then she picked up her handbag and walked down the stairs.

'Bye, Hilda,' she called.

'Watch what you're doing, and if you see Hetty, tell her what I said about Bob!' Hilda snapped.

Elsie stepped out into the sunshine, heading to Stan's house with a spring in her step.

Chapter Twenty-Six

When Elsie reached Stan's house she found him in the front garden on his knees, pruning flowers and clipping shrubs. Next to him lay his big black dog Patch. Stan wore his flat cap and a black waistcoat over a shirt with rolled-up sleeves.

'Morning, Stan!' she called cheerily.

He doffed his cap. 'Morning, Elsie. How are you?'

Elsie walked up the path admiring his handiwork. 'Your garden looks beautiful. I don't know where you get the patience.'

Stan's hazel eyes twinkled. 'I could teach you, if you'd like?'

Elsie shook her head. 'No thanks, Stan. Gardening's not my cup of tea. The only thing I'm good at is cooking.'

Stan wiped his brow. 'Come inside and you can give me my first lesson. I've been looking forward to this.'

He began to rise from the ground and Elsie held out her hand to help him. They held onto each other for a few seconds longer than needed, and she looked into his eyes.

'I've been looking forward to it too.'

Once inside, Stan boiled the kettle to make tea. Patch lay in the doorway to the kitchen, watching Elsie as she walked to the pantry and looked inside. In the pantry at Elm Street, she and Hetty kept tins of food, a box of tea, a jar of jam and a plate of sliced meat. Potatoes, carrots and other vegetables they'd bought at the market were also stored there. However, Stan's pantry was bare. Elsie was shocked. She stared at the empty shelves and wondered if he kept his food elsewhere.

'Stan, where are the ingredients we need to make the casserole and pie?' she asked.

Stan scratched his head and looked a little lost.

'Stan?' Elsie said gently.

'Ah yes,' he said, looking sheepish. 'Well, I'm not the sort of fella who likes going to the shops. I hope you don't mind me asking, Elsie, but if you've got enough time today, could you come to the market with me and we'll buy what we need? I haven't a clue about anything other than gardening. I could talk all day about evergreens and deciduous trees, perennials and annuals. But I'm no good at anything to do with food.'

'But you grew vegetables at the factory during the war.'

'Aye, I can grow them, I just can't cook them,' Stan replied. 'I'm sorry to have to ask, Elsie. I know you must have more exciting things to do, and you won't want to spend all day with me.'

Elsie set her bag on a chair and walked towards him. 'Well, that's where you're wrong, Stan Chapman. Because I can't think of anything I'd rather do than spend my day off work with you.'

Stan took a step closer. 'Really?' he whispered.

'Really,' Elsie replied.

He took her hands in his and gazed deep into her eyes. 'Look, Elsie, I need to say something before we go any further. The last time we spoke to each other, from our hearts, you said you wanted excitement. Now, you know I can't offer you that. But what I can offer is friendship, security... and love.'

'I don't know what I want any more, Stan. One day I think I want to leave Chester-le-Street and see the bright lights of Newcastle. Then the next I want to stay here in this town that I love.'

He gently squeezed her hands. 'Then how about we take things slowly again. Today we'll go to the market and you can teach me to cook. Next week I'll buy train tickets to Newcastle and we can visit the big city together.'

Elsie's eyes opened wide. 'You'd do that for me?'

'I'd do it for *us*. I want to see what life is like outside of this town just as much as you do, although I'd never move away. I love Chester-le-Street. I've got a job I adore, and while my gardens here are small, they give me pleasure. Plus, I've got family living on this side of the river. I don't want to be too far away.'

'I understand,' Elsie replied. 'But I don't have anyone here, you see. That's why I itch to move away. Since Aunt Jean left, there's only Hetty and Hilda, and we're all squashed into the house on Elm Street.'

'How is Hilda these days?' Stan asked.

Elsie smiled. 'She's as belligerent as ever. I swear it's what keeps her going. Physically she's getting a little stronger. She's even talking about moving to a house in Elisabethville.' She clamped her hand over her mouth. 'Oh! I shouldn't have said that. Hetty was told it in confidence and asked me to keep quiet. Me and my big mouth!'

Celebrations at the Toffee Factory

Stan's face creased into a smile. 'I won't breathe a word; you know you can trust me, right?'

Elsie looked into his weather-beaten face. She knew without a doubt that on this matter, or any other, she could trust Stan with all of her heart. Stan leaned towards her for a kiss, and Elsie leaned in too, but the kettle's whistle from the hearth stopped them dead. Elsie steadied herself and sat down at the kitchen table, watching Stan as he made the tea.

Over the next half an hour, they drank tea and talked about the toffee factory.

'I heard rumours the place might close down,' Stan said darkly.

'I heard those rumours too, but I know Anne and Mr Jack will be doing all they can to save it. I won't believe we're closing until I hear it from Mr Jack himself.'

'How's life in the slab room?' he asked.

Elsie took a sip from her mug. 'It's hard work. Oh, not as hard as your work turning soil and shifting rocks in your wheelbarrow. But it's demanding, unrelenting. We've got freshly made toffee coming in all the time, and it has to be levelled before it sets and goes hard. As soon as we've cut it into pieces, it leaves the belt at one end and a new batch of toffee is poured on the other. Everyone's careful, of course, as we know how dangerous the hot toffee is. If it touches your skin . . .' She grimaced. 'I've seen some bad accidents. The doc's had to rush girls to hospital, and one girl had to have a skin graft. Some get so badly burned they never return to work.'

'Does the toffee spill often?' Stan asked.

Elsie nodded. 'More often than it should. Some of the sugar boilers are in a rush to get it onto the slabs. Most of them are precise in their work, but there's one or two who don't care, they just slop it down.'

'You should tell Mrs Perkins.'

Elsie shrugged. She doubted the supervisor would listen to her; the pair of them were always at odds.

'The floor in the slab room gets sticky with toffee. Mrs Perkins gave us a stern talking-to about keeping it clean, but it's not our fault. Some of the sugar boilers need to be more careful when they're pouring.'

Stan was silent for a moment.

'I know Ken Baker, the supervisor in the sugar-boiling room. I could have a word with him if you like?'

Elsie was grateful for his support. 'I don't want to get anyone into trouble, but thank you for offering,' she said.

Stan refilled their mugs, then his face clouded over. 'Speaking of sugar boilers who worked there, Frankie's not been causing you any problems lately, has he?'

'No, I haven't seen him since the fight at the Lambton Arms.'

'If he turns up, and you ever need me, just shout.'

Elsie patted his hand. 'I will, thank you.'

Stan sat up straight in his seat. 'Elsie, may I please ask a question?'

She looked at him, startled by his formal tone. 'Go on,' she said.

'May I . . . I mean . . . only if you'd like to, of course. And I realise you might already have plans, but if you don't . . . well, it's just that you didn't give me an answer when I asked you last time.'

'Stan, just tell me what it is,' she said softly.

'Well, it's the peace celebrations,' he said. 'I wondered

if you'd like to go with me, together, the two of us. Perhaps we could start again and call it a date?'

Elsie felt a warm, comforting sensation inside that made her feel confident in her reply. 'A date sounds good to me.'

When the day of the peace celebrations dawned, Hetty woke to sunshine streaming in through her bedroom window. She looked out of the curtains to see a clear blue sky. She hadn't slept well the previous night, partly due to excitement about the celebrations and partly due to knowing that Dirk would announce his leaving date that day. She knelt on her bed and looked out of the window. Beneath the blue sky, the view from her room was made up of chimney pots and rooftops. She wondered what Dirk was doing right at that moment. Was he thinking of her as she was of him?

'What am I going to do?' she whispered.

There was a knock at her bedroom door.

'Come in, Elsie,' she said.

Elsie entered with a mug of tea. 'Here, get this down you. I'm cooking bacon and eggs for breakfast. Oh, Hetty, isn't it a wonderful day? There'll be marching bands at the castle, and a parade. I'm going to wear my red skirt.'

Hetty took the mug, then sat on the side of her bed.

'What's up? Aren't you excited?' Elsie asked.

Hetty patted the bed and Elsie sat down. 'It's Dirk. Today I find out the date he's leaving.'

'I'm sorry, love. I know how much you like him.'

'I love him, Elsie. He means everything to me. He's supported me after what happened with Hilda, and Dan. He's been faithful and true. I want a future with him, but it's impossible. I haven't allowed myself to think past the end of each day when we're together.'

Elsie squeezed her hand. 'You've made the most of each moment together, and that's more than some people get. I know it's hard, but Dirk has another life in Belgium. He has family there, and friends, and a job to go to, working in his parents' chocolate shop. They speak a language we don't understand. They're different. He's different. You have to let him go. There's no other way.'

Hetty sipped her hot tea. 'I know all of this. It's kept me awake at night. It's on my mind when I'm at work at the factory, and when I'm cleaning at the castle. It's all I can think about. I've been hoping for a miracle, but I know I've been kidding myself. Dirk has to return. I understand that, of course, but it doesn't mean it doesn't hurt.'

Chapter Twenty-Seven

Little work was done that day at the factory or anywhere else in town. The day was for celebrating soldiers who'd returned safely from war, and for remembering those who had died. Jack's toffee factory had set up a large blue canvas tent in the grounds of Lumley Castle, offering free toffees for all. And at Anne's suggestion, there was to be a fancy-dress competition, with a prize for the girl who dressed most like Lady Tina, the face of their most successful brand. Hetty had been asked to judge and pick the lucky winner. The prize was a tin of Jack's luxury toffee, wrapped in a blue ribbon and bow.

After ensuring Hilda had eaten breakfast, Hetty and Elsie headed to the castle arm-in-arm.

'I don't like leaving Hilda alone. She should be with us today, enjoying herself,' Elsie said as they walked in the sunshine.

Hetty shot her a look. 'I don't think Hilda's ever enjoyed herself. Nothing about today could put a smile on her face.'

'You can be harsh, Hetty. I'm not sure she deserves that,' Elsie chided, but Hetty remained firm.

'You weren't brought up by her, Elsie. She's mellowed over the years and you're seeing her now when she's weak. Her vicious tongue doesn't cut like it did and I've hardened myself to it. I went through hell with her for years when I thought she was my mum. She always put me down, and in front of other people too. I don't want to see her suffer, of course. But neither will I allow her to stop me from getting on with my life.'

They walked on in silence.

'Has Dirk told you when the houses in Elisabethville might be available for locals to move into?' Elsie said at last.

Hetty shook her head. 'Not yet. He said he'd let me know as soon as they're ready so we can take Hilda for a look around. I'm still not sure we're doing the right thing by moving her. If she stays here, she's got neighbours who call during the day when we're at work. Who will call if she moves? She'll know no one at Elisabethville.'

'You've got a point,' Elsie agreed. 'Do you think they'll still keep that name for the village when local people move in? It was named after the Belgian queen.'

Hetty shrugged. Talking about Hilda always made her feel sad. The woman had ruled her life with a rod of iron and a sharp tongue, always telling her she wasn't good enough, pretty enough, smart enough. The last thing she wanted to do, today of all days, was think about that. She felt bad enough knowing what lay ahead with Dirk. She hung on tight to Elsie's arm, turned her face to the sun and pressed her eyes closed, feeling the warmth on her skin and hearing the birds sing in the trees.

She was brought out of her reverie when Elsie screamed.

'Oh look, Hetty. Look!'

Hetty opened her eyes to see a small group of factory girls walking ahead. All of them were dressed in bonnets and gowns, their faces made up with powder and rouge.

'They must be taking part in the Lady Tina competition!' Elsie looked at Hetty. 'You're going to have your work cut out trying to choose a winner. They all look amazing. And there'll be loads more turning up.'

'I wish my heart was in it,' Hetty muttered.

'Still thinking about Dirk?' Elsie asked.

But Hetty didn't answer, keeping her gaze ahead as the castle loomed into view.

To reach the castle grounds, they crossed Lumley Bridge then began to climb the grassy banks. Ahead of them were brass bands and soldiers marching. The men saluted one another, then marched on, arms swinging by their sides. Hetty saw a group wearing the uniform of the Durham Light Infantry, and one man in particular caught her eye. She recognised the way he walked, his straight back, his long face. It was Bob. He seemed not to have noticed her, and she hurried on, not wanting to catch his eye. Flags and banners fluttered in a gentle breeze. Children ran in circles holding hands, and couples danced together. The fields around the castle were dotted with marquees and tents. Everyone wore their best summer clothes, pretty dresses for the girls, and hats with flowing ribbons. The men and boys wore suits and ties.

'Seems strange to be heading to the castle without going to work,' Hetty said.

Elsie leaned into her. 'Is it true there's a ghost at the castle?'

Hetty tutted. 'Only if you're daft enough to believe in

such things. But yes, there's a myth that Lily of Lumley haunts it. I've never seen her myself. Mind you, Mrs Doughty is scarier than any ghost. Did you know we can go inside the castle today?'

Elsie's eyes lit up, excited. 'Really?'

Hetty nodded. 'Some of the private rooms are open. I'll take you inside. We can visit the ballroom. Oh, you should see it, Elsie. It's like nothing you've seen before, so ornate and pretty. I can take you into the dining parlour and drawing room too. Even the music room will be open today.'

'Where do the staff sleep?' Elsie asked.

'Staff quarters are on the top floor. The rooms up there aren't as grand as the ones open today.'

Elsie pointed ahead. 'Look, there's the Jack's toffee tent.'

They headed to the tent and helped themselves to handfuls of toffee. Elsie stuffed one straight in her mouth while Hetty placed hers in her skirt pocket.

'I'll keep them for later,' she said.

She saw Mr Jack deep in conversation with a gentleman dressed in a fine suit and top hat. Next to him was Anne, talking to a lady Hetty presumed was the gentleman's wife. She and Elsie watched as Anne smiled at the woman in front of her, offering her a tin of best toffee wrapped in blue ribbon. Hetty waved in her direction, hoping she might notice, but Anne was too busy to see.

'Morning, ladies,' a voice boomed behind them.

Hetty spun around and saw Stan Chapman with a large black dog at his side. He raised his cap to them both.

'Morning, Stan,' she said. She glanced at Elsie, surprised to see her looking so coy. Was she imagining it, or was her friend blushing? She looked from Elsie to Stan and back again, noticing they couldn't keep their eyes off each other. She suddenly felt surplus to requirements.

'I think I'll go and listen to the brass band,' she said.

'You don't need to go on my account,' Stan said.

Hetty smiled. 'Oh, I think I do.' She looked at Elsie. 'I'll see you later for the guided tour of the castle I promised.'

Stan's dog began whining, so Stan made a fuss of him for a few moments. While he was distracted, Elsie reached for Hetty's hands.

'Thank you, my friend,' she whispered.

'I thought you wanted excitement, not a factory gardener?' Hetty whispered back.

'Well, I thought I knew what I wanted, but it turns out I've got a lot to learn.'

Hetty kissed Elsie on the cheek, then wandered in the direction of the marching bands. The music filled her soul, urged her on, and she began swaying in time to the trombones and trumpets, cornets and drums. And then her heart lifted when she spotted Dirk. How handsome he looked in his very best suit. His blue eyes sparkled in the sunshine, and he looked as happy as she felt. She walked to him, ready to hold him tight. When they reached each other, he gathered her into his arms.

'Hetty, my darling,' he breathed.

'Isn't this a wonderful day, Dirk? Isn't it marvellous? The music, the colours, it's magical.'

'Hetty, I'm afraid the news we've dreaded has arrived. I've been told the date I'm to leave.'

'Not yet, Dirk. Please don't tell me yet,' she begged.

Dirk pulled her close. The music played, bands marched,

children laughed and screamed and ran. Women and men walked arm-in-arm, picnic blankets were laid on the grass, beer bottles were opened, sandwiches eaten. But Hetty saw nothing of this. She let herself be held, never wanting to let him go.

'I demand you take your hands off my fiancée!' a voice yelled.

Hetty felt Dirk's arms fall. At first she couldn't make out what was happening. Was this part of the fun of the day? Was it a soldier who'd drunk too much beer? But sadly, it was no joke. For there was Bob, fists raised in a fighting stance, hopping from foot to foot like a boxer in a ring.

'That is my girlfriend, sir, and if you don't let her go, I will fight you!' he yelled at Dirk.

'Bob! Stop it!' Hetty cried.

Dirk was taken aback. He stepped away from Bob and held his hands up in surrender.

'I don't want to fight,' he said, shaking his head. Then he looked at Hetty. 'But neither will I give up the love of my life.'

Hetty didn't know if she was coming or going. She didn't like the aggressive look on Bob's face. He seemed ready to exchange punches, moving side to side, putting up his fists. Around them, people stopped to watch, thinking this a game, part of the celebrations. Some people were even laughing.

'Bob, what are you doing? You're making a fool of yourself,' she said.

Dirk stepped in front of her to protect her. He tried to reason with Bob, but Bob was so fired up, he wasn't willing to listen. He lashed out with a punch that caught Dirk in the face. Dirk reeled from the impact, and Bob tried to hit him again, but Hetty threw herself against his legs in an attempt to topple him.

'Stop it! Bob, stop it!'

She managed to push him to one side but was no match for his brute strength. Then two sugar boilers from the factory waded in and pulled him away.

'She's mine, I tell you!' Bob screamed as the sugar boilers led him away.

Hetty ran to Dirk and winced when she saw the side of his face starting to swell. The crowd around them who'd thought the fight was for fun began to disperse, shaking their heads and tutting. Then Hetty saw Mr Jack striding towards her with a face like thunder.

'Hetty Lawson, what's got into you! You're the face of Lady Tina toffee and I will not have you or any of my girls involved in a brawl like a common fishwife. You've brought shame on the toffee factory. You're an absolute disgrace!'

Chapter Twenty-Eight

Dirk immediately jumped to Hetty's defence. He pointed at Bob, who was struggling with the sugar boilers trying to lead him away.

'Sir, that is the man you should be angry with. Miss Lawson is not at fault.'

Hetty was mortified. A crowd of people were watching; she recognised some of them from the toffee factory. Mr Jack was joined by the gentleman he'd been talking to, and she saw Anne striding towards them too, followed by the older woman, well dressed in a smart skirt suit. Dirk moved to her side, and she felt his protective arm around her shoulder as he continued to remonstrate with the factory owner.

'That man attacked me!' he cried. 'If anyone is a disgrace, sir, it is him, not Miss Lawson. She's innocent.'

Hetty felt him gently squeeze her shoulder. 'Are you all right?' he asked.

She nodded. 'Are you?'

He didn't get a chance to reply as Anne stepped forward.

'Hetty? Who's been fighting?'

Everyone was staring at Hetty: Dirk, Mr Jack, Anne, the sugar boilers struggling to control Bob, the well-dressed gentleman and lady, the men and women in the crowd. She didn't know what to do. This wasn't how she'd hoped her day would unfold. One minute she'd been enjoying Dirk's company, the next Bob had appeared from nowhere, ready to fight. She turned to Anne to tell her what had happened, but knowing that everyone's eyes were on her, waiting, her mouth went dry. No words came out.

Anne began to disperse the gathering. 'There are free toffees for all in Jack's toffee tent – it's the big blue tent at the top of the hill,' she called out.

'Free toffees?' a murmur went up. Slowly the crowd began to thin as men and women walked and children ran to the tent.

Mr Jack cleared his throat. 'Let's return to the toffee tent, Sir Michael,' he said to the gentleman at his side. The two of them walked off, and Hetty heard Mr Jack apologising for what they'd just witnessed. The well-dressed lady who'd been with Anne walked behind the men. As the crowd thinned out, Hetty saw Bob, still being held by the sugar boilers, one gripping each arm. He looked subdued; he'd given up fighting now.

'Take him away,' Anne ordered.

'Hetty! I'll always love you!' Bob called over his shoulder.

Hetty turned her eyes to Dirk. 'I'm sorry you were caught up in this,' she said, kissing his swollen cheek gently.

Anne shooed away the last of the stragglers from the crowd. When the last of them had gone, she reached for Hetty's hand.

'You weren't hurt, were you?' she asked. She looked at Dirk. 'Oh dear, it looks like you were hit.'

'We're fine, just a little shaken up,' Hetty replied. 'It was just as Dirk told Mr Jack. I wasn't involved. I tried to break it up. I'm distraught that Mr Jack called me a disgrace to the factory, and in front of everyone too.'

Anne's face softened. 'Don't worry, I'll speak to him later and tell him what really happened.' She cast a worried look at the toffee tent, where Mr Jack and his well-heeled guests were heading. 'He's on edge today. He overreacted because he's anxious.'

Hetty was surprised to hear this. 'Mr Jack, anxious? I would never have known; he always seems so sure of himself.'

Anne sighed. 'Well, he's nervous today. I can't go into detail, but we're hosting some very important people in the toffee tent. There's a lot riding on how our visitors see the factory represented. William's trying to impress them; we both are. The last thing they needed to see was one of our girls involved in a brawl.'

Dirk shook his head. 'But Hetty wasn't at fault, I've already said so.'

'And I'll make sure my husband and our guests know the truth. Now, if you'll both excuse me, I need to get back to Sir Michael and his wife.'

Anne marched off towards the tent, leaving Hetty and Dirk alone. Hetty flopped to the ground and sat on the warm grass. Dipping her hand into her pocket, she pulled out two toffees. She offered one to Dirk, and he took it and sat next to her. Together they unwrapped the toffees, the silver and blue wrappers glinting in the sunshine. For a few moments they didn't speak, as they enjoyed the creamy, buttery toffee, which melted in their mouths. Dirk laid his arm around Hetty's shoulders again, and she snuggled into his side.

'I will do my best to protect you from Bob,' he said at last.

'I know you will, Dirk. And I thank you for the sentiment, but I need to get used to dealing with his outbursts . . . I mean, after you've gone.'

Dirk dropped his arm from her shoulders and felt in his jacket pocket, pulling out a letter and showing it to Hetty. She frowned as she tried to make sense of it.

'It's written in a foreign language,' she said.

He placed his finger under a sentence halfway down the sheet. 'See this word?' he said. Hetty peered at it; nothing about it seemed familiar. 'That's the word for Friday. And then you have the date.'

She saw the two-digit number as clear as day.

'You're going so soon?' she gasped.

Dirk folded the letter and returned it to his pocket. 'Yes. My tickets have been booked on the railway to Hull and on the ship to Belgium. It's final, Hetty. This is it.'

Hetty slid her arm around his waist. She felt raw inside, empty. There was so much, too much, she wanted to say but she knew that words couldn't stop him leaving. They sat in silence for a few moments as the date settled in her mind. She had just two more weeks with him.

'I've always known this moment would arrive,' she said at last. 'Do you know, I thought I'd feel different once I knew the date.'

'Different how?' Dirk asked.

'I thought I'd be crying, hysterical. But instead I feel empty and lost.'

She pressed her eyes shut to stop her tears. When she opened them, she saw that Dirk had picked up one of the silver and blue toffee wrappers. She watched his long, slim fingers twist the wrapper, playing with it, toying with the shape, bending and turning it. Then he brought the two ends of the tight roll together and twisted them to make a ring. Holding it in his hand, he stood, then dropped to one knee, presenting the blue and silver ring to her as if it were a precious gem.

'Hetty, my darling, would you marry me?'

Hetty looked from the makeshift ring to Dirk. Marry him? She was confused. Was he poking fun? Then she realised how serious he looked.

'Marry you?' she whispered.

'Yes please,' he replied with a smile.

'Marry you?' she said again, trying to process what was happening.

'I would like it very much. I have thought about it for a very long time,' he replied. He was still on bended knee and began to lose his balance, teetering from side to side and finally flopping back down at her side.

'But how...? What...?' she stuttered. 'We can't... can we? I mean... what about your boat ticket to Belgium? What about returning home?'

Her heart began to pound. Marrying Dirk was something she'd never allowed herself to think of. All she'd ever dared do was enjoy each precious moment with him, knowing it would end one day. And now he had proposed, and everything had shifted. Suddenly she felt as if nothing would ever be the same again. The more she thought it over, the more her future began to fall into place and her life began to make sense. They wouldn't have to separate. Her heart lifted, and she wiped away a tear. They could be together after all!

'So you'll stay in England?'

Dirk turned his blue eyes to her. 'No, I must return home, but I thought...' his face began to colour, 'perhaps you could come with me.'

Hetty's eyes opened wide. 'Go with you to Belgium? Me?' she cried.

Dirk turned the paper ring in his fingers. Hetty looked at him again, then at the ring, which was being bent out of shape as he played with it. She took his hand, brought it to her lips and kissed the back of it.

'Dirk, this is a shock. Your proposal has come out of the blue.'

'It's no surprise to me, Hetty, nor to my heart,' he replied.

Hetty struggled to find the right words. 'I can't move to Belgium. I can't speak the language.'

'Then I'll teach you,' he said excitedly. 'There are tutors there who will help.'

Her head spun. This was too much. 'I won't know anyone,' she said.

'You'll make friends, everyone will love you. My sister will take you under her wing.'

'I can't leave Hilda,' she continued, but as those words left her lips, she knew she was grasping at reasons not to go, using Hilda as an excuse to cover her fear of the unknown.

'I understand,' Dirk replied softly.

Hetty took a breath. Dirk's proposal had knocked her for six.

'I've spent so long thinking of how I'd say goodbye to

you, readying myself to say farewell. And now your proposal . . . well, it's a shock, Dirk. It's huge. I'm not sure I'm ready. I want to say yes, of course; with all my heart I want to accept. But moving to Belgium . . . well, I need time to think,' she said.

'Alas, we don't have a lot of time,' he replied. 'It was receiving my leaving date that made me realise more than anything that I want to spend the rest of my life with you. But I must return home, Hetty. My parents need me.'

Hetty closed her eyes, forcing herself to think. If she moved with Dirk to Belgium, she'd be with the love of her life, but she'd be in a strange land. However, if she stayed in Chester-le-Street, what then? She and Elsie would continue looking after Hilda. She'd eke out a living somehow. She shivered when she thought of Mrs Doughty, and the cavernous kitchen where she cleaned. In town, she'd need to steer clear of Bob if she wanted to stay out of trouble. Hilda was a bad-tempered, critical woman to live with. And Dan, the boy she'd thought of as her brother, was dead. Plus, Elsie wouldn't hang around for ever; she'd want her own life away from here one day.

She mused on all this while Dirk stared ahead, fiddling with the paper ring. Her mind whirled and she forced herself to concentrate hard. She couldn't leave Elsie to look after Hilda, that wouldn't be fair. But if she could arrange for Hilda to move to Elisabethville, to a house with a garden, electricity and running water, that'd be something. So many thoughts crowded her mind, and she turned to Dirk, full of questions.

'If . . . if I say yes, Dirk, where would I work? Where would we live? How would we cope? What if I get homesick and can't settle into a new life?'

He kissed her on the lips. 'You are full of questions, Hetty Lawson, and I will answer each one. But first you must answer one of mine that you seem to have forgotten.' He held the silver and blue ring as if it was a jewel. 'Will you marry me, Hetty Lawson?'

Hetty swallowed a lump in her throat. She was so choked with emotion she couldn't speak at first, and when she did, she could only manage a whisper.

'Yes.'

Dirk slipped the toffee-wrapper ring onto her finger, then he leaned towards her and their lips met in a lingering kiss.

Chapter Twenty-Nine

Later that day, in the kitchen at Elm Street, Hetty and Elsie had a heart-to-heart.

'Married?' Elsie screamed. 'You're getting married? When? How?'

'Keep your voice down and I'll tell you everything,' Hetty said.

There was a loud bang against the wall that divided the kitchen from the front room, where Hilda lay in bed.

'Be quiet, the pair of you! I can't hear myself think in here!' she yelled.

Hetty and Elsie shared a look and Hetty rolled her eyes. Then Elsie sat in a chair at the kitchen table while Hetty walked to the pantry, where there was a small bottle of brandy. She pulled it out, found two teacups and poured a little brandy into each. She handed Elsie a cup, then raised her own.

'A toast, to the future. To us,' she said.

'To our future!' Elsie downed her brandy in a single gulp, then leaned forward with her elbows on the table. 'Tell me everything, Hetty. Right from the start.'

Hetty took her time telling the story, luxuriating in

every detail of Dirk's proposal. She even showed Elsie the ring he'd created from the toffee wrapper. 'He says he'll buy me a real one, of course,' she added, which made Elsie laugh.

When she'd finished, Elsie sat back in her seat and crossed her arms. 'You've got less than two weeks to get married before you leave for Belgium. It's not possible. No one can do it in that time.'

Hetty sighed. She and Dirk had talked through this many times that afternoon. 'It'll be difficult, but not impossible,' she said. 'Keep your fingers crossed we can find someone who'll marry us. Mind you, even if we do, everyone around here will be full of gossip. They'll have me down as being pregnant.'

Elsie's eyes darkened. 'You're not, are you?'

Hetty's cheeks turned pink. 'You should know me better by now,' she replied sharply. She reached for Elsie's hands. 'Be happy for me, Elsie,' she said.

Elsie squeezed her hands. 'Of course I'm happy for you. It's just . . .'

'What?'

'I'll miss you. You've been more than a friend to me since I moved here. We've been like sisters. You're my family now.'

'And you're mine,' Hetty replied with a catch in her voice.

'I don't want to think about you moving away,' Elsie said sadly.

'Dirk says we can take Hilda to look at the accommodation at Elisabethville. We could go tomorrow after work, if you'd like. Do you think she'll be well enough for the short walk to the bus stop?'

Elsie nodded. 'She's more than well enough. She's a lot better and more active than she lets us think. I caught her the other day standing by the window, chatting to the woman down the street. When she saw me watching, she scuttled back to bed, pulled the eiderdown up and said she wasn't feeling good. She asked me to make her a cup of tea. And while I was doing that, she asked for a sandwich too.'

Hetty smiled. 'It sounds like she's getting wily in her old age. She's mellowed a lot since you moved in. I think your direct approach suits her. After the upbringing she gave me, I walk on eggshells when I'm with her.'

'I'll be happy to continue looking after her if we move to Elisabethville. But won't you miss her?' Elsie asked.

Now it was Hetty's turn to sit back and cross her arms. 'No,' she said quietly. 'But I'll do the decent thing and go and tell her my news.'

'Good luck,' Elsie said.

Hetty raised her cup and gulped the last of the brandy. Then she braced herself and knocked at the door. 'Can I come in?' she asked.

'Aye,' Hilda replied.

Hetty pushed open the door. The room was dark, and she could just make out Hilda propped up in her bed.

'Oh, it's you,' the woman moaned. 'I was hoping it was Elsie. She normally helps me to the netty before she turns in for the night. Then she turns down my bed, makes sure the fire's out and settles me in. That's more than you ever do.'

Hetty was determined not to let the criticism provoke her. She pulled up a chair to the side of the bed and sat down.

'What are you doing? It's too late to sit there,' Hilda barked.

'I'm leaving,' Hetty said. At that moment, in the front room at Elm Street, her decision on her future was cemented.

'Where are you going at this time of night?' Hilda said. 'If you're off to see your Belgian man, you'll get talked about. Mind you, you'll be used to that by now. I still can't believe you've got the nerve to court a foreign fella. Do you know what they say around here about you? Do you?'

Hetty let her carry on, hoping she'd run out of steam, but Hilda showed no sign of slowing.

'All the comments I hear about you reflect badly on me, you know. So don't think that what you do doesn't come home to roost, because it does. And it's me who takes the harsh words. Do you know how many people have told me that Bob's back in town? Well, do you? And they all want to know why you haven't taken up with him again.' With each word, the woman sounded more spiteful and bitter. 'All the neighbours stop at the window and look in when they walk along the street. They tell me I'm being kept in here like a prisoner. Well, that's gratitude for you. I've looked after you ever since your mother died when you were a kid, and you lock me up in here and don't have a kind word to say and—'

'You've never been locked in. You know the door's always open,' Hetty muttered.

She stood and turned away from the bed. In the darkness, Hilda was still going strong, shouting insults, blaming Hetty for wrongs she had never committed. Hetty paused at the door.

'Hilda, I came to tell you I'm leaving, but I can see that whatever I do, it will never matter to you,' she said.

Even as she walked out of the room, and closed the door behind her, Hilda's criticisms carried on, and any lingering guilt that Hetty felt about leaving her disappeared into the night.

The following morning, Anne parked William's car in front of reception.

'Well done, Anne. Your driving is coming on a treat,' he said.

'There's no need to sound so surprised, dear,' she replied with a half-smile.

Before William alighted from the car, he turned to her. 'You will speak to Hetty Lawson about what happened yesterday at the peace celebrations, won't you? Having one of our factory girls involved in a fight isn't the impression I wanted to give Sir Michael and Lady Bennett. Sir Michael is still grieving the recent loss of his dear father. Nonetheless, his company is one of our biggest creditors and I needed to soften him up. I'm afraid Hetty's behaviour has jeopardised that.'

Anne's face clouded over. 'It was hardly Hetty's fault, dear. But yes, as you spent the whole of last night insisting on it, I'll speak to her this morning. I'll ask Mrs Perkins to send her in after I've spoken to Meg about organising a conference for wholesalers. We should bring them all into the factory, let them see what we do here and aim to increase their orders.'

'An excellent idea,' William said.

'Plus there's something else I want to speak to Hetty about.'

'Oh?' William said, but Anne batted his query away.

'It's nothing to bother yourself with, dear. You keep your mind on wooing our creditors and I'll take care of the girls.'

William rushed ahead through reception, but Anne stopped by Jacob's desk to collect letters and documents marked for her attention.

'How's Meg?' she asked.

'Oh, she's fine, Mrs Jack. Thank you for asking. She and I had a wonderful day yesterday at the peace celebrations.'

'Very good, Jacob. Miss Lawson will be arriving for a meeting with me this morning. Please send her straight through to my office.'

'Yes, Mrs Jack,' he replied.

Later that morning, Anne was reading an article in the regional newspaper about poor sales at Mayfair Toffee. She was cutting it out to show William when there was a knock at her door.

'Come in,' she called.

The door opened and Hetty walked in. Anne beckoned her inside.

'Have a seat, Hetty.'

Hetty looked unusually nervous, she thought. 'Please don't be worried,' Anne reassured her.

'Mrs Perkins told me you'd asked to see me. I haven't done anything wrong, have I?'

Anne looked at her across her desk. 'We're friends, Hetty, so I'm not going to beat around the bush. It's about what happened yesterday at the peace celebration.'

'Oh no.' Hetty groaned. She covered her face with her hands, then peeked at Anne through her fingers.

'My husband insists I give you a talking-to,' Anne said. 'So consider yourself talked to and we'll speak no more about it. I'm going through the motions here. Jacob will have seen you come in, and he'll tell Meg, who'll tell Mr Jack, so everyone will know we had a meeting. What they'll never know is that I won't tell you off or sack you.'

'Sack me?' Hetty cried.

'That's what William wanted to do. He was embarrassed in front of some bigwigs he's trying to impress. If I'm honest, we're desperate to court them for the sake of the factory.'

Hetty hung her head. 'And the stupid fight ruined it for everyone. I wasn't involved, Anne, I told you.'

Anne stood and began pacing the floor, from the window overlooking the rose gardens back to her desk. 'I know you weren't. But my husband is old fashioned. He likes his factory girls to be seen and not heard. He's still living in the past, when girls wore long skirts that trailed the floors and got stuck to the toffee. The modern girl is different, more forward thinking. She's going to have to stand her ground when the soldiers return to work and we go back to full production.'

She continued pacing, thinking carefully about something that had been on her mind for some time.

'There will be many challenges supporting the girls through this change. It won't be easy. Some of the men returning will be injured, others will have seen things that have destroyed their minds. The girls will need to learn to be strong and adapt as the men slot back into their old roles. They will need someone to guide them. I was hoping you might rise to that challenge.'

Hetty sat up straight. 'Me?'

Anne stopped pacing and looked at her. 'You're the one I trust most. You've got a good head on your shoulders. The other girls admire you. And you've had your likeness on our tins of Lady Tina. What better advertisement for our brand than to promote you as the new supervisor?'

Hetty rocked back in her seat. 'Supervisor? I don't understand.'

Anne took her seat at her desk. 'I am going to tell you something now in strict confidence.'

Hetty leaned forward.

'Mrs Perkins is leaving. She has handed in her notice and will be gone by the end of the summer. I'd been thinking of recruiting a new supervisor from outside the factory. But the more I think about it, the more I realise a girl from inside is a much better choice. Not only that, but that girl should be someone I trust. It'll be more money, of course. More responsibility. More power.'

Hetty was silent for a moment.

'Anne, I'm flattered, truly I am. But I can't accept, I'm afraid.'

Anne was taken aback. 'Why ever not?' she asked.

Hetty had planned to tell Anne about Dirk's proposal and her move to Belgium at dinner time in the canteen, but the opportunity was too good to miss. Her face broke into a wide smile as she told Anne her wedding news.

Chapter Thirty

'You're doing *what*?' Anne cried.

'I said I'm getting married and moving to—' Hetty began. But Anne had already thrown her arms around her and was squeezing the life out of her.

When she finally released her, the two girls looked at each other for a very long time.

'So, your Belgian man finally proposed,' Anne said matter-of-factly. 'Well, I'm not surprised. From all you've told me about him, he adores you. But I'm surprised you agreed to move all the way to Belgium. Are you sure you want to live abroad?'

Hetty laid her hand on her heart. 'I've never felt so sure about anything,' she said. 'I want to be with him, it's as simple as that. I love him, Anne, just as you love Mr Jack, and I want a family of my own. Besides, I've nothing to keep me here in Chester-le-Street.'

Anne looked kindly at her. 'Not even a new job as a supervisor?'

'Like I said, I'm flattered you thought of me, but no, not even the toffee factory can keep me from leaving with Dirk.'

'But Belgium is so far away,' Anne said.

Hetty sat up straight in her seat. 'It helps to know I won't be the only girl from Chester-le-Street who's left with a Belgian man. A few others have already gone who've been married to their fellas for months. Oh, I know there'll be a lot to learn. I'll have to master a new language, make new friends and find a job . . .' A thought occurred to her. 'Speaking of jobs, how do I hand in my notice? Should I write a letter?'

Anne waved her hand dismissively. 'No need. I'll ensure things are done correctly. When are you planning to leave?'

'Two weeks' time,' Hetty said.

Anne's mouth opened in shock. 'Two weeks? But that hardly gives me time to arrange a collection for your leaving gift.'

'I don't need anything, Anne. Please don't go to any trouble.'

'Two weeks?' Anne cried again. 'You can't get married in two weeks, it's not possible.'

Hetty gave a wry smile. 'That's what Elsie said. But we're determined to find a way. We're going to visit every vicar in the county. There must be someone prepared to marry us at short notice. I can't travel to Belgium with Dirk without being his wife, it wouldn't be right. But I don't need gifts, Anne. I need to travel light. Just a suitcase, that's all.'

'Then I wish you both well, my friend. And if you need any help for your wedding day, let me know. I'm sure Elsie will help too. Between us we'll give you a send-off to make you proud.'

Hetty's eyes filled with tears, and she reached out to hug Anne. 'I'm going to miss you so much.'

Anne dipped into her pocket and pulled out a folded linen handkerchief. She gently dabbed Hetty's eyes. 'I'll write every week, with news from the factory.'

'And of Dinah too, I hope,' Hetty said.

She pulled herself together.

'I should return to the slab room before Mrs Perkins creates a fuss and says I've been gone too long.'

'Don't let on that you know she's leaving. She doesn't want it announced until we've found her replacement.'

'You can trust me,' Hetty replied. 'And again, I'm flattered you offered me the job. Do you have other girls in mind?'

Anne tapped her fingers against her chin. 'Well, there is someone, but I'm not sure about her loyalty to the factory. I'll need to give it a lot more thought.'

Elsie noticed Hetty return to the slab room and watched as she slipped her feet into her clogs and made her way to the cooling table. She was gently nudged along the table as Hetty pushed her way in just as one of the sugar boilers emptied a pan of boiling toffee. Some of the hot, liquid toffee slopped to the floor and Elsie's face dropped.

'Hey, you, we have to clean that up!' she cried, but the man ignored her and walked away with his empty pan. She turned to Hetty. 'I'll start clearing it up before it hardens.'

She began scraping the toffee from the floor, bristling as she did so, annoyed with the sugar boilers again. She crouched as she worked, being careful not to fall on her knees in case she became stuck. It was one thing being lifted out of clogs, another thing entirely being forced to remove her overalls because they were stuck to the floor.

There was a swish of blue material at her side. She didn't need to look up to know Mrs Perkins was there.

'Elsie Cooper, make sure you remove all of that toffee. The floor in here is a mess. I almost got stuck to the floor myself.'

Elsie was relieved when the supervisor walked off and left her to get on with her work. Once the floor was clear, she lifted her bucket and walked to the edge of the slab room, where broken, unusable toffee was thrown away. She emptied the bucket and began walking back to the table where she and Hetty worked, just as another sugar boiler emptied his pan of hot toffee. More of it slopped to the floor.

Elsie was furious. 'Mrs Perkins!' she called, but the supervisor was nowhere to be seen. She called out to the sugar boiler as he was heading off with his empty pan, but he didn't turn around or reply. She was incensed.

As she looked around the room for Mrs Perkins, to ask her to have a word with the sugar boilers, she took a step in the wrong direction and ended up in the hot toffee herself. Her clog stuck tight; she couldn't move her right foot. Then her left foot dropped into the toffee too.

'I'm stuck!' she called. It was the standard cry that the girls had been trained to give if ever they were stuck to the floor. It was the first time it'd happened to Elsie. She was normally much more careful, but the altercation with the sugar boiler had unsettled her enough to cause a misstep. 'I'm stuck!' she called again, wondering why no one was coming to her aid. 'This isn't funny! Why won't anyone help?' she cried in desperation.

It was then that she saw Stan. He was in his flat cap, boots and gardening clothes, and was heading towards her with a determined look on his face.

Chapter Thirty-One

'Stan? What are you doing here?' Elsie asked.

When he reached her, he whispered in her ear, 'Put your arm around my shoulders.'

Elsie was stunned but did as he asked. Stan lifted her and her feet slipped out of her clogs. She was being carried in his strong arms and saw she was headed to the slab-room door. She couldn't believe it. Normally it would take two sugar boilers, one on each side, to lift a girl from her clogs. As he walked from the room with Elsie in his arms, she looked at Hetty, who was smiling and giving him a round of applause. Some of the other girls broke into applause too, amused by what had happened. Elsie knew all eyes were on her and Stan, but far from being embarrassed, she was happy she was being watched.

'A little birdie told me that you'd always wanted to be lifted out of your clogs by a man with strong arms and a true heart,' he whispered.

'Was that little birdie called Hetty?' Elsie replied. 'I hope you don't get into trouble with old Perkins for this.'

At the slab-room door, Stan set Elsie back on her feet.

She looked into his hazel eyes, then reached up and kissed him on his cheek.

'You're a smashing man, Stan Chapman.'

'You're not so bad yourself, Elsie Cooper. It's dinner time and carrying you out here has given me an appetite. Want to join me in the canteen?'

Elsie looked behind her and saw Hetty waving her away.

'That'd be great, Stan, thanks.'

She slipped her feet into her shoes and set off across the cobbles to reach the canteen. But then Stan stopped dead.

'Let's push the boat out and eat dinner in the café on Front Street instead. My treat.' He offered her his arm and they left the factory grounds.

Elsie and Stan had arranged to meet after work so that he could walk her home. The quickest route home for Elsie was along the back lane. It was where courting couples met in the dark, and sometimes stolen goods were exchanged in the shadows. She felt a little nervous as she waited. She saw shapes move along the lane and assumed it was a couple enjoying a kiss. But then she heard a man's voice. He was talking about the toffee factory, then she heard eggs being mentioned. Eggs? She cocked her ear and took a step further into the lane. Keeping herself pinned to the wall and out of sight, she stayed quiet, hardly daring to breathe in case she was heard. She could clearly hear two men, and she leaned forward slightly. One was Mr Burl from the factory. He was handing over a file of papers, still talking about eggs. Nothing about this made sense. The only eggs at the factory were those fried with bacon and served in the canteen.

Suddenly she heard footsteps heading her way and moved further into the shadows. Mr Burl strode out of the lane, looking around to ensure he wasn't being followed, then made his way back to the factory. Elsie's heart was beating fast. She had no idea what was going on, but any business conducted in the back lane was bound to be shady. Why was Mr Burl there? What was in the folder? And who was the other man?

She wavered, wondering what to do next. She knew that she needed to tell Anne what she'd overheard, but if she went back into the factory and Stan couldn't find her, he might assume she didn't want him to walk her home. The truth was, she'd been looking forward to it.

As she waited, undecided, another man appeared from the gloom of the lane and began walking quickly away in the other direction. He was tall, with white hair, and was wearing a smart coat. As she watched, he turned around to glance behind him and she caught a glimpse of his face. He was older than she'd expected. Then a thought struck her. She remembered the night of the fight at the Lambton Arms, when she'd been on her date with the sugar boiler who'd run away at the first sign of trouble. The pub had been busy, but she remembered seeing Mr Burl because she was surprised he chose to socialise in such a rough place.

Stan bounded up to her, out of breath. 'Sorry I'm late,' he said. He offered her his arm, but Elsie shook her head.

'I'm sorry, Stan, I can't go home.'

'What's wrong?' he asked, worried.

She pointed along the lane. 'There was a man . . .'

Stan's eyes narrowed. 'He didn't hurt you, did he?'

'No, it wasn't like that. It's complicated. I need to see

Anne, right now. I'm sorry, Stan. I'll explain when I see you next.' She began to run towards the factory.

'Elsie!' Stan called, but his voice was lost on the wind.

She burst into reception and startled Jacob when she didn't stop.

'Hey, you, girl! You can't run in here.'

'I need to see Anne . . . I mean Mrs Jack. I need to tell her something, it's urgent.'

Jacob peered down his nose. 'Do you have an appointment?'

Elsie ignored him and ran straight to the door that led to the corridor and Anne's office. She heard Jacob call after her, but she didn't care. She knew in her heart that something wasn't right. When she reached Anne's office, the door was closed. She took a breath to steady herself, then knocked. Without waiting to be invited, she pushed the door open and was disappointed to find Anne's secretary Meg there alone.

'Where's Mrs Jack? It's urgent that I see her,' she gasped.

'She's with her husband in his office,' Meg replied. 'But you can't see her without an appointment.'

Elsie turned and ran along the corridor to Mr Jack's office. The door was open, and she saw Anne and Mr Jack putting on their coats, getting ready to leave. She knocked at the open door, and they both turned to face her.

'This is most unusual,' Mr Jack muttered.

'Elsie, what is it?' Anne said kindly.

Elsie stepped forward gingerly. She straightened her spine and looked at Anne, then at Mr Jack.

'I've just seen something peculiar in the back lane,' she began.

Anne's face clouded over. 'Go on.'

'Will this take long?' Mr Jack said. 'We need to get home in time for dinner with Sir Michael and Lady Bennett.'

Anne shot him an annoyed look. 'Be quiet, dear. I'm sure Elsie wouldn't be here unless it was important. Please, take a seat, Elsie.'

Elsie moved to the chair at Mr Jack's desk but didn't sit down. She couldn't, she was full of nervous energy. Instead, she gripped the back of the chair with both hands and began her tale.

'I was waiting for . . .' She paused. She didn't know if Mr Jack would approve of a factory girl becoming too friendly with the head gardener. 'Waiting for a friend. I sometimes walk home along the back lane because it's quicker, although I know I shouldn't because it's dark without the gas lamps lit. But I knew I'd be safe with my friend, only he didn't turn up when he should, and that's when it happened.'

Mr Jack tapped his watch impatiently.

'What did?' Anne asked, ignoring him.

'I saw something I shouldn't,' Elsie continued. 'It involved Mr Burl. I hope you don't think I'm speaking out of turn. And perhaps it was nothing. He might have had a reason to be in the back lane. I might have things wrong. But it looked very much like he was handing over a folder of papers to another man. And he was acting suspicious, glancing around him, being secretive.'

Anne's face turned to thunder. 'Mr Burl? Are you sure?'

'I'm certain,' Elsie said.

'Could you hear anything he said to this other man?' Anne asked.

Mr Jack yawned theatrically. 'Really, my dear. This is

factory girl gossip. We should be heading home. I don't want to be late for dinner with such important people.'

Anne gently laid her hand on her husband's arm. 'Wait just a moment. Did you hear anything, Elsie?'

'Why, yes, there was talk of eggs, which I thought rather strange.'

Anne and Mr Jack looked at each other.

'Eggs?' they both said at once.

Mr Jack walked around the desk to stand near Elsie. 'Elsie, tell us everything.'

'Well, that was it. I wondered if the man was a grocer. Why else would Mr Burl talk to him about eggs?'

'And you say you saw him hand the man a folder?'

Elsie nodded. 'Yes, exactly that.'

'Did you get a look at the other man?' Mr Jack asked.

'Just briefly. He was tall, elderly and—'

'Did he have white hair?'

'Why, yes, he did,' Elsie replied.

Mr Jack banged his fist against the desktop, which made her jump in surprise.

'William, do you know who it is?' Anne asked, but he didn't reply.

'I haven't got anyone into trouble, have I?' Elsie said nervously. 'I had to come and tell you because it looked suspicious. We all know what goes on in the back lane. It's all shady business, stolen goods changing hands and girls kissing sugar boilers. Mr Burl looked furtive; it made me wonder what he was doing. He kept glancing around as if scared of being seen.'

'Did he see you?' Anne asked.

'I don't think so. I kept myself against the wall. The

other man didn't notice me either. But I've seen them together before. It was in the Lambton Arms.'

Mr Jack rubbed his chin. 'Thank you, Elsie. This is very helpful.'

Elsie looked at Anne. 'Is there anything else you need to know?'

Anne took her arm and led her to the door. 'You can go, Elsie. Thank you for letting us know. It'll remain confidential.'

Elsie left the office with her heart pounding. She made her way slowly along the corridor to reception and out to the cobbled yard for the walk home, avoiding the back lane this time.

Anne sank into the nearest chair and stared at her husband in disbelief. He was perched on the edge of his desk.

'Are you thinking what I'm thinking, Anne?'

'That Mr Burl could have taken the notes from Meg's office about the toffee eggs – yes, I am,' she said. 'But what was he doing handing them over to this man in the back lane?'

'That's what I'm trying to work out,' William replied. 'Why would he give away secrets about our new novelty line? He knows the information is confidential and under strict embargo. It doesn't make sense.'

Anne spoke slowly. 'Unless Burl has become so dissatisfied with the way the factory is being run that he wants to hurt us.'

'No, Anne, he'd never do that,' William said.

Anne stood her ground. 'We view the man differently, my dear. To you, Mr Burl is a long-standing colleague and friend. To me, he's someone who's caused nothing

Celebrations at the Toffee Factory

but trouble. I fear he is now revealing his ugly side. You saw how irate he became in the board meeting when talk turned to the toffee eggs. What if the man he gave the papers to is someone who wants to go into competition with us?'

William leapt off the desk and began pacing the room, fiddling with his blue bow tie. 'I hope you're wrong, dear, but you may have hit upon something. There is someone who holds a grudge against us, against me. Someone who would pay good money to Mr Burl for those notes. They included production and set-up fees, finance projections, recipes, even creative designs. Oh, Anne, if I'm right, we need to stop whoever has them. Our factory is on the edge of bankruptcy and ruin. You know how hard we're working to reverse that. Conferences for wholesalers, dinner with our creditors, we're doing all we can. But if details of the new novelty toffee get out, we'll be ruined. If another factory starts making toffee eggs before we do, we can't claim we're the first in the country to make them. We need to stop this, Anne, or we'll be ruined. All our good work will be for nothing.'

Anne caught his arm to stop him from pacing. 'Your comment to Elsie earlier about the man with white hair . . . Do you know who he is?'

William nodded. 'I suspect it might be Bertram Dalton. The description fits him perfectly. He always swore he'd wreak revenge on me after I married you in favour of his daughter.'

'But that's absurd!' Anne cried.

'He never wanted me as his son-in-law; he just wanted the factory. He planned to demolish it and clear the land to rebuild. So when I called off my engagement to

Lucinda, he swore retaliation. But this isn't about Bertram's crushed ego at the shame of a broken engagement in his family. It's about business, and he intends to hit me where it hurts. Well, I won't stand for it. This evening, after dinner with Sir Michael, I'll visit Dalton to tell him that I know what he's up to. If he refuses to give up the notes, I'll report him to the authorities. But what on earth will I do about Mr Burl?'

Anne's face clouded over. 'Just you leave him to me.'

Chapter Thirty-Two

When Elsie returned to Elm Street, Hetty was working at the hearth, preparing tea, boiling a pan of water on the fire and peeling potatoes.

'You're late, is everything all right?' she asked when Elsie walked in.

Elsie flopped into the nearest chair. 'I had to stay behind at the factory to talk to Anne.'

Hetty's face dropped. 'Oh, Elsie. You haven't been getting in trouble with Mrs Perkins again? I keep telling you to do up your overall, but you never listen. I knew she'd report you.'

'No, it wasn't that,' Elsie said.

She removed her coat and slipped her feet from her shoes. Then she walked to the hearth and sat next to Hetty to help peel potatoes. As the girls worked together, preparing the evening meal, Elsie told Hetty all that had happened at work. Hetty's eyebrows rose in surprise.

'Eggs? Why on earth would they talk about eggs?'

Elsie shrugged. 'Maybe Mr Burl's a secret chicken farmer,' she said, which made Hetty giggle. 'But he looked furtive in the back lane and the other fella couldn't get away quick enough. He almost ran along the lane when Mr Burl handed him the folder. Anyway, it's been quite a day, with one thing and another.'

'You mean Stan coming into the slab room and carrying you away in his arms?'

Elsie smiled widely. 'How did he know I was stuck to the floor?'

Hetty grinned. 'I spotted him outside the slab room, so when I saw you were stuck, I rushed out to tell him. You'd mentioned how much you wanted to be lifted out of your clogs and into someone's arms. I couldn't think of anyone better than Stan. You seem to be getting on well.'

Elsie worked on the potato in her hand, turning it and scraping the skin to reveal the white flesh.

'We rub along together. I wouldn't say there's much passion or excitement, but I can live with that.'

'Are you sure? Not so long ago you were crying out for excitement, and you claimed Stan was too dull.'

Elsie was silent a moment. She thought about Stan's strong arms when he'd lifted and carried her. She thought about their dinner in the café that he'd paid for, even insisting they had a pudding afterwards. She was glad his appetite had returned and that he'd stopped work to eat dinner. He said she was a good influence on him. She thought about his weather-beaten face, his hazel eyes, the loving way he tended his garden, the flowers he nurtured to bloom and thrive. And she would never forget the day he'd walked into the river to save her life.

'He's a good man. Solid. Dependable. A girl could do a lot worse. Besides, he says he'll take me for a day out to Newcastle and he's going to buy our train tickets.'

'I wish you well, Elsie. He's a really good man.'

'We've both done well with fellas,' Elsie mused. 'What time are we meeting Dirk at Elisabethville tonight to look at a house with Hilda?'

Hetty glanced at the clock. 'I told him we'd meet him in an hour. Which means we'd better get these potatoes on to boil.'

'Don't you think it'll be ironic if Hilda moves to Elisabethville?' Elsie said with a grin. 'I mean, she's been less than polite about the Belgians.'

'Less than polite? That's putting it mildly!' Hetty said. 'She's been downright nasty about them. She never has a nice word to say about anyone. If she does end up living there, I hope she eats her words. Oh, by the way, there's a letter for you.'

Elsie put the pan of potatoes on the fire, then stood and picked up the letter from the mantelpiece. She studied the handwriting on the front and noted the postmark.

'It's from Aunt Jean in London.'

She slid her nail under the envelope flap, tore it open, then pulled out the letter inside and began to read. She was expecting the usual news from Jean's life in London, about walks in the park with Binty, her dog. But this letter was different, the news more serious. Elsie couldn't take it in; it didn't seem real. She started again, forcing herself to slow down and read carefully. She was concentrating so hard, she didn't realise Hetty was staring.

'What is it, love? You look like you've seen a ghost.'

Elsie looked up. 'It's Jean . . . she wants to know how to send me a postal order. The man she's been working for passed away and left her some money in his will. She wants to send some of it to me. I'm not sure I understand.'

Hetty moved to stand next to her, and Elsie felt her arm around her shoulders. Together the girls read the letter, then Elsie laid it on the table.

'I don't know what to do,' she said.

Hetty tapped it. 'Anne will know. She might even go to the bank with you, if you ask.'

Elsie's hand began to shake. 'Look at this final line. I'm going to need more than Anne's help with this.'

With money comes opportunity, Elsie. Use it wisely. A chance like this comes once in a girl's life. Buy your freedom, if you can.

Elsie looked into her friend's kind face. She felt tears prick her eyes. 'She's telling me to leave Frankie. I mean, really leave him. Oh, Hetty, I don't know how.'

Hetty pulled up a chair. 'Speak to Anne, she's the only one we know who can help. She knows things we don't, she's clever and smart. She'll know about . . .' She paused.

Elsie looked at her. 'Divorce,' she said quietly.

Hetty nodded. 'There's no shame in it, Elsie. The war's changed things. Women can go to court to start divorce these days.'

Elsie put her head in her hands. 'Not women like me. Not a girl who works in a toffee factory.'

Hetty reached for her hand. 'Frankie's brother and his wife will support you and attest to your character. If Frankie shows up sober in court it'll be a miracle. No judge in the land would force you to stay married to him after what he did.'

Elsie's head dropped, and her tears began. Hetty gently wrapped her arms around her.

'I'll help you, Elsie. I'll do all I can. We'll get rid of the stench of Frankie Ireland from your life, and when we do...'

Elsie looked up, waiting expectantly, wanting and needing to hear what Hetty said.

'When we do, you'll be free. If it's Stan you want, you can have him. You could even marry him if you wanted to.'

Elsie wiped her eyes and managed a smile. 'Think of the gossip that'd cause around here,' she said.

'Ah, but you won't be living around here if you move to Elisabethville with Hilda,' Hetty said. 'It'd be a brand-new start. You'll be living in a new area with new neighbours and friends.'

Elsie sat up straight in her seat. 'But the friend I care about more than anyone else won't be here to share my new life. She'll be living in Belgium, and I'll miss her each day.'

'I'll miss you too, Elsie. You've taught me about resilience and independence, and about looking out for myself.'

Elsie dabbed her eyes with a handkerchief. 'And you've taught me about family and love. You brought me into your home and cared for me when I needed it most. Oh, I'm rambling now. Jean's letter has knocked me for six. There's so much to think about, but you're right, Anne's the woman to ask for advice. I don't imagine that divorce will be easy or quick. It might take months, even years.'

Hetty patted her hand. 'And you've got all the time in the world.'

Chapter Thirty-Three

Later that night, Elsie, Hetty and Hilda walked slowly home from the bus stop after their visit to Elisabethville. The visit had perked Hilda up, and she'd talked non-stop on the journey home.

'I've never seen anything like it before. The house had an indoor netty, and lamps coming on at the flick of a switch. I'm taken aback with the quality of it all. I didn't expect that,' she said.

When they reached the terraced house on Elm Street, the girls headed to the kitchen. Normally Hilda would retreat straight to her room and to bed. But she was fired up by what she'd seen and wanted to talk. They all removed their coats and sat at the table.

'Will I tell Dirk you want to move there?' Hetty asked.

'I haven't made my mind up yet,' Hilda huffed.

'Don't rush her,' Elsie said gently.

'The house will need cleaning,' Hilda said.

'You know Elsie and I will do that for you.'

'And the garden's a mess,' she continued.

'I'm sure Stan would help with that,' Elsie chipped in. 'But the house itself was grand, wasn't it?'

Hilda looked around the small kitchen. 'Anywhere has to be better than here. It holds too many bad memories.'

Elsie noticed she glared at Hetty as she said this, and also noticed that Hetty feigned not to notice.

'Stan said he'd be able to get a van from work to help move the furniture,' she said.

Hilda shot her a look. 'Who's this Stan you keep talking about?'

Elsie lifted her chin. 'He's the gardener at the toffee factory and a good friend.'

'I don't want him coming round unannounced to the new house if we move,' Hilda said.

Elsie caught Hetty's eye, and the girls shared a smile.

'Look, Hilda. Do you want to move or not? Dirk needs a definite answer tomorrow,' Hetty said.

'I'll think about it overnight,' Hilda said. Then she pushed herself up from her chair and walked off to her room.

'Do you think she'll take the house?' Elsie asked once she was out of earshot.

Hetty shrugged. 'You never know with Hilda. One minute she wants one thing, the next she wants another.'

Elsie felt her friend's eyes on her. 'What is it?' she asked.

Hetty sat back in her chair. 'I feel dreadful about leaving you to look after her. Here I am planning to travel to another country, getting married to Dirk as soon as we find someone to carry out the wedding. And you're . . .'

'Stuck?' Elsie said with a smile.

'No, that's not what I meant. It's just that Hilda's a negative woman while you're the opposite. You always see the good in people. You're a ray of sunshine compared to her rainy day. I've lived with her gloom all my life and I won't miss it one bit. But I'm worried about you and the toll that looking after her might take.'

'Listen to me, Hetty. Have I ever once complained about looking after her?'

'Well, no, but—'

Elsie held up her hand. 'Have I ever moaned about her? Called her names?'

Hetty shook her head.

'Now, I don't think Hilda and I will ever be best friends, but I'm happy. Looking after her gives me a purpose, a reason to come home from work. I enjoy baking and cooking. Since moving in here, I've learned how to manage a house. After living in that rotten flat with Aunt Jean for years, I craved a home of my own. And now that I've got it, that home comes with Hilda as part of the deal. I'll look after her. You don't need to worry.'

'And what if you and Stan start courting strong, what then?' Hetty asked.

Elsie smiled. 'Stan has his own house. Oh, it's not much of one and it needs a woman's touch. But it's there if we need privacy, or I need time away from Hilda's sharp tongue.'

'Thank you, Elsie. I hope you know how grateful I am.'

Elsie was silent for a moment, then she turned her gaze to Hetty once more.

'You've got a good man in Dirk Horta. I just wish Belgium wasn't so far away.'

'You could always come to visit,' Hetty offered

'Perhaps I could, if Aunt Jean's money stretches that far.'

'Pay for your freedom first,' Hetty said.

'Oh, I will. I'll speak to Anne and take her advice on what I need to do. Divorce is a scary road to travel on when I haven't a clue what to do. Whether Frankie will be sober enough to sign documents remains to be seen. But I'm determined. And you know me, when I put my mind to something, I always get what I want.'

The following day, the toffee factory was closed. Hetty was at work at Lumley Castle, where talk was of the peace celebrations and how much the staff had enjoyed the day. Elsie stayed at home to talk to Hilda about the practical details of moving, as she had now made her decision to take the house in Elisabethville. However, although the factory was silent, Anne and William were there, as always, working hard behind the scenes, devising more ways to pay off the debts. William worked in his office, while Anne worked in Meg's, with the connecting door ajar. Dinah was sitting on the carpeted floor, happily drawing. William was composing a letter.

'I'm writing to our solicitor to instruct him to send a letter to Bertram Dalton,' he called to Anne. 'The scoundrel refused to see me when I called at his home. He needs to understand the seriousness of his actions in regard to taking the notes about our new novelty line.'

'And I'll tackle Mr Burl,' she replied.

'Did you sack Hetty Lawson?' William asked.

Anne looked up from the report she was writing. She stood, smoothed down her skirt and walked through to her husband's office. She'd heard his question clearly but needed time to compose her reply.

'Sorry, dear?'

'I said, did you sack Hetty Lawson as we discussed? The girl who caused a fracas at the peace celebration in front of Sir Michael and Lady Bennett.'

Anne stood in front of William's desk so that he had to look up at her as she delivered her reply. 'No, I didn't sack her.'

'But I said—'

'I know what you said, dear. But Hetty wasn't involved in the fight. It was two men who were fighting, neither of whom had any connection to the toffee factory.'

William sighed. 'So the girl told you she wasn't involved, and you were fool enough to believe her.'

Anne put her hands on her hips. 'Now look here,' she said angrily. 'Hetty is a good friend, and if she said she wasn't involved in the fight, I believe her. She's an honest girl and a hard worker, one of the best we've got. She's so impressive I even offered her the role of supervisor to replace Mrs Perkins.'

'You did what?' William exploded, leaping from his seat.

'Oh, sit down, dear,' Anne said softly, indicating their daughter, who was now watching them argue.

Subdued, William did as he was told, but he shook his head disapprovingly. 'Anne, Hetty Lawson is the face of Lady Tina, our leading brand of toffee. We can't have any whiff of scandal about her, or it'll reflect badly on the brand, the factory and the future.'

Anne sat opposite him. 'There is no scandal, dear, and I will not be drawn further on the subject. Besides, Hetty will soon be leaving us.'

William leaned forward. 'She hasn't been poached by a rival firm, has she?'

'No, she's getting married and moving overseas.'

He tapped his pen against his chin, taking this in. 'Where overseas?'

'Ghent, in Belgium. Her chap's family own a chocolate

shop, where I understand she will work with her new husband. Remarkably, the street where the shop stands remains almost intact after the war. So as far as Hetty is concerned, please can we drop the subject?'

Dinah came to Anne, climbed into her lap and put her small pudgy arms around her neck. Anne nuzzled against the child.

'I've been giving a lot of thought to the Lady Tina brand,' she began. An idea had been slowly burning in her for some time. She knew she'd have to take this carefully and slowly. 'We know that Mayfair Toffee has been suffering low sales for some time and is in the process of running the business down.'

'What does Mayfair Toffee have to do with Lady Tina?' William asked.

'Do you remember the newspaper article I showed you about poor sales at Mayfair?'

William nodded, and Anne carried on.

'Well, as you suggested, I delved a little deeper into which of their brands was suffering most. It turns out it's their brand they call Old-Fashioned Delight, and its tin has a picture of a woman on the front, not unlike our Lady Tina – a woman with a parasol and bonnet, a sentimental picture to evoke nostalgia.'

William leaned forward. 'What are you saying?'

Anne gently moved a lock of Dinah's hair behind her tiny ear. 'I'm saying that if our factory carries on as it is, we may well limp out of the dire situation we find ourselves in with our debts.'

William leaned forward. 'Don't forget we have the eggs, Anne, the eggs.'

Anne gave a wry smile. 'How could I forget about

those? But perhaps we need to bring about even more changes.'

William narrowed his eyes. 'What kind of changes?'

Anne was in her stride now. 'We could bring a new partner to the board, a partner who's prepared to invest.'

She paused and looked at William, knowing she had his full attention.

'At the peace celebration, Lady Bennett more than hinted that Sir Michael had expressed interest in investing in our factory. Remember, he has the money from the sale of his late father's land.'

William's eyes shone with excitement. 'Go on, dear,' he urged.

'I suggest that Lady Tina has had her day.'

'But—'

Anne held up her hand. 'Listen to me. War has changed everything, not least the way we women think of ourselves. We don't want to be presented with old-fashioned parasols and bonnets when we buy a sweet treat. We want a toffee brand that reflects the changes war has brought. A brand that promotes optimism, the future, family and love. We need a new toffee line, not just novelty eggs. Oh, they'll sell well, I'm sure, and by Easter next year we'll be the talk of the country, the only toffee factory to produce such a line.'

'As long as Bertram Dalton doesn't get there first.'

'Our solicitor will deal with him,' Anne said sternly. 'Dalton knows nothing of the toffee industry or confectionery. We're the experts, and you, my dear, are the toffee king.'

William began to fiddle with his bow tie. 'You flatter me, dear,' he said.

'Of course I do. You're my husband and I love you. And I want the world to know how wonderful Jack's toffee is. But we're going to need more innovation if we want to cause a stir. I suggest a new line of toffee aimed at the modern woman. One that suggests affection, devotion, loyalty, a kinship bond, and above all the importance of family.'

William narrowed his eyes. 'I'm not sure about this, Anne. You know the costs involved in production when we bring out a new line. What if we get it wrong?'

'Before we do anything, we must ask Mr Gerard and his team for creative advice. We'll even ask Sir Michael for his input, to flatter his ego. It might prove just the thing to bring him into our world. We could offer him a seat on the board in exchange for his investment.'

William tapped his fingers against the desk. 'His wife is rather charming too. Perhaps we could offer to put her likeness on the tins?'

But Anne shook her head. 'No, she's too old. We need a face that suggests optimism and a bright future ahead, trust, security and love.'

'Mama!' Dinah said.

Anne turned to look at her daughter. At the same time, William's eyes lit up. The two of them exchanged a smile.

'I think we've just found the face of our new brand,' Anne said.

Chapter Thirty-Four

At the weekend, the weather was sunny and bright. At home on Elm Street, Hetty was getting ready to spend the day with Dirk. Their plan was to visit churches to ask if they could be married at short notice. She wasn't sure their madcap plan would work, but what else could they do? The thought of travelling to Belgium as an unmarried woman shamed her, although Dirk assured her that he'd be the perfect gentleman. He even suggested they could marry in Belgium instead. However, Hetty wanted a clear conscience as she left her old life as Miss Lawson and started her new one as Mrs Horta. She liked the way it sounded when she said the name out loud.

As she dressed, she heard a noise from downstairs. It was an unfamiliar noise, and it took her a few moments to realise it was Hilda laughing.

A few minutes later, as she was brushing her hair, she heard a knock at the front door. She ran to the landing in time to see Elsie open the door. Her heart lifted when she saw Dirk on the doorstep. How handsome he looked in his suit.

'I'll be down in a moment!' she called.

She picked up her handbag and jacket and ran downstairs to the kitchen, but there was no one there. Then she heard the sound of Hilda's laughter again, coming from the front room. She heard Dirk laughing too, and Elsie. Going to Hilda's room, she saw Hilda sitting in a chair by her bed. When Hetty walked in, Dirk greeted her with a kiss on both cheeks, then laid his arm around her shoulders.

'Shall we make the most of the nice weather?' he asked, gesturing to the window.

'Yes, let's go,' Hetty said, feeling suddenly uncomfortable about the shared joke that she was no part of.

'Just a moment,' Hilda called.

Hetty braced herself for whatever criticism was sure to come her way. But when she looked at Hilda, she saw that she seemed relaxed and calm. Her gaze fell on Elsie's make-up bag by the bed.

'Oh, we've had some fun putting powder and rouge on this morning, haven't we, Hilda?' Elsie joked.

'Such fun,' Hilda replied.

Hetty was stunned. She couldn't remember the word *fun* leaving Hilda's mouth before. She was even more surprised when Hilda asked Elsie to help her out of her chair. With Elsie supporting her, the woman walked to Hetty and Dirk.

'Elsie tells me you're off to plan your wedding.'

'That is right, Mrs Lawson,' Dirk said politely.

Hilda nodded, keeping her gaze on Hetty. 'Well, I have a little put by; some savings . . .' She swallowed hard. 'It's yours if you need it, for the wedding.'

Hetty couldn't move. Her feet were stuck to the floor. Hilda had never done or said anything nice to her, and she didn't know how to react.

It was Dirk who broke the silence with effusive thanks. He stepped forward and awkwardly put his arms around Hilda, trying to hug her, but Hilda's body didn't move and she kept her eyes on Hetty.

'That's wonderful news,' Elsie said. Hetty knew her friend was egging her on, trying to pull her out of her shock.

'Yes,' was all Hetty could manage. She looked from Dirk to Hilda and Elsie. All of them were staring at her, waiting for her response. She felt numb and couldn't speak.

'It's a very generous offer, Mrs Lawson,' Dirk said, and he took Hetty's hand and gently squeezed it. 'Isn't it, Hetty?'

Hetty felt the pressure of his hand. She opened her mouth to say something, but she still couldn't find the words. Then Hilda took a step forward and kissed her on her cheek. Hetty's jaw dropped. She heard Elsie gasp and saw her hand fly to her mouth.

'Hetty?' Dirk said.

Hetty had trouble snapping out of her thoughts. She felt Hilda's hand on her arm.

'Thank you,' she managed at last. 'Thank you very much.'

She was overcome with shock and emotion. This was the first time in her life that she and Hilda had made a connection. And it seemed it was because of Elsie. She walked to her friend and hugged her.

'Thank you,' she whispered.

'Don't thank me,' Elsie replied. 'It was her idea. The move to the new house has got her all fired up. She's really excited.'

Hilda waved her hand at Hetty, as if dismissing her. 'Go, the two of you. Go now and find a vicar. Stop hanging around; you're making my room look untidy.'

Hetty gave a wry smile. The old Hilda was back.

She and Dirk headed outside. They held hands as they walked and chatted excitedly about Hilda's offer, about the train journey to Hull and the journey by ship to Belgium. Dirk talked about his family, about how much he knew Hetty would be welcomed and loved. He'd already written to tell them that she had accepted his proposal and that she would return with him to Ghent.

When they reached Front Street, Hetty assumed they'd head to the nearest church and keep going until they found a vicar willing to marry them before they left the country. However, Dirk had other plans.

'Please, Hetty, come to the river and sit with me for a while.'

'But we don't have time,' she protested.

'Please, come this way, it won't take long,' he begged.

Hetty followed him to a bench and sat down. He dipped his hand into his jacket pocket and brought out a small black box. Inside was a plain silver band.

'This is to replace our toffee-wrapper ring.'

He lifted the ring out of the box and slid it onto Hetty's finger. It was a perfect fit.

'I bought it at the market in Durham from a silversmith. I hope you like it.'

Hetty lifted her left hand and marvelled at the slim band.

'There is no diamond, I'm afraid. I could not afford it, but there are many diamond shops in Antwerp, a short train ride from Ghent. We could visit there one day,' he added.

'Oh, Dirk, it's beautiful,' she said.

Dirk slid the empty box into his pocket, then stood and held out his hand for Hetty, and together they walked to St Cuthbert's church. Inside, the vicar was laying hymn books on pews. In the middle of the aisle was a spray of summer roses in a vase. Sunlight streamed through stained-glass windows, casting multicoloured shadows on the floor.

'Good morning, you're a little early for the service,' the vicar said.

Dirk took hold of Hetty's hand and began to tell him of their plan.

'We're leaving soon for Belgium, you see. We have the tickets already,' Hetty added once he had finished.

The vicar rubbed his chin. 'This is most unusual,' he said. 'Alas, I cannot sanction a marriage in such a short space of time. There are procedures to be followed; the banns must be read in advance.'

'We're sorry,' Hetty mumbled. She pulled Dirk's hand. 'Come, let's go. The reverend is busy, and we have a lot to do.'

'You could perhaps try the Methodist church,' said the vicar kindly. 'I know the minister there has more liberal views. Or St John's church in Birtley, though I fear you will receive the same response there as I have given you.'

Hetty and Dirk left with heavy hearts. They walked quickly to the Methodist church, but were told nothing could be done at such short notice. They tried a third church, where the vicar advised them to make an appointment to come back in two weeks.

'I'm sorry, we don't have that much time,' Hetty said.

At the next church they tried, they were greeted by enthusiastic hymn-singing, and the vicar was clearly too busy to talk. And when they took the bus to Birtley, they found that St John's church was closed. They looked at one another in dismay.

'What are we going to do?' Hetty asked.

Dirk turned his face to her, and she looked into his deep blue eyes. 'We could have a civil wedding, Hetty. Would you mind very much if we didn't get married in church?'

'I suppose . . .' she began. The truth was, she'd always dreamed of a church wedding. 'Under the circumstances, it may be our only choice.'

Dirk thought for a moment. 'Then we need to visit Chester-le-Street town hall. But I must tell you something, Hetty. If by some miracle we can get a special licence for a civil wedding, it means that our marriage won't be recognised in the eyes of the Church.' He looked at her seriously. 'I don't know if I could live with that. Could you?'

Hetty knew she couldn't. Before she had a chance to reply, however, Dirk continued.

'We could have a church service in Ghent, though, with all of my family around us.'

'Oh, Dirk, that'd be wonderful,' she said.

They hurried to the bus stop to return to Chester-le-Street. When they arrived, they ran to the town hall. The office there was sparse and barren, unlike the warm, welcoming churches. An officious man with a pince-nez looked down at them when they approached.

'We would like to know how we can be married here,' Dirk said. Hetty heard the desperation in his voice.

The man at the desk nodded slowly. 'You wish to have a non-religious civil marriage here in the register office?'

'Yes please, as quickly as possible,' Hetty said.

'I see,' said the man, although Hetty was concerned that he didn't seem in any way rushed. She grew impatient as he took his time. 'Well, the Marriage Act of 1836 allows this, of course. But I'm afraid we can't offer you an appointment today.'

'What about tomorrow?' she asked hopefully.

The man tried to suppress a smile. 'I'm afraid we're not open on Sunday. However, there has been a cancellation . . .'

He turned away and pulled a heavy book from a shelf. He placed it on the desk and opened it. Hetty and Dirk held hands. Hetty's heart was beating hard. The man slowly turned the pages of the book, running his finger down each one until he found what he was looking for.

'Ah yes, here it is. A week on Friday. Does that suit?'

Hetty and Dirk looked at each other. Hetty's heart dropped to the floor.

'Next Friday? But that's the day we leave for Belgium.'

Dirk's face clouded over, and he turned to the man. 'Are you sure there isn't another appointment before then?'

The man gave him a hard stare. 'Quite certain, sir, yes.'

'What time is the appointment?' Dirk asked.

'Dirk, we can't delay leaving. The tickets are booked.'

The man returned his gaze to the ledger. 'It's the first appointment of the day, at nine a.m., sir.'

Hetty's heart suddenly lifted. 'That would give us just enough time to reach the railway station for our train,' she said.

Dirk's blue eyes shone with excitement. 'We'll take the appointment. Thank you.'

The man took their names and entered them into his book. He gave them details of what to expect at their appointment along with a bill to be settled, then sent them on their way.

Chapter Thirty-Five

Later that week, Anne drove to the factory. She parked squarely on the cobbles and turned to her husband with a satisfied grin.

'I think my driving and parking are almost on a par with yours now, dear.'

William could only agree. 'That's because you had me as your instructor,' he said. He leaned across and gave her a peck on the cheek. 'Come on, let's go. There's a lot to do today. We need to meet with Mr Gerard and his creative team to discuss the novelty eggs.'

Anne thought for a moment. 'Is it really wise to carry on with that line while Bertram Dalton is being investigated by our solicitor?' she asked, concerned.

'Of course it's wise. We should . . .' he allowed himself a little smile, 'crack on with it. In fact, I think it's an eggs-cellent idea!'

Anne grimaced. 'Oh dear. You're going to be insufferable. But seriously, I'm worried that Dalton will beat us to production of the eggs.'

'We'll scramble his egg plans!' William carried on. 'He poached our idea!'

Anne sighed and shot her husband a look.

'Sorry, dear, I'm getting carried away,' he replied with a cheeky smile.

'You eggs-asperate me at times,' she teased. 'I mean it, though. Shouldn't we wait until we receive confirmation from the solicitor that Bertram Dalton will go no further?'

William's eyes twinkled with mischief. 'Our solicitor is one of the best in the north. He won't let us down. Not only will he stop Bertram from producing our toffee eggs, but he'll also bring him to court for being in receipt of stolen goods, namely Mr Gerard's notes.'

'My heart is set on getting rid of Burl, William. He betrayed us and should be sacked.'

'Let's not be hasty. He has been with me for years and I'd like to hear what he has to say before I make a decision. Though I have to admit his behaviour lately is becoming untenable. I don't think I'll ever forgive him for the way he spoke to you.'

'You're being too lenient. Just because he has been loyal to you doesn't mean he should get away with stealing confidential notes and handing them to an outsider,' Anne replied sternly.

She stepped out of the car and picked up her briefcase from the back seat. William was already striding into the factory. When Anne entered the reception, she saw Jacob at his desk.

'Morning, Jacob,' she called.

He raised his head and forced a smile. Anne had known him since the first day she'd started work at the factory, and she could count on the fingers of one hand the number of times she'd seen him offer a genuine smile.

'Has Mr Burl turned up for work yet?' she asked.

'No, Mrs Jack. I haven't seen him.'

Anne walked to her office and took off her coat and hat. She had a pressing list of appointments and a full in-tray of work. However, knowing she had to tackle Mr Burl about what Elsie had seen in the back lane lay heavy on her mind. She hadn't slept well because of it.

Meg appeared at her office door. 'Mrs Jack? Would you like me to bring you a cup of coffee?'

'Good morning, Meg. Yes please. And could you ask Mr Burl's secretary to send him to my office as soon as he arrives.'

'Yes, Mrs Jack,' Meg said.

Anne sat for a moment going over what she and William had discussed. Then she began to go through the pile of letters that Meg had left for her attention. After a while, there was a knock at the door. Her heart beat a little faster, and she stood, thinking it the best way to present herself to Mr Burl. She'd invite him in and ask him to sit down, while she remained standing so that she'd have the advantage. She wouldn't beat around the bush. She'd tell him straight that he'd been seen in the back lane with Bertram Dalton. She'd tell him that she knew he'd handed over confidential documents. She'd watch his body language for signs as to whether he was telling the truth.

She straightened her spine and pushed her glasses up to the bridge of her nose. She was ready to give him hell.

'Come in,' she said.

But it wasn't Mr Burl who entered, it was Meg, carrying a tray with a coffee pot and a blue mug on it. Anne felt deflated, and her shoulders slumped. She'd been ready for a fight and now the energy drained from her.

Meg approached her desk and set down the tray. 'I'm afraid Mr Burl hasn't arrived yet,' she said.

'Then he's late!' Anne barked.

Meg jumped back in surprise. 'Are you all right, Mrs Jack? If you don't mind me saying so, Mr Jack is also on edge this morning.'

Anne sighed heavily. 'Yes, I'm fine, Meg, thank you. We've both got a few things on our minds.'

'Anything I can help with?' Meg asked.

Anne looked into her eager face and softened. 'Nothing that anyone can help with, I'm afraid. This is something that Mr Jack and I need to concentrate on.'

'Don't forget you have a meeting in half an hour with Mr Gerard and his creative team. It will be held in Mr Jack's office.'

Before Anne headed to the meeting with Mr Gerard, she marched to the shared office where Mr Burl's desk was, but he wasn't there. She asked his secretary where he was, but the poor girl was at a loss.

'I'm sorry, Mrs Jack. He should be here. There's nothing in his diary to indicate he had a meeting elsewhere.'

Anne made her way to William's office, taking deep breaths with each step she took, trying to calm her anger. If Mr Burl wasn't at work, where was he? Was he up to no good with Bertram Dalton? Were they colluding right at that moment, plotting against the factory? She suddenly felt dizzy and stopped dead, leaning her hand against the wall. Her heart was beating fast and she needed to calm down. When she felt steadier, she walked on.

William's office door was ajar, and she saw him sitting with Mr Gerard and two young men from the artwork department. Meg was at his side with her notepad and pencil. Elderly Mr Gerard rose slowly from his seat when Anne entered, and went to her to kiss her cheek.

'Good morning, Anne,' he said.

Anne acknowledged the men at the table. 'Good morning, gentlemen,' she said as she sat.

Over the next hour, the novelty eggs were discussed from a creative point of view. The size of the eggs was paramount; they needed to fit into a child's hand yet be hearty enough to satisfy a hungry man. Packaging colours were debated, with the blue of the factory logo being the obvious choice. Then Mr Gerard suggested a long list of names for the new product. However, William settled on the simple but effective *Jack's Toffee Egg*.

'The novelty is in the product. We don't need a fancy name,' he said.

Anne watched as Meg scribbled notes. She remembered when she'd been William's secretary, recalling how hard it had been for her to capture notes from meetings where creative ideas twisted and turned from Mr Gerard's mind.

Soon talk turned to Anne's idea of another new line of toffee, this time aimed at the modern woman. William leaned forward and looked hard at Mr Gerard and his men.

'This is Mrs Jack's idea. I'd like her to take full credit.'

Mr Gerard was enthusiastic. 'Why, it's one of the best ideas I've heard. Anne's right. We need to change things around. Stay still and we stagnate. I'm all for bringing in fresh ideas.'

'Even if it means getting rid of Lady Tina?' William asked.

Now it was Anne's turn to interject. 'Just hold on a minute. I never said anything about stopping production of Lady Tina. She may be the old lady of our toffee production but she's a classic! We must keep it running, it's our most successful line. I propose that the new toffee runs alongside it, like Lady Tina's younger, brighter sister.'

'Genius!' Mr Gerard cried.

'I agree. I'd buy it,' a little voice said.

Anne looked at Meg. Had the comment really come from her? She normally never said a word in meetings, and nor was she expected to. Her role was to bring in coffee, serve it and make notes.

'Go on, Meg,' Anne encouraged her.

Meg sat up straight in her seat. 'I said I'd buy it. If it's a new toffee for the modern woman, now that war's over, it's a celebration of life.'

One of Mr Gerard's men frowned. 'We've already shelved one idea for Sweets of Peace. How will this new line be different?'

'Because it will be aimed at families with the promise of a bright future. William and I have already discussed this,' Anne said.

William thought for a moment, then turned to Meg. 'And you say you'd buy it?'

'Yes, sir,' Meg replied. 'As would all of my friends, I'm sure.' She dropped her gaze to the table, and Anne saw her face redden.

'Go on, Meg, please,' she said.

Meg gulped. 'Well, I keep my ears open, and I hear things in the factory from the girls. They say Lady Tina has had her day.'

William gasped. 'But she's our best-selling brand!'

'If you don't mind me saying, sir, Lady Tina is old fashioned and out of step with modern thinking. People keep buying it because they love the taste, it's the best in the country. But the picture on the tin, well, it was fine before the war, when people needed nostalgia and a sense of safety looking back at the past. But now our past includes the war years, and no one wants to look back on that.'

'Indeed,' Mr Gerard said sagely.

'We need to look to the future, William, in all areas of our work,' Anne urged.

William sank back in his seat. 'Are you writing this down, Meg?' he asked.

Meg looked up from her pad, where she was scribbling furiously. 'Yes, sir.'

William fiddled with his blue bow tie, then turned his gaze to Mr Gerard's men. 'Work with the finance team, draw up detailed costings for this new line.'

'Yes, sir. Would you also like us to draft ideas for the picture of a modern woman on the tin? I understand there's a very attractive girl at the factory, Elsie Cooper, who was approached to be the face of Sweets of Peace. Should we approach her again to be the face of this new brand?'

Anne and William shared a look. Anne saw William's face soften and a smile reach his lips.

'There's no need to ask Elsie, or any of the girls. Our daughter Dinah's likeness will be painted on the tins. She will represent the future.'

Mr Gerard clapped his hands with glee. 'That's a perfect idea; I couldn't have thought of better myself!'

When the meeting ended, Mr Gerard dismissed his men. Once they'd left the office, he looked seriously at William.

'We've been friends since you were a boy. Be honest

with me. Are you sure the factory can afford to produce two new lines? We both know how precarious our finances are. The toffee eggs will sell well on pure novelty alone, but a new line of sweets in addition to this ... are you sure the factory can stretch to it?'

William looked at Anne, then reached for her hand.

'There is the possibility of investment. Anne and I are taking things slowly with the person involved. I can't say any more right now. Trust me, Mr Gerard. I feel certain that all will be well.'

'I hope you're right,' Mr Gerard replied.

Chapter Thirty-Six

Once Mr Gerard left the office, Meg began to clear the coffee pot and mugs then walked off to the kitchen. This left Anne and William to talk alone.

'Mr Gerard's right, William. I'm concerned too that we may be going too far too soon. We're not out of the woods yet, we're still paying off our debts.'

'Have faith in me, Anne,' he said.

'I trust you, of course, but I feel nervous that we're over-extending production when we should be reining it in.'

William gently took hold of her hand. 'I know there's a long way to go and it may come to nothing, but we have Sir Michael's interest in investing. It would be a huge boost. In fact, it could change everything.'

'*If* it happens,' Anne said sagely.

William nodded slowly. 'You're right, of course. I need to speak to Sir Michael in private. I'll invite him for a tour of the factory and see if he mentions investing. Oh, I know we could carry on without his help, but we would struggle. However, with his investment, just think what we could do.'

Anne looked at her husband and saw his eyes sparkle.

She leaned across the desk and kissed him. 'Your optimism is one of the many reasons I love you, Mr Jack.'

'And I love you too, Mrs Jack,' he replied. But then his face clouded over. 'However, there is unfinished business. We need to discuss Mayfair Toffee again.'

Anne stood and beckoned William to follow her. 'We can't talk here. Meg could return any moment and overhear us, and I'm not sure I trust her completely. She seems a little flighty at times.'

She led the way along the caramel-coloured corridor with its brown wooden walls and thick carpet. When she reached her own office, she closed the door. She pulled two chairs close, then she and William sat down with their heads together.

'Did you find out the date when Mayfair Toffee is due to close?' William asked.

'Within a year. I haven't cut off correspondence with them yet.'

He rubbed his chin. 'Then write to them today. Ask for another appointment and pretend you want to know more about the job they offered you. Stall for time. Tell them you're considering your position. And when they call you in to meet them again, don't act suspicious.'

Anne was confused. 'Suspicious?'

William's hand flew to his blue bow tie, and he fiddled nervously with it. 'Didn't I tell you?'

'Tell me what?' she said.

When he didn't respond, Anne narrowed her eyes. 'William?' she said sternly. 'I know that look on your face. You're up to something – what is it?'

A smile played around his lips. 'I'm planning to buy Mayfair Toffee, dear.'

Anne's jaw dropped. 'You're *what*?' she cried.

'Are you certain I didn't tell you?' William said. He scratched his head.

'I think I'd remember if you had. Have you completely lost your mind? What's the point in buying a failing toffee factory?'

'Mayfair Toffee is failing because they're not keeping up with trends.'

'We can't afford to buy a factory. Where will the money come from? We have trouble enough keeping this one afloat! Have you gone completely mad?'

William paused and twisted his bow tie again. 'Buying Mayfair Toffee is a dream I harbour.'

Anne raised her eyebrows. 'Since when? Oh, William, it's all wrong. It's crazy.'

'It's the right thing to do, Anne, if – and only if – Sir Michael invests.'

Anne was silent a moment, letting the shock news sink in.

'Have you talked to your father about this?'

'Not yet. I was hoping you'd come with me when I speak to him.'

Anne felt angry with William for not telling her about his idea, but she also felt something else, something she couldn't place at first. She stood and began pacing, letting the shock news sink in. And as she did, she slowly began to realise what a great opportunity this would be for the factory, for Jack's brand of toffee, for their workforce and for the future. She stopped pacing and turned to him. His face was expectant.

'Well, what do you think?' he said.

Anne tried to suppress a smile, because she was still

annoyed at her husband for not talking this through with her before. But the world of possibilities it could open up, combined with William's enthusiasm, proved too hard to resist. She flew to his side.

'I think it's the craziest idea you've ever had. But I also think it might work.'

'Only with Sir Michael's investment, of course,' William said more soberly. 'I'm not entirely reckless.'

As Anne kissed him on his lips, there was a knock at the door. She leapt back.

'Come in,' she said, smoothing her hair behind her ears.

Meg popped her head around the door. 'Mr Jack, there's a messenger boy from the solicitor's office in reception. He asks if you would have time to meet the solicitor this morning in his office on Front Street. He says it's about the matter you recently wrote to him about and it's urgent.'

Anne and William exchanged a look.

'Tell him I'll be there in half an hour,' William replied.

He stood and walked out of the office, but Meg remained at the door.

'What is it, Meg?' Anne asked.

The secretary gripped her hands together. 'It's Mr Burl, he's in his office.'

'Can you ask him to come and see me,' Anne said.

'I did, Mrs Jack, but he refused.'

'Oh, did he now?' Anne said, her tone darkening. 'Right. Then there's only one thing for it.'

She marched out of her office, past Meg and along the corridor to the shared office where Mr Burl's desk was. The door was closed. She raised her hand to push it, but at the last minute she stopped. She knew her feelings were running away with her, and she had no proof of what Mr Burl had done. She couldn't go into his office with all guns blazing, accusing him of theft, of passing on confidential notes, when she only had Elsie's word. Oh, she believed Elsie, of course. But if she was to tackle Mr Burl on this matter, she needed solid proof. She had to wait until William returned from his meeting with the solicitor, when news about Bertram Dalton would be confirmed.

The wait was interminable. An hour ticked by, then another. When William returned, he walked into her office.

'What did the solicitor say?' she asked immediately.

He sank into a chair. He looked done in, she thought.

'William?' she said gently.

'It's as we thought, Anne. Bertram Dalton has admitted he took the notes about the toffee eggs. However, he claimed it was done in a spirit of collaboration with Mr Burl and that Mr Burl had cleared it with me first. The coward blamed Mr Burl for everything. The solicitor has taken a written statement from him and our notes have been returned. He has sworn in writing that he won't go into competition with us to make the eggs or any other toffee product. The man's a fool, he knows nothing about confectionery. The solicitor pointed out to him the scandal it would cause if any of this got out and made its way to court.'

Anne could feel her legs start to tremble, and she walked to her chair and sat down. She looked across the desk at William.

'Do you realise that Elsie Cooper has saved us? If she hadn't seen Mr Burl and Bertram Dalton in the back lane, we might have lost the new novelty line. Even if Bertram didn't go into production, he could have sold the notes. Elsie has kept us from ruin.'

'We should offer her something for her vigilance – a tin of best toffee perhaps?' William suggested, but Anne shook her head.

'I have something better in mind. But first, now that we know the truth, I need to visit Mr Burl.'

'Anne, be careful. He's not going to take it well, being reprimanded by a woman.'

'Oh, I'm not going to reprimand him,' she said. 'I'm going to sack him.'

She expected William to argue, knowing that his long friendship with Mr Burl often blinkered him to the man's faults. She was ready to stand her ground if he protested. When he didn't, she took heart. She placed her hand on his shoulder.

'Would you still like me to report back to you after I've spoken to him? Earlier, you said you'd decide what to do depending on how he reacted to being confronted.'

William covered her hand with his own. 'No, Anne. Now that Elsie's words have been confirmed by the solicitor, you know what you need to do.'

Anne squared her shoulders and with a determined look on her face left her office and marched off to see Mr Burl.

Chapter Thirty-Seven

Anne gritted her teeth as she strode along the corridor. She kept her back straight and focused on the task ahead. When she reached Mr Burl's office, she knocked on the door but didn't wait for a reply before she pushed it open and walked in. Mr Burl looked up from his desk, startled.

'I need to speak to you, Mr Burl,' she said. She looked around the office. 'Alone.'

The three other men in the room rose and hurried out. Anne closed the door behind her, then walked to Mr Burl's desk.

An evil grin came to his face. He leaned back in his chair and crossed his arms. 'Take a seat,' he said. But Anne remained standing, looking down on him.

'We have never got along, Mr Burl.'

Mr Burl's face remained impassive.

'From the first day I began work at the factory as William's secretary, you went out of your way to make things difficult for me.'

He opened his mouth to speak, but Anne cut him off.

'Oh, I know why it happened. It was your ex-fiancée, Miss Brabin, who told me. She'd been led to believe by you that the role of William's secretary was hers. You told her you'd put in a good word for her. And so the fact that I was appointed instead of her caused problems in your relationship, and she ended the engagement.'

Mr Burl's face darkened. 'What happened in my private life is no business of yours...' He seemed to remember whom he was speaking to. 'With all due respect, Mrs Jack.'

'Oh, but it became my business, Mr Burl,' she said. She stood her ground, feet pressed to the carpet, her back straight and breathing even. 'When your fiancée left you, you blamed me. You went out of your way to cause problems for me. You tried to make me look foolish in front of William and the management board.'

Mr Burl sneered. 'You didn't need my help to make you look foolish. You managed to do that very well on your own.'

Anne felt heat rise around her neck, and her face flushed with anger. She was determined not to give him the satisfaction of knowing his words stung. She pushed her glasses up to the bridge of her nose.

'I recall, Mr Burl, that you once suggested that the reason I joined the factory was to find myself a husband. You even said I'd gone after William from the very first day and begged him to call off his engagement to Lucinda Dalton.'

'Well, didn't you?' he leered. He leapt from his seat. 'Mrs Jack, what is this about? You've interrupted my work and given me a dressing-down about my private life. Now, if you don't mind, I'm a busy man with many appointments. I have the quarterly finance report to work through, an agenda to set, and my secretary will be here any moment for our daily meeting.'

'Sit down,' Anne said firmly.

Mr Burl remained standing. 'I beg your pardon?'

'I said, sit down.'

'Now look here—'

'Sit!' Anne barked.

It took a few seconds, but Mr Burl finally, reluctantly, sat. Anne could feel her face burning. She clenched her fists, then released her fingers, trying to compose herself.

'Mr Burl, I mentioned the name Lucinda Dalton just now. No doubt she is a lady you are familiar with.'

A puzzled look crossed his face. 'I know of her, of course. She was engaged to Mr Jack before you came along.'

'And you also know her father, Bertram. Is that right?'

Mr Burl's left eye began to twitch. 'Who?'

Anne shook her head. 'Don't play the innocent, Mr Burl. I know that you and Bertram Dalton have become rather close.'

'Nonsense!' he cried, but he shrank away as if trying to press his body into his chair.

'Oh, but it's not nonsense, is it? You see, you've been spotted together twice.'

Mr Burl's face turned white. 'How dare you come in here and make accusations against me.'

Anne paused for a moment.

'Accusations, Mr Burl? Why, I haven't accused you of anything . . . yet.'

His eye twitched again. 'What is this about?'

'It's about you and Bertram Dalton, Mr Burl. It's about you taking . . . no, let's call it what it was . . . stealing confidential notes from the factory. The confidential notes that were discussed in private at a board meeting you attended where our new novelty line was proposed.'

With every word, Anne saw Mr Burl shrink further back. His face crumpled in on itself, his eye twitching uncontrollably.

'I'm not taking this from you. I demand to speak to Mr Jack!'

'You can demand as much as you like, but my husband won't see you today. Or tomorrow. Or the day after. He's known you for decades and thought of you as a trusted colleague and friend. That's why your betrayal of him and the factory has hurt him deeply.'

'I'll speak to him man-to-man,' Mr Burl said, but Anne could tell the fire had gone out of him, and he was trying to negotiate his way out of the situation.

'No you won't,' she said. She leaned forward and placed her hands on the desk, looking him straight in the eye. He leaned further back in his chair.

'I think you know what I'm going to say next, Mr Burl,' she said calmly. 'Or would you like me to spell it out for you?'

She held his gaze for a few uncomfortable seconds, unsure what he might do. She knew he wouldn't dare lash out at her, although she saw the anger in his eyes.

'You're sacking me?' he cried.

Anne took her hands off the desk and stood up straight. 'Yes, Mr Burl, that's exactly what I'm doing, and it comes with my husband's blessing.'

'William would never sanction this!' he cried.

'He already has,' Anne replied. She looked around the office and pointed at an empty chair. 'I'll sit here and wait while you pack up your belongings. I need to ensure you don't take anything you're not entitled to. No folders, files or notes.'

She walked to the chair, smoothed her skirt and sat down. She was beginning to feel sick and too hot. She crossed her legs at the ankles and waited, but Mr Burl didn't move.

'In your own time, Mr Burl,' she said.

She waited a few moments more, watching him like a hawk. She'd expected him to clear his desk, open drawers and empty shelves, but he didn't. He simply picked up his briefcase, pulled his coat and hat from the coat stand and walked to the door. He paused on the threshold and turned to face her.

'This factory was ruined the day you were taken on.'

Anne let the comment go; it was water off a duck's back, nothing more than a parting shot from a brute of a man. She followed him out to the corridor and walked a few paces behind him. His secretary came towards them.

'Mr Burl, where are you going? What about our meeting?'

He swept past her without a word and strode through the reception, where Jacob was working on his ledger. When he reached the door to head outside, Anne stopped him.

'Mr Burl, please hand over your keys.'

Jacob looked up from his work. Mr Burl's face was like thunder. Anne remained calm while he delved into his coat pocket then thrust the keys into her hand. She stood at the door, watching as he walked out onto the cobbled courtyard then through the factory gates. When she was certain he'd gone, she collapsed into the nearest chair.

Her legs began to tremble, her heart beating too fast. She put her head in her hands.

Jacob rushed to her with a jug of water and a glass. 'Mrs Jack, are you all right?'

He filled the glass with water and handed it to her. Anne sipped at it slowly.

'I'm fine, Jacob. Or at least I will be.'

'Mrs Jack . . . Mr Burl handed over his keys. Does this mean . . .?'

Anne turned her gaze to Jacob's pinched face.

'Yes, Jacob. He's gone. Finally.'

She took another sip of water, then a deep breath, trying to calm her racing heart. She and William had decided that the incident with Mr Burl and Bertram Dalton must remain in confidence. It was for the ears of board members only. Elsie had been sworn to secrecy too about what she'd seen in the back lane.

'Let's just say he didn't have the best interests of the factory at heart,' she went on.

She stood unsteadily, and Jacob caught her by the arm.

'Please, let me help, Mrs Jack,' he offered. He took the glass from her free hand and placed it on his desk. Then he led her to William's office. Thanking him profusely, she expected him to leave to return to his work, but he hovered in the corridor.

'Mrs Jack, there are certain things . . . problems that I was aware of about Mr Burl,' he whispered. 'Meg told me many times when she worked for him how much of a brute he was and how badly he treated his staff. He was a monster with the girls in the typing pool. He often had them in tears. Even the supervisor, Miss Briggs.'

Anne patted Jacob's hand. 'I know all of this, and

I tackled him about it many times. I think we gave him too many second chances. Let's be grateful now that he's finally gone.'

'Who will replace him?' he asked.

'There are many good men at the factory we can choose from,' Anne replied confidently.

Jacob walked away, and Anne let herself into William's office. She found him pacing the floor, hands behind his back, dictating a letter. Meg sat at the side of his desk, scribbling in her notepad. When Anne entered, the secretary looked up

'Mrs Jack, are you all right? You look as white as a sheet.'

Anne suddenly felt very tired. She put it down to the adrenaline of her encounter with Mr Burl leaving her in a great rush. She'd never sacked anyone before; it had taken a lot out of her. She felt hot and sweaty too. She sat down, picked up a confectionery trade magazine and used it to fan her face. William rushed to her side.

'What is it, dear?'

'He's gone,' she said.

She tried to quell a building sense of nausea. She felt William's hand on her arm, saw Meg's face swim in front of her. Her hand fell to her side, the water glass dropped to the floor, then everything faded to black.

Chapter Thirty-Eight

Anne opened her eyes to see two faces peering at her. She closed her eyes again, trying to work out what was going on, then slowly opened the right one. She saw William looking at her with concern.

'Anne, dear? Speak to me, darling.'

She opened her left eye and saw Meg hovering with a glass of water.

'Here, Mrs Jack, take a sip.'

Anne focused on William's face. 'What happened?'

'You fainted, dear. I'm going to take you home.'

Anne could feel the hard chair underneath her and knew her feet were firmly planted on the floor.

'Did I fall onto the floor, and you helped me into this chair?'

'No, dear, you seem to have blacked out in your chair. The stress and exertion of sacking Mr Burl must have got to you.'

Anne took the glass of water from Meg. 'Yes, I remember sacking Mr Burl, then I spoke to Jacob and came in here . . .'

'That's when you blacked out,' Meg said, worried. 'The factory doctor's on his way.'

Anne sat up straight in her seat. 'I don't need to see the doctor. I'm perfectly all right, just a little overwrought after what happened with Mr Burl.'

There was a knock at the door, and the doctor, a strapping young man fresh out of medical school at the University of Durham, walked in. Despite Anne's protests, he checked her over thoroughly. All done, he pronounced her blood pressure too low.

'I suggest you go home and rest, Mrs Jack,' he said.

'That's exactly what I think too,' William said. He held out his arm. 'Come, dear, I'll drive you home now.'

But Anne didn't move. She looked from the doctor to her husband.

'I'm feeling perfectly fine and I don't want to go home. I have a lot of work to do.'

'Anne, please do as the doctor suggests,' William said.

'Mrs Jack, I think you ought to take his advice,' Meg added.

Anne flapped her hands at them all, growing irritated with the fuss. 'I'm going nowhere.' She looked at Meg. 'Meg, dear, would you prepare a pot of coffee and bring some toffee cake from the canteen.'

'Yes, Mrs Jack,' Meg replied, turning to the door.

Anne looked at her husband. 'William, I want to stay here. I'll take a breath of fresh air in the gardens after I've had my coffee and cake.'

William threw up his hands in exasperation. 'You're a stubborn woman, Anne Jack. I know that once you've set your mind on something, nothing I say will change it.'

He looked at the doctor. 'Maybe you can talk some sense into my wife so that she goes home to rest.'

'Mr Jack, sir, with respect, could I please speak to your wife alone?'

'Please go, William, I'll be fine,' Anne said.

William left the office and closed the door behind him. Anne looked into the handsome face and deep-brown eyes of the factory doctor.

'Your husband is right, Mrs Jack. You really should go home.'

Anne thought for a moment.

'This is the first time in my life that I've fainted, Doctor. I was in a highly nervous state after a bruising encounter with my least favourite member of staff. Now he's gone and I feel a lot better. In fact . . .' She put her hand on the arm of the chair and pushed herself up to stand. She pressed her feet into the carpet and took a deep breath. 'See, I'm as steady as a rock. I feel fine.'

'No dizziness?' he asked.

She shook her head.

'Nausea?'

'It's gone.'

The doctor began to close up his bag, then turned back to Anne. He cast a glance at the office door before he spoke again.

'Mrs Jack, I have a personal question for you.' He pulled at his shirt collar and gave a little cough. 'I must ask, given the circumstances of your fainting episode and nausea . . . You also said that you'd been feeling rather hot, and I wondered . . .'

Suddenly Anne had a feeling she knew where this was leading. She'd suffered the same symptoms twice before.

'You're wondering if I might be pregnant,' she said quietly.

The doctor nodded. 'Yes, I am.'

She sat down, her head reeling. She was silent a moment, trying to figure things out. And with a growing realisation, the truth of her fainting spell and the nausea began to make sense. She went over dates and events of the last few weeks. In addition to feeling queasy each time Edith cooked kippers at home, when she'd normally devour them, she'd also felt physical changes inside her. They were all signs she should have recognised, but she'd been too focused on the factory, too busy to think of herself. She slapped her hand against her forehead.

'How could I not have known?' she whispered.

'Mrs Jack, you must let me know if you fall ill again. Please go home to rest.'

But Anne felt too distracted to rest. The feeling of tiredness and nausea she'd suffered after speaking to Mr Burl now turned to a building sense of excitement as the truth of her pregnancy sank in.

'I'll be fine, Doctor.'

The doctor looked uncertain. 'Perhaps I should speak to your husband again . . .'

'You'll do no such thing,' she said firmly. 'If I say I'm well enough to remain at work, taking things easy for the rest of the day, then that's exactly what I will do. Be assured that if and when I feel too ill to be at work, I'll go home.'

The doctor hesitated a moment, then headed to the door.

'As you wish, Mrs Jack,' he said politely.

Anne sat in the silence of William's office letting the news sink in. She laid her hands on her stomach, thinking of a brother or sister for Dinah, another grandchild for Albert and Clara. Thinking also of her baby boy, living in Scotland with Mr and Mrs Matthews. Her mind turned to the letter she'd received from them and the words within. *Everyone is fine.* A warmth spread through her each time she thought of the letter. She had no need to worry any more. Then, being practical, for that was her way, she turned her focus to the future. Another baby would mean more work for Edith. She decided to speak to William about giving their housekeeper a pay rise. Thoughts whirled around her mind as the door swung open.

'We're going to have another baby!' she called out, but it wasn't William who walked into the office. It was hard to know who got the bigger shock.

'Oh, Mrs Jack, that's wonderful news,' Meg said as she placed the tray with the coffee pot and a slab of toffee cake on William's desk.

Anne stood, feeling embarrassed. 'I'm sorry, Meg. I was expecting my husband.'

Meg backed out. 'He's on his way now, I'll leave the two of you to talk.' She put her finger to her lips. 'And your secret is safe with me.'

As Meg left the office, William entered.

'You look a bit better, dear. Your face has more colour.'

This time, instead of blurting out the words, Anne took her time, relishing the thought of delivering news that she knew William would welcome. She walked to the desk and poured the coffee.

'I've got something to tell you, dear,' she began, handing him a mug.

'Oh?' William said.

'You might want to sit down.'

He sat and listened as Anne explained what the doctor had said. As she spoke, his eyes began to twinkle and his face became animated, then he rushed around his desk to hold her in his arms.

'My darling Anne, how I love you.' He looked at her with concern. 'Surely this is more reason for you to go home to rest.'

Anne patted his hand. 'No, dear. I feel perfectly well, and I intend to stay here. I'll be fine with a piece of toffee cake inside me with my mug of coffee. Then I'll take a walk in the gardens. A breath of fresh air is all I need to set me up for the afternoon.'

'You'll have dinner too, of course,' William said, worried.

Anne kissed him again. 'Of course I will, especially now that I'm eating for two.'

Elsie was sitting on a bench in the factory garden. The sun was in her eyes, and she kept squinting. She'd hoped to see Stan and spend her dinner break with him. She'd even cooked him a beef pie, which she'd wrapped in paper, but there was no sign of him or his team. She guessed they must be working in the greenhouses or potting sheds.

She turned her face to the sun, letting its rays warm her and enjoying the peace and quiet of the gardens. She heard birds singing in the trees and could smell the sweet perfume from the roses surrounding the bench. She looked at the red rose planted in memory of Anabel, the girl who'd lost her life on the factory floor. Next to it was the recently installed war memorial, engraved with a list of names of factory men who'd died in the war. She closed her eyes and sent up a silent prayer for them all.

By now more girls were coming outdoors, some to sit on the grass or on a bench to eat their dinner, others to head to a café on Front Street. Elsie had already finished the sandwich she'd brought for her dinner. She thought about Hetty, who'd headed to the town hall with Dirk to arrange the papers she needed in order to travel to Belgium. Each time she thought about her friend, she felt a bittersweet mix of happiness, jealousy and loss. Happiness because Hetty had found a good man in Dirk and was to be wed. Jealousy because marriage was something that hadn't worked for Elsie. She'd married the wrong man; everyone had warned her about Frankie, but she'd been too reckless to care what they said. And she also felt a growing sense of loss, knowing that Hetty would be gone in just over a week.

Lost in her thoughts, she didn't notice a figure walking towards her. It was only when Anne was almost right by her side that she looked up, startled.

'Sorry, Anne, I didn't see you, the sun was in my eyes.' She moved along the bench so Anne could sit down.

'How are you, Elsie?' Anne asked.

'I'm well. I was just thinking about life, you know, and about losing Hetty.'

Anne nodded. 'You two are best friends, of course you'll miss her. I'll miss her too. But we'll still have each other. I'm glad we're back to being friends now. I can't apologise enough about how I acted over the situation with the brooch.'

'Don't mention it, Anne. Although I still can't believe you thought I was after your husband. He's really not my type.'

Both women laughed, then Elsie composed herself and turned to Anne.

'Anne, there's something I need to speak to you about. Could I ask you a favour, please?'

'You can ask me anything, Elsie, you know that.'

Elsie took a moment to think about how best to ask for help.

'Well, my aunt Jean wants to send me something. I hoped . . . well, I didn't want to presume, but Hetty suggested you might be able to advise me.'

She noticed that Anne didn't appear to be listening; she was shading her eyes from the sun with her hand.

'Oh blimey, they weren't expected today,' she cried.

Elsie craned her neck to see who Anne was talking about. 'Who is it?'

But Anne didn't reply. She stood.

'I'm sorry, Elsie, I need to go.' And with that, she hurried away.

Chapter Thirty-Nine

Elsie watched as Anne walked away to greet a well-dressed couple who were strolling arm-in-arm in the factory garden. After a few moments, she turned back and pointed and waved. Elsie tentatively raised her hand and waved back, wondering what was going on. She was even more surprised when Anne headed back to the factory and the couple in their fancy clothes started walking towards her. She sat up straight on the bench and brushed away the crumbs from her sandwich, then fastened the top button of her overall, smiling brightly as they approached.

The gentleman was tall and slim and wore a long black coat and shiny shoes. He held out his hand. Elsie didn't know if she should stand to shake it or remain seated. In her indecision, she half rose from her seat.

'Good afternoon, my dear. Mrs Jack tells me that your name is Elsie Cooper,' he said politely. 'I'm Michael Bennett.'

Elsie shook his hand then sat down. She looked from the gentleman to his wife. She was a stout woman, and shorter than her husband. Her dark hair was curled stylishly around her attractive face.

'And this is my wife Beryl.'

Elsie shook her petite hand. 'Would you like to sit down?' she offered, thinking it the polite thing to do.

The couple sat, the gentleman in the middle, a respectable distance from Elsie, with his wife on his other side.

'Most pleasant,' he said, surveying the grounds.

'The gardens are very well kept. The head gardener is called Stan Chapman. He does a wonderful job,' Elsie enthused.

'The rose bushes are particularly beautiful,' Beryl agreed.

Elsie couldn't think straight. Why had Anne pointed her out to the couple, and who were they? As she tried to make sense of it, Beryl continued.

'The large red rose is spectacular.'

'It was planted in memory of one of the factory girls who died in an accident. She was called Anabel and her brother said red roses were her favourite. When the gardens were dug over for vegetables during the war, Anabel's rose was the only shrub not dug up. Mrs Jack insisted it remained as a tribute to a wonderful girl. Next to it is the memorial stone with the names of all our factory men who died in the war. It's only recently been unveiled.'

Elsie realised she was talking too much because she was nervous. She tried to breathe slowly to calm her racing heart.

'Most commendable,' Michael said.

'We spoke to Mrs Jack just now,' Beryl chipped in. 'She recommended we wait in reception while she goes to find her husband. He wasn't expecting us, you see. But I care nothing for sitting indoors on such a sunny day. Besides, I wanted a chance to meet one of the girls who work here before I take an informal look around the factory grounds.'

Michael turned to Elsie. 'Tell me, my dear. What work do you do?'

Elsie told the couple all about her work in the slab room, explaining how her role smoothing and cutting toffee was just one part of a long chain in the toffee-making process. Michael asked several questions, and she was impressed by his knowledge of the confectionery business. She noticed too that all the time he spoke, he held his wife's hand. It was a gesture that warmed her heart. Her nerves calmed and she felt at ease.

'And what do you do outside of work?' Beryl asked.

'I look after my friend's aunt, who's not well,' Elsie replied. 'We're moving house soon,' she added. 'I like to walk along the river, too. It's pretty there.' She thought of the time she spent with Stan. 'I sometimes walk with a friend and his dog.'

Beryl turned so that she was fully facing her. 'And what about recreation opportunities for the factory girls?' she asked.

Elsie racked her brains. 'Recreation? Well, there's the canteen. The girls who work in there cook a lovely cheese pie, it's my favourite thing to eat.'

She noticed Michael and Beryl exchange a smile and wondered if she'd said the wrong thing. Beryl shook her head.

'No, dear. What I meant was, are there any field games played by the girls after work each day?'

Elsie smiled. 'Field games? No. The only running we do at the factory is to see who can get out of the gates first when the whistle blows.'

Her comment made the couple laugh.

'Most unusual,' Michael said at last.

'Unusual, sir?' Elsie asked.

'Yes, I've found that during the war, many women working in munitions factories came together to form football teams. Some of the teams play at a high level now. Although the munitions factories are no longer needed, several of the women's football teams have carried on. In Sunderland there's a very good team called the Southwick Lilies.'

'They're excellent,' Beryl added. 'It's the fresh air, you see. Working in the munitions factories there was no ventilation, and girls needed to get away from the dust and noise. Fresh air and exercise were just what was needed.'

'Ah, we don't have problems like that at Jack's toffee factory,' Elsie said. 'The rooms are ventilated, noise is minimal and there's not a speck of dust.'

'Most heartening to hear,' Michael said.

'Oh, and the smell of toffee when it's being made is so delicious it sends you to heaven,' Elsie continued.

'How delightful,' Michael said.

Elsie thought for a moment. 'Sometimes, on a sunny day, girls play tag and run around the gardens at dinner time. But we've never had organised games. I'm not sure Mr Jack would approve.'

'I can't see why not. He's an open-minded man,' Beryl said.

Elsie saw Meg walking towards them. Michael and Beryl stood when they spotted her.

'It's been most pleasant talking to you, Miss Cooper,' Beryl said.

'Most illuminating,' Michael added.

Elsie watched as Meg politely greeted the couple.

'Sir Michael, Lady Bennett. Mr Jack would be delighted to see you. Please, follow me to the office, I'll take you there right now.'

Elsie rocked back in her seat. Sir? Lady? She looked at Meg, hoping for some kind of explanation, but the secretary walked away with the couple, leaving Elsie in shock.

After a few moments, she decided to head to the canteen for a cup of tea before her dinner break ended. She was delighted to bump into Hetty walking through the factory gates.

'How did it go at the town hall?' she asked.

Hetty sighed. 'Not good. There are so many forms to be filled and stamped, and of course it's all a rush because we're leaving next week. My head's spinning. I'm worried we won't get the paperwork done. If we don't, I'll have to travel to Ghent on my own, without Dirk, and I'm not sure I'm brave enough.'

Elsie gave a cheeky wink. 'You're Hetty Lawson and you're brave enough to take on the world. I've got every faith in you.'

Hetty held up crossed fingers. 'I hope so. The stress of it keeps me awake. I thought getting married was supposed to be the happiest day of your life, but when I think about the red tape involved in leaving the country, it overshadows thoughts of our wedding.'

Elsie slipped her arm through her friend's. 'Then let's go and take your mind off it with a cup of tea. We'll talk about something more important than red tape.'

'What's that?'

'Why, what you're going to wear on your wedding day, of course.'

The girls walked into the canteen and Elsie was stunned to see Anne sitting at a table with Mr Jack and the couple she'd just been talking to. She noticed that Michael, or Sir Michael as she now knew him to be, was tucking into a slice of cheese pie. She and Hetty took their mugs of tea to a free table.

'Come on, then, what are you planning to wear?' Elsie asked.

The girls discussed everything from dresses, shoes, coats and hats to trains and boats to Belgium. They were still deep in conversation when Anne appeared at their table and slid into an empty chair.

'Oh my word, what a day,' she sighed.

Elsie looked around, wondering where Mr Jack and their guests had gone. 'Have Sir Michael and his wife left?' she asked.

'William has taken them on a tour of the factory. Sir Michael was keen to see the slab room after hearing all about it from you. He was quite taken with your enthusiasm. He was also singing the praises of the cheese pie, and said you'd recommended it. Thank you, Elsie, for speaking to him and his wife. I appreciate it.' Anne leaned forward and spoke in a low voice. 'The two of them could be very important to the future of the factory. That's all I can say for now.'

'His wife asked me if the girls here play sports. She seems very keen on women's football.'

'She's a huge advocate of team sports, football especially,' Anne said.

Elsie pushed her empty mug to one side. 'It seems a good idea for girls to get together outside of work. Especially now that soldiers are coming back to the factory.

Some of the girls are going to feel they're being pushed out of their jobs.'

'Which they are,' Hetty chipped in.

'Exactly!' Elsie said. 'Team sports could keep the girls united, even those who lose their jobs. If we start a football team, it'd give them somewhere to meet on evenings and weekends.'

'I'm not a fan of football,' Hetty said, shaking her head.

'Me neither,' Elsie said. 'But I am a fan of girls helping each other, meeting friends and playing together.'

'You might be on to something,' Anne said. 'Fresh air, exercise and friendship could lead to better productivity at work. I'll speak to William about it. Leave it with me for now.' She put her hand to her stomach.

'Are you feeling all right?' Elsie asked.

Anne looked from Elsie to Hetty. 'I'm feeling a little shaken, to be honest. I had a difficult morning; I had to sack a senior member of staff.'

Elsie gasped. 'No!'

'Who was it?' Hetty whispered.

'I can't say until news of his replacement is announced,' Anne said. 'Afterwards I had a bit of a funny turn .'

'What do you mean, a funny turn?' asked Elsie.

Anne glanced behind her to ensure she wasn't overheard. 'Girls, I've got some exciting news!'

Chapter Forty

Later that day, Elsie and Hetty were hard at work in the slab room. Elsie was concentrating on smoothing the hot, liquid toffee, being careful not to let it touch her skin. She and Hetty worked side by side, in tune with each other, pulling the levelling bar across the toffee, then bringing down the cutter. On it went, smoothing and levelling, cutting and sending the toffee to be wrapped. When one slab of toffee had been cut and cleared, the girls waited for another sugar boiler to come into the room with his pan.

Elsie recognised the man immediately and knew him to be one of the least careful when it came to pouring toffee on the slab. But she was ready for him. As he approached with his pan, she spoke firmly before he could hoist it to his shoulder.

'Be careful this time,' she warned.

He looked at her and scowled, clearly affronted to be addressed by one of the girls. 'I'm always careful,' he hissed.

But Elsie stood her ground. 'No you're not. You spill more toffee on the floor than you pour on the slab. The girls get stuck to the floor when that happens.'

'So what?' he said. He hoisted the pan to his shoulder and steadied himself, ready to pour.

'It stops production when one of the girls gets stuck and has to be lifted out of her clogs. Your carelessness causes all kinds of problems. And it's a waste of toffee when half of it ends on the floor. I'm sure our supervisor won't be happy if she finds out you've messed up again. She could report you to Mr Jack.'

Elsie noticed that the girls at the slab had paused in their work and were watching. She knew they were waiting for the toffee to be poured, but she became aware of something more. It took her a second to realise what was going on. One by one, they took a step forward so that they stood shoulder-to-shoulder with her. She took courage from their support, placing her hands on her hips and glaring at the sugar boiler, who'd begun to struggle with the weight of the pan.

'Pour it carefully,' she said.

He glanced at her, and his face blanched when he noticed the crowd of girls surrounding her. Tilting his shoulder forward so that the pan moved, he began to pour the hot toffee slowly and cautiously, and this time all of it went on the slab. When he was done, he turned on his heel and walked quickly out of the room.

'Well done, Elsie. I don't think he'll give us any more problems,' Hetty said.

Elsie turned to face the girls. 'Thanks, everyone. I couldn't have done that without your support.'

As they all started stretching and levelling the toffee before it turned cool and hard, Mrs Perkins appeared.

'Good work, Elsie,' she said, then she walked off to attend to a problem elsewhere in the room.

Elsie felt her face grow hot. She turned to Hetty. 'That's the first time in all the years I've worked here that Mrs Perkins has said anything nice.'

Hetty gave a wry smile. 'Maybe she's going dotty in her old age.'

The afternoon passed quickly. At the end of the day, as the girls slipped out of their clogs and into their shoes, Mrs Perkins appeared again.

'Elsie, could I have a word?'

Elsie looked at Hetty. 'You go home; I'll catch up.'

The supervisor waited until the rush of girls leaving had thinned to a few stragglers. Then she took Elsie to one side.

'Mrs Jack would like to see you.'

'Now? But I need to get home,' Elsie said.

Mrs Perkins' brow creased. 'Elsie Cooper . . .' she began.

Elsie's shoulders dropped. It was never good news when Mrs Perkins used her full name.

'. . . when Mrs Jack asks to see one of my girls, then that's exactly what she gets. Run along to reception. And make sure your overall buttons are fastened.'

Elsie looked at her top button. It was already fastened; she remembered doing it up when she'd spoken to Sir Michael and his wife at dinner time.

As she stood patiently in front of Jacob's desk, she wondered what Anne wanted. She knew she wasn't to receive a warning for being in Mrs Perkins' bad books this time. Eventually he looked up.

'Yes?' he said.

'I'm Elsie Cooper and Mrs Jack has asked to see me,' she said politely.

Celebrations at the Toffee Factory

'Take a seat, Miss Cooper,' he replied.

Elsie headed to one of four chairs along the wall and sat down while Jacob walked from the room. Left alone, she took a minute to gaze at the plush surroundings of the reception, which had been fitted out to impress factory guests. She was feeling nervous and took a deep breath, but her heart was still going like the clappers.

After a while, the door swung open and Anne walked in. She beckoned to Elsie. 'This way, please.'

Elsie followed her along the corridor to her office.

'Have a seat,' Anne said.

Elsie sat opposite Anne at her desk. 'What have I done wrong?' she blurted out. She couldn't keep quiet any more.

A smile came to Anne's face. 'Wrong? You've done nothing wrong. In fact, it's just the opposite.'

Elsie raised her eyebrows. 'Oh?'

Anne laid her hands on the desk and looked at her. 'Mrs Perkins came to see me this afternoon and told me you'd tackled one of the sugar boilers. I understand there's been a long-running problem with some of the men being careless with the toffee.'

Elsie sat up straight in her seat. 'The girls keep getting stuck to the floor and you know how much time it takes to lift them out of their clogs. It stops production and it's a waste of toffee. Mrs Perkins has mentioned it to the sugar boilers a few times, but they never take much notice. So I dealt with it myself. I hope I didn't speak out of turn.'

'You did the right thing. Mrs Perkins was impressed by the way you handled it. You were firm with the man. You didn't raise your voice or get angry, the way some other girls would.'

Anne leaned back in her seat. She pushed her glasses up to the bridge of her nose.

'There's a maturity about the way you behave at work these days, Elsie. It suits you.'

Elsie received the compliment with a smile and felt her heart swell with pride as Anne carried on.

'Mrs Perkins will be leaving us this summer. She's moving away.'

Elsie's mouth opened in shock at the news. 'But why are you telling me?'

Anne studied her. 'Because I've been looking for someone to replace her as supervisor in the slab room. I've been receiving regular reports from Mrs Perkins about who she thinks might be up to the job. You see, we need someone not only with knowledge of the factory but with a talent for managing the girls. We need someone with authority, someone the girls look up to. I think we've finally found that person in you.'

'Me?' Elsie cried. 'You want *me* to be the supervisor?'

Her heart began to pound. Her mouth went dry and she gripped the arms of her chair. All of a sudden she felt anxious and nervous, overcome with fear, and before she knew what was happening, words tumbled from her mouth.

'No. No, I can't. I'm not up to it, Anne. I can't manage the girls. I haven't a clue.'

'Mrs Perkins will take you under her wing during the few weeks she has left,' Anne said evenly.

But Elsie was shaking her head. 'No, Anne. Please, not me. Choose someone else. I'm not good at being in charge. I don't have the aptitude.'

'Yes you do,' Anne said. 'And you've also got the

maturity. Oh, I won't pretend you've always had it; you've certainly made mistakes over the years.'

Elsie's heart was beating so hard she felt it might burst from her chest. She swallowed and forced herself to concentrate.

'Since you moved in with Hetty, though, you've changed. You're responsible now, respectable. You're a woman who knows her own mind.'

'Anne, please, I don't think I can,' Elsie said again.

'Well *I* think you can, if you put your mind to it,' Anne said gently. 'And Mr Jack agrees. He trusts you, Elsie. Why else did he choose you, of all the girls, to buy the necklace for me? And he's impressed with you too after you met Sir Michael and Lady Bennett today. They spoke highly of you. Plus, Mr Jack and I wish to reward your loyalty. If you hadn't come to us to report what you saw in the back lane, I shudder to think what might have happened. Please, at least think about my offer.'

Elsie twisted her hands together. 'I'm not sure I want to manage the other girls. They're my friends. What will they think if I start telling them what to do?'

'The girls respect you, Elsie. You've been through a lot in your personal life . . .'

Elsie raised her eyes to Anne, and they shared a look. She was relieved when Anne moved the subject away from Frankie.

'On a practical level, the hours would be longer. You'd need to arrive each morning before the girls, and you'd be the last to leave the slab room at night. Of course, promotion to supervisor would mean you'd be paid more.'

Elsie let Anne's words sink in, but she still had trouble seeing herself in charge of other girls.

'Surely with all the men returning from war, one of them could take over from Mrs Perkins instead,' she said.

Anne pushed a lock of hair behind her ear. 'Mr Jack and I have other plans for the returning soldiers. They'll work elsewhere, but I can't go into details right now. I need a woman to supervise the girls, Elsie, and I want that woman to be you. So do Mr Jack and Mrs Perkins. We've discussed it thoroughly today.'

Elsie looked into Anne's kind face. 'I'm honoured you thought of me. And I'm flattered that you asked. But I honestly don't think I'm cut out for it.' She could feel her heart hammering under her overall.

'Promise me you'll think about it for a few days,' Anne said. 'Perhaps you can give me your answer by the end of the week.'

Elsie bit her lip. Considering the generous offer was the very least she could do, although she still felt the role was beyond her.

'I promise I will,' she said.

Chapter Forty-One

That night while Elsie and Hetty were peeling and chopping onions, Elsie told Hetty about Anne's offer. Hetty said she was pleased for her, of course, but Elsie sensed a hesitancy.

'There's something you're not telling me,' she said when she could bear it no more.

Hetty carried on chopping. Elsie gently laid her hand on her friend's arm to stop her.

'You don't think I'm good enough for the role, is that it? You think I'm too flighty and too flirty with the factory men. Oh, I know what people think of me. People would laugh at me behind my back if I accepted the job. They'd say: "Look at Lady Muck. Who does she think she is?"'

Hetty shook her head. 'No, Elsie, you're wrong. No one would laugh or talk about you. You're more than capable of being a supervisor. The girls at work who know you, who *really* know you, know you've got the right temperament for the work. Anne wouldn't have asked you if she didn't think you had what it takes.'

'Then why are you being . . . I don't know . . . distant?'

Elsie said sadly. 'You don't seem happy about me being offered the job. I need your advice, but you're holding something back. I've known you long enough to know how your mind works.'

Hetty put down the knife. 'I wasn't going to tell you, Elsie, but I can see how upset you are.'

'Tell me what?'

Hetty sighed. 'Anne asked me if I wanted the job,' she said.

Elsie sank back in her chair. Her face fell.

'I turned it down because I'm leaving. Not even the offer of being a supervisor could stop me from being with Dirk.'

'Oh, I see,' Elsie said.

'I'm sorry, Elsie. I wouldn't have told you if you hadn't pushed me. I hate keeping secrets, but Anne swore me to secrecy because she didn't want the girls knowing that Mrs Perkins is leaving. The news will be announced once a replacement is found.'

Elsie looked at her. 'Would you have taken the job, if you were staying?'

Hetty turned away, picked up her knife again and began scraping potatoes.

'Hetty?' Elsie said softly.

'We always need more money in this house,' Hetty replied.

Elsie let this sink in.

'So you *would* have taken it. Well, when you put it like that, it would be wrong of me to turn it down. Hilda and I are going to need all the money we can get when we move. There might be new curtains to buy or a new mat for the door. And there'll be bus fares to pay from Elisabethville to the factory.'

'Elsie, love, don't rush into accepting it if your heart isn't in it,' Hetty said.

'I don't think my heart's got anything to do with it, do you? It's my purse I need to think about now.'

The girls exchanged a smile.

'You know you'll be a great supervisor,' Hetty said.

'I'll be fair,' Elsie said decisively.

'But firm,' Hetty added.

'I won't be cruel like Mrs Perkins used to be when we first started work. I'll be good to the girls. I'll take them under my wing. I'll warn them which of the sugar boilers to avoid and let them know which ones are good men.'

'See, you *can* do it, Elsie, if you put your mind to it.'

Elsie sighed loudly. 'I'm trying to convince myself. I'm still not sure about it, you know.'

'Then don't rush into a decision. Didn't you say Anne has given you a few days to think it over? You need to do what's right for you.'

'I need to think of my future. But more than anything, I need to do what's right for the girls. Am I the best person to lead them, to teach them and to reprimand them? I'm hardly a good example, coming in late some days, swanning off to the gardens to look at the men, getting stuck to the floor in my clogs. Mind you, I enjoyed being lifted out by Stan.' Elsie smiled at the memory, then turned to Hetty, suddenly serious. 'Do you really think I can do it?'

'I know you can. You'll be a good example. You'll keep the girls from harm, you'll show them how to stand up for themselves if the sugar boilers are careless. They'll look up to you in a way that we never did to Mrs Perkins. You're one of the girls, Elsie. You know the pitfalls and pleasures of working in the slab room and you've worked in the wrapping room too. You've also packed and weighed more tins of toffee than you can remember. We learned each role as we went, helping each other. We even created shortcuts when what Mrs Perkins told us seemed long winded or old fashioned.'

Elsie dropped her gaze. 'I'm still not sure. You see, that's why Anne asked you first. You make decisions without going to and fro. You're dependable, respectable Hetty Lawson.'

She felt Hetty's hands on her shoulders.

'Look at me,' Hetty said.

Elsie looked at her friend's face and saw that Hetty's eyes were sparkling.

'You're an amazing woman, Elsie Cooper. Not only are you my best friend, and I'm going to miss you dearly when I leave, but . . .' Hetty's voice caught in her throat, 'the girls in the slab room will be lucky to have you in charge. You can guide them. Make sure that none of them are put upon. You can keep them safe, make sure they don't end up like poor Anabel. You've got a good friend in Anne, so if there are problems, you can go straight to her. And I'm sure Mrs Perkins will be on hand to train you before she leaves.'

'Yes, Anne told me she'd offered to do that.'

Hetty let her hands drop. 'Have you spoken to Stan about this?'

'No. I planned to talk to him tonight. I'm meeting him on the riverside for a walk with his dog.'

'He'll stick by you whatever you decide.'

Elsie wrapped her arms around Hetty. 'Thanks, Hetty. I wish I had your courage. It's strange that both you and Anne think I'm brave enough.'

'You're braver than you realise, Elsie. Besides, if I can leave Chester-le-Street and head overseas to a foreign land where I don't know anyone and can't understand the language, I'm sure you're brave enough to start a new job. And if you've got the stomach to handle Hilda, you can handle anyone.'

Elsie laughed out loud. 'When you put it like that, a new job doesn't seem so scary.'

Later that night, Elsie wrapped up in her coat, as the night had turned cool, and headed to the riverside. When she reached the bench where they'd agreed to meet, she saw Stan and her heart skipped. The sight of him cheered her and made her feel safe. She walked quietly behind him, put her arms around him and planted a kiss on the top of his head. He spun around and held her, and they kissed for a very long time. Patch wagged his tail at the sound of Elsie's voice, and Elsie made a fuss of the dog before the three of them set off. As they walked, she held hands with Stan and they chatted non-stop. She told him about her day at the factory, then about the job offer.

'When do you start?' he asked, as if it were a done deal.

Elsie shot him a look. 'I haven't accepted yet. I don't know if I can do it.'

Stan stopped walking, and Patch ran rings around them. 'Elsie Cooper, you can do anything you want. You're the most remarkable woman I've met. The girls in the factory idolise you. Can't you see it? Some of them even dress like you. They open their buttons on their overalls the same way that you do. They style their hair the same way. I sometimes overhear groups of them chatting in the garden at dinner time. You should hear what some of they say.'

Elsie was horrified. She put her hands over her ears. 'I don't want to know,' she cried.

Gently Stan took hold of her hands and brought them to his heart. 'They respect you, Elsie. They know what you've been through with Frankie.'

Elsie grimaced at the sound of her husband's name. Would there ever come a time when it didn't strike fear into her?

'They know you went through a bad time, and they admire you for turning your life around. You inspire them, and that's one heck of a reason to accept the new job. And of course, there's the increase in your pay packet that I'm sure will come your way.'

'Hetty thinks I can do it too,' she said softly. 'Although she was offered the job before me.'

'She's got her face on the tins of Lady Tina toffee, that's why,' Stan said. 'It's only natural the factory wanted to promote her. But the fact is, Elsie, they've offered the job to you. So don't feel second-best to Hetty, or anyone else. You go for it, girl, if that's what you want.'

Elsie felt a lump in her throat as Stan's words went to her heart. They walked on, the moon's reflection in the river turning her mood sentimental. She stole a look at Stan's rugged face and reached again for his hand.

'Stan?'

'What, love?'

'Do you know anything about postal orders?'

He scratched his head. 'Nothing. Why do you ask?'

Elsie told him about the money that Aunt Jean had offered.

'She says I should buy my freedom,' she said.

Stan gave her a quizzical look. 'What do you mean?'

Elsie pulled him close. She could feel the warmth from his body and his breath on her face. 'What I mean is that once I have the money from Jean, I could use it to buy something I'd only dared dream of before.' She looked into his hazel eyes. 'I could divorce Frankie and get him out of my life at last.'

She heard him gasp.

'It won't be easy,' she continued. 'And it won't be quick. But I'll have the money to do it. And when I'm free, Stan... when I'm free...'

'However long it takes, I'll wait,' he whispered.

'Thank you,' Elsie said.

Then, under the light of the moon, she drew him to her in a loving embrace.

Chapter Forty-Two

Anne was in the living room at Albert and Clara's house. She was playing a game with her mother-in-law and Dinah while William talked business with his father. When there was a pause in conversation, she looked up. Holding Dinah's hand, she nodded at her husband. William cleared his throat.

'Father, Mother,' he began.

Clara and Albert looked at him.

'Anne and I have news for you.' He reached for her hand. 'We're going to have another child.'

Clara threw her arms around Anne. 'Congratulations to you both,' she said, wiping away a tear.

'Well done to the pair of you,' Albert said. 'We must celebrate. Let's open a new bottle of brandy.'

'Not for me, Albert,' Anne said quickly. Just as with Edith's kippers, the smell of brandy now turned her stomach.

'Dinah's to have a little brother or sister, how beautiful,' Clara said. She swept the child up in her arms and kissed her. Anne relished seeing her daughter enjoying cuddles and fuss from her grandmother.

Albert handed brandy glasses to Clara and William, then William raised his in a toast.

'To Anne and our new baby,' he said.

'And to the factory. We have news on that front too,' Anne said, casting a glance at her husband. 'Don't we, dear?'

William sat up straight and carefully placed his glass on a side table.

'What is it?' Albert said.

William looked from his mother to his father. 'You'll remember that some time ago I met with Sir Michael.'

Albert nodded. 'Yes, I do recall you mentioned it. Sir Michael is one of the best sorts of men. Your mother and I have known him and Beryl since before we were married. I was a good friend of his father's too, before he passed away.'

'Beryl is too sports-minded for my liking,' Clara said with distaste.

Anne let the comment slide and prompted William to carry on. Once he began to speak about Sir Michael's proposed investment, Albert perched on the edge of his seat. His eyes shone with excitement, just as William's did. Anne watched father and son talk through the pros and cons of taking such an investment. And then William gave his parents the news that had shocked Anne when she'd first heard it.

'And if Sir Michael signs on the dotted line and we secure his investment, I'm going to buy Mayfair Toffee.'

'The brand name?' Albert asked in surprise.

William shook his head. 'No, Father, I'm going to buy the factory. It's failing and on its knees. It likely won't last another year.'

'Why buy something that isn't successful?' Albert asked.

'Because I'm going to turn it around. They're failing because they haven't kept pace with modern tastes or procedures. They've rested on their laurels too long.'

Albert stood and began pacing. Anne watched him. It was the same way of walking and thinking that she'd seen William do a thousand times. He asked question after question and William fully answered each one. Albert continued pacing, pausing to point out hypothetical problems and potential bumps in the road that could derail William's plan. Anne knew he was testing his son's resolve and business sense. At each turn, William replied with a well-thought-out response. Anne's heart swelled with love and pride. Albert looked gravely at his son.

'Are you certain we can afford it?'

William didn't hesitate in his reply.

'Yes, we can afford it, Father.'

'*Only* if Sir Michael invests,' Anne chipped in, shooting her husband a look, knowing his enthusiasm was running away with him. William pretended not to notice and carried straight on.

'We have men coming back from war and I want to employ as many as I can at Mayfair Toffee's building. Anne and I have even come up with an idea for a new brand of toffee aimed at the modern woman. Such buyers are our future.' Here he glanced at his daughter and smiled before he continued. 'I also plan to install machines that are all the rage in the Swiss confectionery trade.'

'Machines?' Clara said, clutching her heart.

'Toffee-wrapping machines, Mother,' William explained.

'Won't that mean that machines will take the place of girls in the wrapping room?' she asked, aghast.

'It will, and that's a good thing.'

Clara stared at her son. 'Now you're not making sense.'

William smiled at her. 'Mother, at the moment, we have hundreds of girls all wrapping by hand. It's laborious work and some of the girls are in pain with crippled hands from the repeated action. When the machines come in, we'll be able to wrap toffees faster and be more productive. We can move girls from the wrapping room to work in the slab room or the packing room. We'll make more toffee, quicker, wrap it faster and send it out to the world more swiftly than we do now. Plus, the girls will learn not only to work the machines but to service them if they break down, refurbish them if we buy secondhand. So you see, we won't need to lose girls when the machines come in. And we'll take on as many of the men returning from war as we can.'

'And you say these men will work at the old Mayfair Toffee building?' Albert asked.

'Yes, Father, that's my plan.'

Albert rubbed his chin, deep in thought. 'Do Mayfair Toffee know of your plan to buy the building and everything in it?'

'Anne and I have made discreet enquiries. I haven't wanted to take things further until Sir Michael's investment is certain, after he's signed the contract.'

Albert smiled widely. 'That's exactly what I would have done, had I still been in charge. You're a chip off the old block.'

Anne sat forward and laid her hand on William's knee.

She looked at Clara. 'There is just one thing more we should add,' she said.

'Ah, yes,' William said, remembering. 'Mother, I know that Lady Bennett's love of sports and team games might not be to your taste.'

Clara grimaced. 'Not one bit. It's unseemly to see young girls working up a sweat.'

'Times are changing. Girls want to be active these days,' William told her.

Now it was Anne's turn to pick up the conversation. She lifted Dinah onto her lap and the child snuggled against her.

'Lady Bennett is very keen for Jack's toffee factory girls to unite in team sports outside of work. In fact, there will be a clause to this effect in the contract if Sir Michael offers investment.'

'What nonsense,' Clara said.

'I think she has a point,' Anne continued. She saw Clara shrink back in her seat, so she spoke carefully, gently, as she outlined the advantages of the idea. 'She suggests we start up a women's football team, not unlike the Southwick Lilies in Sunderland. It means the girls will unite in team spirit outside of the factory. They'll make new friends too. It will lead to better productivity at work.'

She could tell Clara was giving this some thought.

'And best of all,' she added with a grin, 'the girls will be dressed in shirts dyed the same shade of blue as the factory logo.'

She waited for Clara to comment, but the older woman remained silent.

'Mother, what do you think?' William said at last.

When Clara began to speak, she was smiling. 'There's one thing you haven't mentioned.'

William looked puzzled. He glanced at Anne and she shrugged, then they both looked at Clara, wondering what she had to say.

'If Sir Michael invests and you buy the factory, you'll have to decorate it in the colours of Jack's toffee factory.' Clara paused and grinned mischievously. 'You're going to need an awful lot of blue paint.'

At the end of the week, Meg stuck her head around Anne's office door.

'Mrs Jack, Elsie Cooper is here to see you. She hasn't got an appointment. Would you like me to send her away?'

'No, ask her to come in, please,' Anne replied.

She straightened papers on her desk and moved an empty coffee pot to a side table. There was a knock at her door.

'Come in, Elsie,' she said.

When Elsie walked in, she seemed more confident and looked more relaxed than Anne had seen her in a while.

'Take a seat,' she said. 'I expect you're here to give me your answer on the offer to replace Mrs Perkins.'

Elsie sat tall in her chair with her hands in her lap. 'I've thought about nothing else since we spoke,' she began.

'And?' Anne asked.

Elsie couldn't keep the smile off her face. 'And I'd like to accept,' she said.

Anne rushed around the desk and hugged her friend tight.

'You won't regret this, Anne, I promise,' Elsie said.

Anne let her go and looked into her dark eyes. 'This is

wonderful news. Now, there's something else you need to know.'

Elsie raised her eyebrows. 'Oh?'

'What do you know about women's football?'

Elsie's eyes narrowed. 'Is this anything to do with Lady Bennett?' she said.

'It's everything to do with her.' Anne lowered her voice. 'What I tell you in here must remain in confidence, Elsie. You can tell Hetty, we can trust her, but apart from that, no one must know. There may be changes at the factory. Big changes, extra premises and . . .' she paused for effect, 'toffee-wrapping machines.'

'Machines?' Elsie gasped. 'But won't that mean girls will be out of work?'

Anne shook her head. 'No. I'll explain everything in full when I can. All you need to know for now is that there is the promise of investment. However, it comes with a proviso. We will be required to start a football team for the girls. All the female supervisors will lead training sessions and be involved in team selection and management. You won't be on your own in this; it's something I'm keen on too. I'm sorry to spring it on you, Elsie, but do you think you'd be up to the task?'

Elsie took a deep breath. 'It sounds like a lot of work, but I'm ready for it.'

'I'll confirm things as soon as I can. We're still at a delicate negotiating stage,' Anne added sagely. She thought of the discussions taking place and the contract that the factory's legal team was in the process of drawing up with the collaboration of Sir Michael and his advisers. She patted Elsie's shoulder, then walked around her desk to return to her seat.

'Could I ask a question, Anne, please?' Elsie said.

Anne smiled. 'After I've just sprung that shock on you, you can ask me anything. In fact, if you asked me for the moon, I'd be inclined to hand it to you, wrapped with blue ribbon, of course. What can I help you with?' She noticed that Elsie's cheeks had coloured.

'I need your advice,' Elsie began.

Anne leaned forward. 'Why, yes, of course, what is it?'

She saw that Elsie was gripping her hands together in her lap and wondered what was so serious that it would cause such discomfort. She smiled warmly, encouraging her to speak. Elsie gave a sharp nod, then the words spilled from her lips.

'Anne, what do you know about postal orders?'

Chapter Forty-Three

When Hetty woke on Monday morning, she lay still in bed, listening to the sound of birds outside the window. Then she heard sounds from the kitchen below and knew it was Elsie cooking. She crossed her fingers and hoped for toast with a mug of steaming hot tea.

By now she could count on one hand the number of days she had left to work at the toffee factory. She'd also handed in her notice at her second job at Lumley Castle and wouldn't return there again. Her leaving had been news that hadn't gone down well with Mrs Doughty, the housekeeper. However, before Hetty had left the castle, Mrs Doughty had taken her to one side and her normally dour expression had lifted.

'Good luck, Hetty,' she'd said, and she'd planted a kiss on Hetty's cheek.

Now, lying in bed, Hetty stretched her arms above her head, and her thoughts, as they always did first thing each morning, turned to Dirk. She wondered what he was doing at Elisabethville. Was he packing his trunk for his return to Belgium? Was he thinking of her? How strange that in just a few days' time she'd be married to him and would be Hetty Lawson no more. Stranger still to think she'd no longer live on Elm Street, or in Chester-le-Street or even in England. No more working at the toffee factory, no more sharing confidences with Elsie, no more friendship with Anne. Oh, how she'd miss them both.

She looked at her suitcase on the floor. It would soon be time to pack, but first she had to decide what to wear for her wedding. Elsie had offered her one of Aunt Jean's dresses. However, Hetty wanted to wear something of her own. Plus, whatever she wore for the wedding would have to travel with her to Belgium. Time would be tight after the ceremony, with no time for celebrations, not even a drink in the Lambton Arms. She and Dirk would need to walk straight to the railway station to catch the train to Hull. If they missed it, they'd miss their boat. There could be no hanging around. She knew she needed to wear something durable and warm, in case the boat journey was cold. She thought of her favourite blue skirt. It was robust and she felt comfortable wearing it. She smiled, hearing Elsie's voice in her head telling her that robust and comfortable never turned a fella's head.

She yawned, then slowly poked a leg out from under the eiderdown and placed her foot on the floor. She swung her other leg out, stood up and stretched, then began to wash and dress, going through the motions, following her daily routine. As she washed in cold water from the jug on her nightstand, she thought how different her new life would be. This time next week, where would she be living? Who would her friends be? What would Dirk's family be like? Thoughts rushed in, threatening to overwhelm her. Each time she thought of the upcoming changes, she felt anxious about the move from everything she knew. However, her heart was set. She was certain that whatever happened in Belgium, Dirk would protect her.

She headed downstairs, greeted Elsie, then called to say good morning to Hilda. But if she'd been hoping for a kind word, she was wrong.

'Shut the door, you're letting the heat out,' Hilda snapped.

Hetty closed the door and walked back to the kitchen.

'How is she?' Elsie asked.

'Same old Hilda, miserable and snappy. I won't miss her one bit.'

Elsie shot her a look. 'You shouldn't be so harsh. She's had a difficult life, as you know.'

Hetty sank into a chair. 'I know only too well, that's the problem. All my life Hilda's taken out her hardship on me.'

'You could at least be grateful that she offered you money for the wedding,' Elsie reminded her.

'Of course I'm grateful, and I've told her so – you were there when I did. She even kissed me on the cheek. It's the first kind thing she's done. And the first time she's kissed me.'

Elsie spun around. 'Really?'

Hetty nodded. 'Life with Hilda was never easy. There was never affection or love, kisses or hugs. Not for me, just for Dan. He couldn't do anything wrong. But that's because he was her son, whereas I turned out to be just a girl she had to bring up because it was expected.'

'But she *did* bring you up,' Elsie said gently. 'She kept you warm, put a roof over your head, cooked for you, fed you. You had your own bedroom. That's more than I ever had. Sometimes I had to sleep on the sofa if Aunt Jean needed the bedroom when she brought a man back.' Her face clouded over at the memory. 'And she always brought a man back,' she continued sadly.

She walked to Hetty and sat next to her.

'But I'm not my aunt Jean and you're not Hilda. We're grown women and we'll forge our own future. Look at you, off to Belgium, and getting married too! As for me, I've got a new job to look forward to.' She bit her lip. 'Although I feel nervous about learning how to use the new machines. Anne has been telling me all about them.'

'What about you and Stan?' Hetty asked.

Elsie smiled widely. 'We're a strong team. We both know where our relationship is headed, in time. There's no hurry. I want... no, I need to learn to manage the new house at Elisabethville and look after Hilda and tend the garden. I'll have to get used to having taps with running water. And electric lights! I still can't believe I'll have such luxury. Oh, Hetty, can you imagine?'

She slapped her hand against her forehead.

'Oh, I forgot to tell you, Anne is going to help me with the money from Aunt Jean.'

Hetty put her hand on Elsie's arm. 'That's great news.'

'She's also taking me to the town hall next month to see what I need to do to begin a divorce. After what Frankie did to me and our child, there's no judge in the land who'd deny me my freedom. At least that's what Anne says.'

'And she's usually right,' Hetty replied.

The girls ate breakfast, then headed out for the walk to work. As they walked, they talked about writing to each other every day once Hetty left.

'I'll send news of Stan, of the gardens at the factory, and of Hilda if you'd like me to.'

'I would, thanks, Elsie,' Hetty replied.

When they reached the toffee factory, they joined the women swarming through the gates. It was usually at this point that Elsie, hidden by the crowd, undid the top button of her overall. But today she walked straight through, keeping her button fastened. Hetty caught her eye, nodded at the button and smiled. Elsie laughed out loud.

'I've got to be respectable now I'm to be a supervisor,' she said with a cheeky grin.

When they reached the cobbled courtyard, Hetty saw Anne waiting at the door to reception.

'Hetty! Elsie!' she called.

The girls walked to her.

'Follow me, please. I need to speak to you both.'

Hetty and Elsie shared a look, and Hetty shrugged.

They followed Anne through reception, where Jacob didn't even lift his head, and along the carpeted corridor. They were expecting to head into Anne's office, but she walked straight past and led them instead to Mr Jack's. Anne stepped inside, while Hetty and Elsie faltered at the threshold.

'Come in, girls, don't be shy,' she said.

They entered the wood-panelled room, where Mr Jack was sitting at his desk. Anne was standing behind him.

'Good morning, Mr Jack,' Hetty and Elsie chorused.

'Please, sit down,' he replied, indicating two chairs opposite him.

Hetty suddenly felt nervous. She looked at Elsie, who was sitting up straight and had an air of confidence about her. Taking heart from her friend's stance, she straightened her shoulders too, planted her boots firmly on the carpet and looked straight at Mr Jack. His round face appeared cheerful, his blue bow tie was straight and he seemed to be in good humour.

'Miss Lawson,' he said, addressing Hetty first, 'I've called you to see me this morning because I've had a rather good idea.'

Hetty looked from up and saw a smirk on Anne's face. 'Sir?' she said, confused.

'When do you leave for Belgium?'

'Friday, sir,' she replied.

'I'm given to understand that your future husband belongs to a family of chocolatiers. Is that correct?'

'Yes, sir. His family own and run a chocolate shop in Ghent.'

'Ah yes, the city of Ghent, a major Belgian port. We could use the warehouses on Korenmarkt, along the River Leie,' he said, absent-mindedly rubbing his chin.

Hetty was impressed with his knowledge of Ghent, which was far in excess of her own. She had no information about her new home other than what Dirk had told her. He'd talked lovingly about its churches and castles, but she couldn't recall a port. She wasn't sure if she was expected to confirm Mr Jack's statement, so she stayed silent.

'And it's a city that escaped the worst of the war invasion,' he continued. 'From newspaper reports, I understand that Ghent did not suffer severe shell damage and in fact came out of the conflict relatively unscathed.'

Now Anne joined the conversation. 'But that doesn't mean that the war was without its consequences for the people who live there, dear,' she added gravely.

Mr Jack turned to Hetty again. 'Do you know whereabouts in Ghent the family chocolate shop is?' he continued.

Hetty knew exactly where it was, for Dirk had spoken about it at length. She tried to remember how to pronounce the name of the street.

'Yes, sir. It's on Donkersteeg. There are more chocolate shops in the city, run by other families, on streets such as Klein Turkije and Ham.' She wondered where the conversation was going, and why he was asking so many questions.

'Why, it sounds perfect,' he said.

Anne placed her hand on his shoulder and looked at Hetty. 'What my husband is trying to say, or rather to ask you, is whether Dirk's family might be interested in being one of the first Belgian stockists of our toffee.'

Hetty rocked back in her seat. 'Oh. I see. Well, I'd need to speak to Dirk, of course.'

'Take all the time you need. Once you're in Belgium, let us know your address and we can send tins of toffees as samples,' Anne said kindly.

Hetty was stunned by the offer. 'Thank you,' she managed to say.

Then Anne turned to Elsie. 'Elsie, you're probably wondering why we called you into this meeting.'

Elsie looked confused. 'I thought I was here to support Hetty,' she said, but Anne shook her head.

'Exciting as it is for Hetty to be heading off for a new life overseas, we also have exciting news for you.'

'For me?'

Hetty noticed Elsie's leg bobbing up and down, a sure sign that she was nervous.

Mr Jack leaned forward. 'Oh yes, Miss Cooper. Something special has arrived at the factory.'

Hetty looked at Anne, who could hardly keep a smile off her face.

'What is it?' Elsie asked.

Mr Jack's eyes were sparkling with joy. 'It's our new toffee-wrapping machine ... and we'd like you to be the first girl to use it.'

Chapter Forty-Four

Hetty went to work in the slab room while Elsie followed Mr Jack and Anne to the wrapping room. She had worked in the wrapping room before, and it was as busy as ever with girls wrapping thousands of toffees by hand. But today there was a hush in the air. The girls turned to stare when she walked in with the toffee factory owner and his wife. At first, she felt nervous, being under scrutiny, but she took a deep breath and held her head high.

'You're going to be a supervisor one day. Might as well start acting the part,' she muttered to herself.

Anne caught her eye and smiled. 'You all right, Elsie?'

Elsie nodded in reply. As confidently as she could, she strode down the aisle, where girls stood motionless in front of tables piled with toffees and papers. Everyone was waiting to see what would happen.

'It appeared overnight. It wasn't there when I left work last night,' one girl whispered as Elsie walked past.

'I'm scared. I'm not touching it,' another one said.

Elsie ignored the idle chatter and kept her gaze fixed on the machine in the corner of the room. She held her breath as she neared it. She'd expected a brute of a thing, bigger and taller than herself, perhaps reaching to the ceiling. She'd thought it would be wider than a slab table, but it looked less threatening than she'd feared. She'd built it up on her mind to be a mechanical monster.

'Here it is,' Mr Jack said with a flourish. He and Anne stood either side of it, proudly presenting their new acquisition.

'You really want *me* to be the first girl to use it?' Elsie said. She looked around the room. 'Shouldn't the supervisor in here learn how to use it first?'

'Sally Porter, the supervisor, hasn't turned up for work again. We might need to think about replacing her. Besides, why shouldn't you be the first to use it? You're the best all-rounder we've got,' Anne said.

Knowing Hetty had been offered the supervisor role first, Elsie bit her tongue to stop herself saying the words *second best*. The old Elsie, the less mature, more reckless Elsie would have said it. She was proud of herself for keeping quiet and enjoyed the feeling of power it gave her.

She eyed the machine carefully, walking around it, peering inside where she could. It was made of metal, box like, with levers and contraptions. She'd seen nothing like it before.

'Can I touch it?' she asked.

Anne nodded. 'Place your hand on the top, never inside.'

Elsie felt the cool metal against her palm, then her fingers followed the machine's hard angles and curves. 'It doesn't scare me,' she said, knowing she was trying to convince herself. 'How does it work?'

'Let me show you,' Mr Jack said. He turned to the girls

who were looking on in wonder. 'Those who want to see the machine in operation, step forward.'

No one moved, although a lot of whispering went on at the wrapping tables. Then, slowly, a girl or two from each table walked towards Elsie. She acknowledged each one with a smile. Some girls held their friends back from approaching the machine.

'Don't go, it could be dangerous,' they warned.

More girls came forward, until there was a small crowd. Mr Jack encouraged everyone to take one step back.

'We need air and space around the machine,' he explained.

When a space had been cleared, he pulled the lever that started the machine. It was much noisier than Elsie had expected. Some of the girls jumped back, startled.

'It wraps twenty sweets a minute,' Mr Jack said over the noise.

Elsie was flabbergasted. 'Twenty?' she cried.

'Oh, it's efficient all right,' he said.

He picked up a pile of wrappers and held them aloft for the girls to see. 'We will be phasing out these waxed wrappers and bringing in new wrappers on a roll, to be used in the machine.'

Elsie watched in awe, committing Mr Jack's words and actions to memory. He scooped up a handful of toffees and placed them into a round metal wheel at the front of the machine. The wheel had small holes in it. He inserted a narrow roll of blue wrapping paper into the back of the machine. Then he turned a handle at the side and the toffees were brushed into the holes of the wheel. They fitted perfectly.

Elsie watched, eyes wide, as the machine took out a

Celebrations at the Toffee Factory

toffee from the wheel and the roll of blue wrapping was pulled from the back. The wrapping twisted itself around the toffee, then the machine lifted the toffee and twisted again. Next, the wrapped sweet was thrown out of a chute, to be neatly caught in a basket. Another toffee was twisted, lifted, twisted again and thrown, then another.

Mr Jack picked up the basket of wrapped toffees and handed it to Elsie. 'Pass it around, Elsie. Let the girls see the quality of the work.'

The basket was passed; toffee wrappers were inspected and the machine was pronounced a success. However, some of the girls weren't impressed.

'I don't like it, it works too fast,' one of them said.

'Mind your hands don't get caught, otherwise your fingers will get wrapped,' warned another.

'It's dangerous. All machines are,' said a third.

Elsie let the chatter go over her head. She was stunned by the machine's efficiency and speed. And yet she couldn't help feeling uneasy that such a machine would take the place of two or three girls. As the girls around her walked back to their tables, she was overcome by sadness.

Anne stepped forward. 'What is it, Elsie? What's wrong?'

Elsie bit her lip. She wasn't used to speaking up to Anne about issues at work. But now that she was going to be a supervisor, she had to look out for the girls.

'It's so quick and efficient, and the girls work much slower,' she said, casting her gaze around the wrapping room. She noticed that some of the girls were nervously eyeing her as she chatted to Anne. She knew she would be talked about. She lifted her head and placed her arms by her sides. She wouldn't show weakness in front of them any more.

'Don't worry, Elsie. No girls will need to leave the factory when the machines come in. We'll train them to fix the machines if they break down. We'll train them to keep them in good running order; the machines will need daily cleaning and attention. We'll need girls to keep the machines supplied with toffees and wrapping rolls. All kinds of jobs will be created.'

'I'm sure you're right, Anne, but it's a very big change that we need to get used to.'

Anne was silent a moment, and when she spoke again, she took Elsie by surprise. 'Would you like to move here to the wrapping room to supervise the girls? Sally Porter has let me down too often with the amount of time she takes off work. She tells me she's ill, but she's been spotted working on the market when she should be here. I need to put her on a final warning. Or would you prefer to stay in the slab room?'

Elsie looked at the girls, many of whom had returned to wrapping toffees by hand. A few more inquisitive ones were still milling around the machine, and she was relieved to note she was no longer the talk of the room. She considered Anne's question for a few moments, than walked back towards the machine.

'Mr Jack said I would be the first girl to use this,' she said.

Mr Jack appeared with a handful of toffees and popped one in his mouth. 'And you will be, Elsie Cooper. Come here.'

Elsie moved to stand next to him. He handed her a roll of wrapping paper and showed her how to correctly insert it. Then he gave her the unwrapped toffees, which she placed into the wheel.

'Press this lever,' he told her. Elsie had to strain to hear him over the noise.

She pressed the lever and marvelled once more as the machine moved toffees into the holes. She was transfixed as she watched it lifting the toffees, twisting the paper and throwing them into the chute. As the basket filled with toffees, her heart soared with pride.

'I can do it!' she cried. She couldn't wait to tell Hetty and Stan.

Mr Jack held out his hand and she shook it heartily.

'I never doubted you for one moment,' he replied.

Elsie looked at Anne. 'I'd like to accept your offer. I want to stay where the factory's future is, here in the wrapping room.'

Chapter Forty-Five

Later that night, at home in the Deanery, William retired to his armchair to read the newspaper. He'd removed his bow tie and the shirt he'd worn for work, and was now looking more relaxed in an old jumper that his mother had knitted. Upstairs, Anne was reading a story to Dinah. When her daughter fell asleep, she joined William in the living room.

The night had turned cool. Edith, always thinking one step ahead, had lit the coal fire, which spread a gentle heat around. Anne sat down on the sofa and picked up a trade magazine that had a feature on new machines for confectionery makers. She was flicking through the pages when William sharply folded his paper and placed it on the arm of his chair. She looked up at him.

'Everything all right, dear?'

He smiled warmly. 'Everything, my dear Anne, is more than all right. In fact, I have some news. I've been burning to tell you all afternoon, but I wanted to choose my moment carefully. Now that we're relaxed by the fire, Dinah's asleep and Edith has taken the rest of the night off, I think it may be the right time to tell you.'

Celebrations at the Toffee Factory

Anne could tell by the mischievous glint in his eye that he was up to something. She walked to his armchair, moved his newspaper away and sat on the arm of the chair, putting her arm around his shoulders. William gave her a peck on the cheek, then stood and walked to the drinks cabinet, taking out a bottle of brandy.

'Not for me, dear,' Anne said.

He looked at her, then put the brandy bottle back on the shelf. 'Me neither,' he said. 'Shall I make tea?'

Anne caught his arm as he began to head out of the room. 'William, you're acting like a coiled spring. Whatever it is, tell me now, before you explode.'

He looked at her sheepishly. 'You know me too well, my love.'

'Come on, out with it,' she said gently.

He cleared his throat. 'Oh, I've been savouring this news since late afternoon.'

'Whatever it is, why didn't you tell me at work, if it's so important?'

'Because this is news that I wanted to share with you alone. I wanted us two to be the only people in the world to know what had happened.'

'William!' Anne exclaimed. 'You're infuriating! Just tell me, for heaven's sake.'

As she waited for him to explain, he did a rather unusual thing. He sat down and reached under the armchair, and when he brought his hand out, he presented her with a slim, narrow box.

'It's yours at last,' he said.

Anne took the box, puzzled. Her husband was certainly in a playful mood. It fitted perfectly into the palm of her left hand, and with the fingers of her right, she lifted the catch. Inside was a beautiful blue and silver necklace. She gasped when she saw it.

'Is this the necklace that . . .? Does this mean . . .?' The questions tumbled out of her mouth one after the other as her head spun. She couldn't stop her mind from racing.

'Anne, dear. I promised you the necklace as a gift to celebrate a special occasion.'

Her heart was beating fast, and she took a deep breath to calm her nerves. 'Does this mean what I think it means?' she whispered, hardly daring to listen to William's reply, for what if she was wrong? But then he smiled, and that was when she knew that she was right.

'Yes, dear. Sir Michael has invested. He signed the contract this afternoon.'

Clasping the box tightly, she flung herself onto William's lap and threw her arms around him. They sat together in his armchair and held each other close. How long they stayed like that was hard to know, but the fire went cold and the embers died as they talked long into the night, going over their plans to spend Sir Michael's money wisely.

'He wants to be involved in the running of the old Mayfair factory,' William said.

'I think you mean the latest addition to Jack's toffee factory.' Anne couldn't hide the glee in her voice.

'I'll have to offer him a seat on the management board, of course. He's very interested in our new line of novelty eggs and wants us to . . .' he gave a cheeky smile, 'crack on with production as soon as we can.'

Anne rolled her eyes.

'Oh, I almost forgot to tell you,' William continued, 'Sir Michael and Lady Bennett have invited us to dine with them at Seaton Hall next week. And speaking of Beryl, we will of course have to acquiesce to her penchant for team sports for the factory girls.'

Anne thought about her conversation with Elsie. 'Leave that to me, it's all under control. Although we will need a name for the football team.'

'How about...' William trailed his hand in the air as if displaying the name, 'the Toffee Factory Girls Football Club?'

But Anne shook her head. 'We'll call them *Jack's* Toffee Factory Girls. Remember, it pays to advertise. I may even play for the team myself.'

William gently laid his hand on her stomach. 'Promise me you'll wait until after our baby is born.'

She snuggled into his side and sighed contentedly. 'What good news this is,' she breathed. 'And I have some news for you too. Mrs Perkins came to see me today, to discuss a private matter.'

'Oh?' William said.

Anne laid the box on the table and pulled back from William. 'What she told me inspired an idea that could bring in extra income to the factory.'

'Extra income? I'm all ears,' William said.

'Well, as you know, Mrs Perkins is leaving to live in Durham with Mrs Fortune. Mrs Fortune owns a property on Victor Street. It was left to her in her brother's will as she was his only family member. If you remember, it's where I used to live when I first moved to Chester-le-Street. I had a nice room that received the afternoon sun.'

'Victor Street?' William said thoughtfully. 'She could earn a pretty penny if she sells up.'

'And she *is* selling up. In fact, she's looking for a buyer right now. That's where I thought we could help.'

'But we don't need another house, Anne. Has the good news about Sir Michael clouded your mind?' he joked.

Anne knew she'd have to play this carefully and slowly to bring William around to the idea that had been forming since Mrs Perkins' visit.

'When I was new to town, and had nowhere to live, Mrs Fortune's house became my sanctuary. I was well fed and looked after, and it provided me with shelter and warmth.' She remembered the small room where she'd lodged. There'd been a single bed and a chest of drawers, nothing more. 'Mind you, Mrs Fortune was inquisitive when I first lived there. She didn't trust me one bit. She used to barge into my room on the slightest pretext, assuming I was entertaining a gentleman.'

William laughed out loud. 'You weren't, were you?'

She threw him a coy look. 'Of course I wasn't. And yet for all her faults, she turned out to be one of the nicest people I've met. I trust her and that's why I think we should speak to her about buying her house.'

William was silent for a long time.

'Anne, we can't afford it,' he said at last.

'We could if we rent out the rooms.'

This caught him off guard. 'Sorry?' he said.

Anne sat up straight. 'Girls like I used to be, coming to town to work at our factory, sometimes need somewhere to live. Somewhere that's safe and warm, and within walking distance of the factory, so they don't need to spend their wages on bus fares.'

She expected William to stop her from carrying on, to

tell her that her idea was nonsense. When he didn't, she took heart and continued.

'We could rent out rooms to girls who need accommodation. We'd charge the going rate, of course, and could put one of the girls, an older one, perhaps, in charge.'

'Elsie Cooper again?' William suggested.

'No, I understand she's moving to live in one of the empty houses at Elisabethville once Hetty leaves for Belgium.'

'Ah, that's a shame. I like Elsie a lot.'

Anne looked at the necklace in the box. 'Yes, I remember that not so long ago, I thought you liked her too much,' she said.

William leaned forward and placed his hand on her arm. 'Wouldn't it be too much trouble for you, buying a property in your condition? You don't need the stress of it with our baby on the way.'

'I'm fine, William, really. Edith is such a big help. I'm one of the lucky ones. I have you, Dinah, Edith, your parents and the factory. I'm surrounded by love and friends. Elsie and I get on well. But some of the girls have nothing, just the wages we pay them. Their home conditions are not our business, of course, but if they need somewhere to live, whether it's a room for a night, a week or a year, we could help them. What do you say? Would you at least consider it?'

William nodded slowly. 'Let me think this over. I have much on my mind after signing the contract today, but I promise you, Anne, I'll consider it carefully, for your sake.'

Anne patted his hand. 'And for the sake of our factory girls.'

She picked up the box and opened it again, marvelling at the way the stones in the necklace shone in the light of the oil lamp.

'This is beautiful, my love,' she said. She stood, leaned over William and kissed him full on the lips. 'I shall wear it with my brooch when we have our celebration dinner with Sir Michael next week.'

Chapter Forty-Six

The morning of Hetty's wedding dawned with a clear blue sky. She was woken by a knock at her bedroom door.

'It's me,' called Elsie.

'Come in, I'm decent.'

Elsie stepped inside carrying a mug of tea, which she placed at Hetty's bedside.

'How are you feeling? Nervous? Excited?'

Hetty pushed herself up to sitting and lifted the mug. 'I'm feeling all kinds of mixed up, but in a good way, if that makes sense.'

'I think I know what you mean,' Elsie replied. 'Now, is there anything you need help with before we set off for the town hall?'

Hetty glanced at her suitcase lying on the floor. 'I think I'm done, Elsie. I'm packed and my papers are in my handbag. Dirk has our travel documents and tickets. All that remains is for me to get up and get dressed.'

Elsie narrowed her eyes. 'Are you sure you want to wear your blue skirt to get married in? One of Aunt Jean's dresses would look prettier.'

'I need to dress sensibly and warmly, Elsie. You know

Dirk and I need to rush to the railway station after we leave the town hall, then I'll be sitting on a train for hours before travelling overseas on the boat. Oh my word, when I say it like that, it makes it all seem real. I can't believe what I've done.'

Elsie sat on the edge of the bed. 'You're not having second thoughts, are you?'

Hetty smiled at her friend. 'Never,' she replied with conviction. 'But I will tell you something. I'm scared about what lies ahead, not just today, but in my new life in Ghent.'

'Dirk will protect you,' Elsie said.

Hetty took a sip of tea. 'That's the one thing I'm certain of. He's a good man. I've done well, haven't I?'

'We both have,' Elsie replied. 'I'll let you finish your tea and get dressed. Stan is coming with your bouquet. He's picking pink and white roses from the factory gardens. I'll dress them in blue ribbon when they arrive and make them look as pretty as you.' She reached in her pocket for a handkerchief to dry her eyes. 'Oh, Hetty, my friend, I'm going to miss you something rotten.'

She stood and walked quickly from the room. Hetty was left with a lump in her throat and tears in her eyes.

She managed to finish her cup of tea, savouring each mouthful, wondering what tea would taste like in Ghent. Did the Belgians even drink tea? She had no clue. She washed and dressed slowly, thinking about Dirk waking up in his room at Elisabethville. He was being accompanied to the wedding by his friend Tomas, who would be travelling to Belgium with them. Tomas was an older man and a little rough around the edges for Hetty's liking, but he was friendly and spoke good English. She slipped on her favourite blue skirt, stockings and shoes and a cream blouse that Anne had given her. It had a lace collar that flattered her neckline. Then she brushed her hair and applied a touch of powder and rouge.

Placing the final items in her suitcase, she fastened its locks, then picked up her handbag and stood in the doorway, looking back into the room. She'd expected to feel sad at leaving it for the last time, but the excitement she felt for the adventure ahead coloured her emotions.

'Bye, room,' she said, then closed the door.

She walked downstairs carrying the heavy suitcase, lumping it into the hallway. There was a knock at the door, and she answered it to find Stan holding a spray of pink and white roses.

'Oh, Stan, these are beautiful, thank you!' She stood to one side to allow him to enter the house. 'Come in. We're just about to have breakfast.'

But Stan stayed where he was. 'Thanks for the offer, but I can't stop. I need to set my team away with work at the factory before I head to the town hall to give you away. I'm as proud as Punch that you asked me.'

Elsie walked into the hall and Hetty saw her eyes light up at the sight of Stan. She walked to him and slid a paper bag into his hand. 'I've made you a beef pie.'

'Thanks, Elsie. What would I do without you?' He kissed Elsie, waved at them both, then walked away.

Hetty brought the bouquet to her nose and buried her face in the flowers. 'The scent is heavenly,' she declared.

'Pass them over and I'll pretty them up with the ribbon,' Elsie said.

Hetty handed her the bouquet. 'I'll say good morning to Hilda,' she said, but before she could reach the door, it opened to reveal Hilda herself. Hetty stopped dead in her tracks. The two women eyed each other cautiously, and Hetty wasn't sure what to say. It was Hilda who broke the impasse.

'So, you're all set to leave, then?' she barked.

'Yes, it seems that I am,' Hetty replied evenly.

Hilda nodded at the bouquet, which was sitting on the kitchen table. 'I hope you haven't been frittering away the money I gave you.'

'Now, Hilda, don't take that tone with Hetty, today of all days,' Elsie chipped in.

Hetty was grateful for her friend's intervention. The last thing she wanted on her wedding day, and on the last day of her old life, was to get into a war of words.

'Stan brought these flowers,' she said. 'The money you gave me is safe. I can't thank you enough for your help.'

'Aye, well, see that you spend it wisely,' Hilda said, more gently.

That was when Hetty noticed that her aunt was smartly dressed in a skirt suit, and was even wearing her good shoes.

'Does this mean . . . ?'

'Yes, I'm coming to your wedding,' Hilda said. 'Now, clear the flowers off the table and let me sit down.'

Hetty was surprised and moved by Hilda's words. She was warmed by the fact that her last day with the woman would contain a little bit of goodwill. She moved the flowers to one side and helped Hilda into a chair. Elsie placed a plate piled with toast on the table, but Hetty found it hard to chew due to the lump in her throat, and each time she looked at Elsie, she saw tears in her friend's eyes. Hilda, however, was greedy for the toast.

'Is there more, Elsie?' she asked.

Elsie picked up the toasting fork, speared a slice of bread and placed it over the fire.

Once breakfast was done, Hilda returned to her room and Hetty helped Elsie wash the breakfast plates.

'You don't need to do this, it's your wedding day,' Elsie said.

'I want to,' Hetty replied. 'I want to remember these things: you cooking breakfast, Hilda . . . well, being Hilda.'

Elsie smiled. 'She'll never change, and anyway, she's not your problem after today. Don't worry about her. You know I'll always have her best interests at heart. And if she ever gets too much to cope with, I'll let off steam at Stan's house or go for a walk by the river.'

Hetty finished drying the plates and hung the tea towel on a peg on the hearth. Then she stood and smoothed down her skirt.

'It's time, Elsie.'

Without a word, Elsie put on her coat and hat. She picked up Hetty's suitcase from the hall and called into Hilda's room. 'Hilda, we're ready to leave.'

After a moment, Hilda emerged in a smart coat and matching hat that Hetty was sure she'd never seen before.

'You look lovely, Hilda,' she said.

'Don't be daft, lass,' the older woman snapped.

Together they set off for the short walk to the town hall. When Elsie struggled with the heavy suitcase, Hetty carried it, swapping the bouquet and the suitcase between them. When they arrived, Hetty couldn't believe what she saw. Her heart began to pound as she took in the sight of a small crowd of people. She saw Anne with Dinah in her arms, standing next to Mr Jack and Mr Gerard. There was Mrs Doughty from Lumley Castle, with her face powdered and rouged. There was Jim and Cathy Ireland from the Lambton Arms, with their three boys dressed in suits. There was Jacob with his arm around Meg. Mrs Perkins and Mrs Fortune were there too, arm-in-arm, each holding a small bouquet of violets. There was Beattie with a handful of girls from the toffee factory that Hetty had worked with since her first day.

She smiled at them all, gripped her bouquet of roses and went to speak to everyone. She saw Stan wrap his arms around Elsie and pull her to him in a bear hug. And then she saw Dirk, walking along Front Street with Tomas. Both men carried suitcases. She handed her bouquet to Elsie and ran to Dirk. He dropped his suitcase on the ground and flung his arms around her.

'You look beautiful,' he breathed against her cheek.

Hetty stood back and looked deep into his blue eyes. 'Everyone came,' she said, indicating her friends. 'They want to see us get married then wave us off at the railway station.'

Tomas picked up Dirk's suitcase and the group headed inside the town hall. Dirk and Hetty were last in. As Dirk went to find the registrar to alert him that they were ready for their appointment, Hetty hung back at the door.

'Hetty?' Dirk said.

'I want to take a last look at Chester-le-Street. I'll just be one moment,' she said.

She stood on the steps of the town hall and looked up and down Front Street. She saw the entrance to Market Lane that led to the factory. She saw the Lambton Arms pub, and memories of her late father rushed at her. She dabbed her eyes with her handkerchief and was about to head inside when she spotted a man on the other side of the road. At his side sat a small black dog that Hetty immediately recognised. From behind, she heard Dirk call her name, then she felt him at her side. He laid his arm around her shoulders.

'Hetty, the registrar is waiting.'

Hetty stood transfixed as Bob walked across the road and headed straight for her, the dog following. Dirk had seen him too, and he stepped forward, on his mettle, in case of trouble. But Bob's expression and body language didn't suggest he was there for a fight. Instead, he held out his hand.

'Look after her, please,' he said to Dirk. He shook Dirk's hand, then held out his hand to Hetty. 'Have a good life, Hetty Lawson.'

Hetty shook his hand, then nodded at the dog sitting at his feet. 'Your dog looks just like mine did. He was called Jet.'

The dog cocked its head to one side. Bob shrugged.

'It's not my dog. It followed me this morning and won't go away.'

As he turned and walked off, Hetty looked at Dirk. 'Life is full of surprises,' she said.

'And we will have plenty more, you and I,' Dirk replied. He kissed her on her cheek, then together they walked into the town hall.

After the ceremony ended, Mr and Mrs Horta made their way up Front Street to the railway station. Tomas walked ahead carrying his and Dirk's suitcases, while Stan carried Hetty's. Hetty linked arms with her new husband.

When they reached the station, the train was waiting and steam filled the platform.

'There's no time to waste,' Tomas said, swinging the suitcases aboard.

Hetty's legs felt weak, and her heart pounded. Around her was a bustle of activity: lovers saying goodbye, mothers bundling children into the train. She began hugging everyone, receiving kisses and good-luck messages. However, Hilda was nowhere to be seen.

'Where is she?' Hetty asked Elsie.

'I'm sorry, love. She went straight home when we came out of the town hall,' Elsie replied.

'I shouldn't be surprised, or disappointed, but I am,' Hetty said sadly.

Elsie handed over a package wrapped in paper and tied with blue ribbon. 'It's a tin of Lady Tina toffee,' she explained. 'I couldn't let you leave without giving you a gift that will always remind you of home.'

Hetty struggled to take the tin as she was still holding the bouquet of roses in her arms. She held them out to Elsie.

'Could you take the flowers, Elsie? I don't mean to sound ungrateful, but they'll wilt and die on the train. Perhaps you could share them with Anne and Hilda.'

Elsie took the roses and pulled out two blooms, one pink and one white. The white one she threaded through Dirk's buttonhole and the pink one she laced into Hetty's fair hair.

'I'll press these and keep them for ever,' Hetty said.

She hugged Elsie and kissed Dinah on her chubby cheek. Mr Jack stepped forward and shook her hand.

'Safe journey, Miss Lawson!' he called.

'She's Mrs Horta now,' Anne reminded him, then she hugged Hetty. 'We'll be in touch about the toffees for the chocolate shop in Ghent.'

Dirk stepped onto the train and held his hand out to Hetty. She took a last look at her friends, forcing herself not to cry, then climbed aboard. As she wound down the window and peered along the platform, she heard a whistle blow. Dirk was behind her, and he had tears in his eyes too. Steam billowed along the platform as the train picked up speed. Elsie, Anne, Mr Jack... everyone waving her off grew smaller as it began to snake away.

'Come, let us sit down, darling wife,' Dirk said. Hetty looked into her husband's blue eyes and trusting face, then took a deep breath and headed to her seat to start the journey to her new life.

On the platform, Mr Jack carried Dinah. Elsie dabbed her tears away.

'What'll I do without her?' she cried.

Anne stepped forward and put her arm around her friend's waist. 'We'll manage together. Do you know what? I might make a trip to Ghent myself one day, if the wholesale business to Belgium takes off. Perhaps you could join me if I can persuade William that a visit would make business sense.'

Elsie's eyes lit up. 'Why, that would be wonderful.'

Anne hugged her tight. 'Come on, let's go to work. There are toffee eggs to be discussed!'

RAISING READERS
Books Build Bright Futures

Dear Reader,

We'd love your attention for one more page to tell you about the crisis in children's reading, and what we can all do.

Studies have shown that reading for fun is the **single biggest predictor of a child's future life chances** – more than family circumstance, parents' educational background or income. It improves academic results, mental health, wealth, communication skills, ambition and happiness.[1]

The number of children reading for fun is in rapid decline. Young people have a lot of competition for their time. In 2024, 1 in 10 children and young people in the UK aged 5 to 18 did not own a single book at home.[2]

Hachette works extensively with schools, libraries and literacy charities, but here are some ways we can all raise more readers:

- Reading to children for just 10 minutes a day makes a difference
- Don't give up if children aren't regular readers – there will be books for them!
- Visit bookshops and libraries to get recommendations
- Encourage them to listen to audiobooks
- Support school libraries
- Give books as gifts

There's a lot more information about how to encourage children to read on our website: **www.RaisingReaders.co.uk**

Thank you for reading.

---

[1] OECD, '21st-Century Readers: Developing Literacy Skills in a Digital World', 2021, https://www.oecd.org/en/publications/21st-century-readers_a83d84cb-en.html

[2] National Literacy Trust, 'Book Ownership in 2024', November 2024, https://literacytrust.org.uk/research-services/research-reports/book-ownership-in-2024